# TRAVELING MONSTERS

*Traveling Monsters* is a work of fiction. Names, places, characters, monsters, and incidents are the products of the author's imagination or are used fictitiously. Any resemblance to actual events, locals, monsters, or persons living or dead, is entirely coincidental.



First Edition

Place of Publication Marina CA
Paperback ISBN:979-8-9885169-0-3
eBook ISBN:979-8-9885169-1-0
Library of Congress Control Number: 2023912166

# TRAVELING MONSTERS

S.A. LUNAMIR

SA Lunamir

A troll rested in a cleaning closet at San Francisco International Airport. Trolls love the dark. This one appears to be eating—worrying the last bit of chewy tendon off a bone.

# CHAPTER 1

# SCARLET

The airport loomed in front of Scarlet Burke as she dragged her luggage behind her. She inhaled a last lung full of fresh air, moist with Bay Area fog. Although the day was gray, it felt warm, like the sun would be out soon. Juan Nieves, her boyfriend, walked close by her side. He took her hand, nervous before the long flight to Spain. The roar of a plane engine preparing for takeoff sounded in the distance.

Scarlet led them toward the counter. She needed to check her large bag. But, of course, the line snaked out twenty people deep. Rummaging in her purse, she pulled out both passports and placed them in a back pocket for easy access. The faster they could get through the airport lines, the sooner they would be on their trip.

Juan's phone rang. He frowned at the screen. "It's my mom."

"Well, take it."

"I told her I'd call her when we got to our gate."

"She's worried."

He grumbled and answered the phone.

Scarlet used the time to look at her phone. She had her presentation on Tuesday; it was her first one at an international conference. Every spare moment she could, she went over the speech. Her heart pounded while re-reading the words—it terrified her to imagine standing on the stage. What if she mixed up numbers—or spoke too fast? She huffed, exasperated. This trip should be exciting, not an anxiety rollercoaster. Her superiors finally showed some confidence in her.

And after the work in Spain finished, she'd get to take an overdue vacation with Juan. They'd spent a few holiday weekends traveling around California, but this would be their first long sojourn. She felt excited about what it could mean for their relationship. It would be a turning point, hopefully for the better.

Juan still spoke to his mom soothingly in Spanish when Scarlet reached the counter. Balancing the phone with his cheek, he picked up her luggage and placed it on the belt.

"That's a light bag," said the clerk.

Scarlet handed over their passports. "Yeah, it's big but not very full. We want to buy souvenirs."

He handed her back the passports with their boarding passes stuck in them. "Tracking number on the back. Have a lovely trip. Security is through there," he said and pointed.

"Thank you. I have one question," she said, barely waiting for the clerk's nod, then continued, "is the flight fully booked? Is there anyone sitting next to us?"

"Let me look," responded the clerk, his fingers typing and eyes scanning the computer screen, "you're in luck. For now, no one is in that third seat. But check again at the gate—it could fill up."

Scarlet's seat was clean although not comfortable, she pushed her backpack down in front of her, limiting her legroom. At the same time, Juan maneuvered his carry-on into the overhead compartment. They were near the back of the plane. Take-off wouldn't be long, with not too many more passengers to wait for. She hoped she could get a nap in. This flight would be the long section of their air travel. There were no direct flights to Malaga, Spain, from SFO. Instead, they had to go north to Stockholm and then fly south to Spain.

Juan buckled in and poked at the screen in front of him. He was responsible for planning most of the vacation portion of their trip, as Scarlet had been too busy with work. A new manager and a presentation to prepare felt almost overwhelming to her. Juan scrolled through a map of Europe, stopping on Florence. He had decided to stick to Italy after they left Spain. They could come back another time to see the rest of Europe.

"Look, they have a whole section on gelato," he said.

Scarlet glanced at the screen. "Do most of your plans for our trip revolve around ice cream?"

"That might be true."

"You sure do know how to make me happy." Scarlet smiled.

Her smile fell off her face when she saw someone attempt to put their luggage in the compartment above their seats. It looked like she meant to sit in the third seat. Not a someone, she realized. A something. It was a troll. Scarlet could see supernatural phenomena. No one else reacted strangely to the troll. Scarlet assumed the other passengers and Juan saw a normal person standing there. The troll struggled to get her things in the overhead compartment—she was too short. Her gray scrunched face was all screwed up. Juan stood to help her.

"That is nice," the troll said in its gravelly voice, handing her bag over to him.

"No problem." Juan stowed the luggage obliviously and sat back down.

Scarlet's face felt hot, and her scalp tingled. Her vision narrowed into a tunnel. She glared furiously at the troll—sure, it was not her seat. The troll had seen Juan and taken advantage of an open spot. Spirits and creatures loved Juan; Scarlet had resisted dating him for six months because of this and the fact that they worked together. The day she first met him a cloud of fluffy yellow spirits fluttered around his head. She remembered how one sat on the shoulder of his white polo, and another bounced on his clipboard as he asked about a flickering fluorescent bulb in her lab. They left promptly in Scarlet's presence, flopping to the ground and skittering under a door. Not only could she see beyond ordinary creatures, but she also seemed to repel them.

If her Great Aunt Lou hadn't been a bit different, too, Scarlet would have thought herself mad. But her aunt explained a few things to her. Perhaps she would have given her more guidance, but she died when Scarlet was eleven.

Whatever repulsive ability she emitted seemed to work on the troll, as it sat as far away in the narrow seat as possible.

Scarlet examined the little gray woman—trolls were bad—she knew that from bedtime stories. But this one was small. She wore a shaggy black coat, the popular kind, and even expensive. She carried a tiny purse, also black, Prada. The troll's skin was a stony gray, her hair the color of raisins. She wore tight black jeans and combat boots. Not regular combat boots, ones with a pattern on them. Scarlet thought they were cute. Everything else looked like it would have been cute five years ago.

Their plane began to taxi; so much for sleep on this plane ride. Scarlet felt another wave of resentment rush over her. She got out her phone to reread her speech but saw an email from James, her new manager. It was labeled as important. She sighed and opened it.

The first six hours in the air were not bad. Juan relaxed a little, eating one of the peanut butter and jelly sandwiches she had packed. She kept crackers in her bag, too, all things easy on nervous digestive systems.

An action movie flashed across the screen in front of Juan, his second of the flight. Green Northern Lights painted the sky outside their window as they entered the Arctic Circle. Scarlet poked him so he could lean over and see them too.

Besides compulsively reading over her presentation again, she read James's message and reviewed the data on her laptop. The actual results of the test contradicted his model. He wanted an explanation, and she put off responding. It would be hard to do respectfully. The results glared at her. Even though things were going relatively well on the plane, she felt her heart pound and the tingles of anger in her hands.

The troll never moved. She looked distorted. The cabin lights were off, but in the weak monitor light, the troll seemed to be a paler shade of gray than earlier. Also, the troll appeared to be melting. The black pants and shaggy jacket she wore puddled in the third seat. At moments like this, Scarlet wondered what everyone else saw. The troll's arms and legs were tucked in at impossible angles. Nothing about her looked close to human.

Juan turned from the green natural spectacle outside their window. "I can hear you sigh, even through my headphones. What's wrong?"

Over half of those sighs were directed at the troll. She needed to be more careful. Juan couldn't know how big of a freak she was. "Just an annoying email."

"James do something wrong again?"

"Eh, probably."

"I don't get it. Doesn't he have a Ph.D? Shouldn't he be better at stuff?"

"Learning stuff and working are totally different skills, babe."

"He had a job before this, though—he told me about it."

"I bet they gave him a good reference to get rid of him," she said. The conversation slowed her heart rate.

That got a laugh out of Juan and a twitch from the troll.

Scarlet closed her laptop and took Juan's hand a little aggressively. There was one more reason for her sighs. She needed to get up. But she did not want to leave Juan alone with a monster. He turned back to his screen, ready to resume his movie. She poked him in the shoulder again. "Hey, wait, I need to pee."

He must come with her. It was the only way she would be able to go. Hopefully, he wouldn't protest. They had both guzzled water earlier in the day.

He turned to the troll, who stirred like she woke from a nap.

"Excuse me. We need to get out."

Scarlet squeezed Juan's hand. The troll got up wordlessly, looking haggard and letting off more than a slight smell of something rotten.

CHAPTER 2

# DONYA

At last, that thing is gone. Donya panted and wiggled around in the seat, feeling singed all over. She tried her best at scheming, but her brain felt dry, while the rest of her felt like she stayed out in the rain all night. She usually liked a drenching, but right now, she was soggy. The young man—she had to get to him. Coming across a human like that as an adult, was a one-in-a-billion chance, and she would not pass it up. If she ate his heart, she would never be troubled by sunlight again. She could spend all day in a bright park, watching children play, waiting for an inattentive parent. It would be glorious. She needed to stop dreaming of all the things that could be. She needed to plan.

Her legs did not want to work, but she stood up anyway. If he comes out of the bathroom first, I'll walk to meet him. I can make it. She steeled herself. The woman is not as awful as I thought—she is only a plump redhead—nothing to get worked up over.

The folding doors opened with a clatter and there he was. Donya's eyes could see every detail despite the extinguished cabin lights. Darkness remained her preferred time. She stumbled her way down the aisle.

"Hey, I decided I should get up too. Can I pass you?" Donya said, forcing the biggest smile possible for her.

"Yeah, sorry we woke you up."

"It is fine. They say it is good to get up and walk. My name is Henicka. What's…"

"Hey, love!" the redhead intruded from behind, throwing her arms around him.

"Oooffff, you're squishing me," he groaned. "She needs to get past us."

"Alright," she said, peering through the darkness, her brown eyes narrowed. Her eyes reminded Donya of something, but she could not place what. Their smells were very distinctive from the other humans on the plane. The man smelled musky like all males but with a clean mineral undertone. The redhead, whose scent wafted from her as she approached, smelled like herb toast.

The two humans backed up a few paces, and their smells diminished. The redhead kept her eyes trained on Donya. They made it to a couple of rows with empty seats on either side and split so she could pass through. Watching them, you could tell the redhead didn't want to let go of him for even a second.

"Thanks," Donya breathed. She wondered if the redhead was some sort of witch. Good thing she did not say anything close to her real name. No, not a witch; her hands held five fingers. Donya felt hot again, hot like she stood in the sun, turned to stone, and now would bake forever.

She made it to the bathroom and slammed the folding door shut. The lights hurt her head, not like the sun hurt, though. She slinked out of her jacket and took off her shirt. Splashing water from the sink all over her long torso helped, she put the toilet seat down and sat to collect herself.

It was much better farther away from them. She could give up. Let the human go. This whole trip had been a mistake. She'd left her cold northern home because there were few humans—every missing one drew so much attention, especially children. She made her way to California, known for sunshine, but it still underwent winters too. A few precious months with less sunlight. She initially planned to spend only one winter. She lost track of time and had been pinned for summer. It took her this whole last winter to get up enough strength to make the trip home. Now she would return a failure.

Not many trolls still lived, maybe only a hundred or two in all the north of Europe. She would certainly be the weakest of them all for a long time. Trying something new was not their way. With all its cold fog and meaty homeless, San Francisco had not been as good as the snow-covered mounds her kind loved best. What could she do? She did not want the others to discover her weakness. Maybe Heldrig… would help? He wasn't a troll but rather a lone Azish Elf. She could strike a deal. They could go halves on all that man's parts. Except for the heart, she got it as a finder's fee.

Heldrig moved around the most of anyone she knew. Donya might be the most well-traveled troll on the continent, but that did not say much. With her mind cleared, at last, she thought up what she needed to do. Not a plan per se, but she knew where she needed to start. The redhead would not stand in her way. If she could get one of their names, it would make tracking them much more straightforward. All she knew now was that they were headed to Italy, Florence in particular.

She stood up, wet her shirt, and wormed back into it. She would not give up. Many days remained in March, and there were still a few weeks of the cold left, even further south. There was enough time to pull this off and arrive home victorious, and maybe depending on how much she ate, as one of the strongest trolls in the north.

Donya did not believe in this sort of omen, but the redhead was in fact in her way. She had changed places with her boyfriend. Donya stayed useless for the rest of the plane ride. Donya suffered. Instead of the heat seeming to be a wave, it felt more like hot coals clawing at her skin in this close proximity. When it was time to disembark, the woman reached out as if to touch her, and she, in a very un-troll-like fashion, squealed and pulled back.

Following them through the airport proved almost impossible, even knowing their scent. The crush of people. The constant horrible heat emanating from the redhead. Even the sun tried to confound her, popping out from behind clouds and making a weak display through the large windows, which she avoided.

Struggling to keep up with them, she wanted to watch them check the board to see their connecting flight. That damn redhead moved fast. She looked down at an app on her phone instead of stopping at any boards. Then the immigration line sprang into existence. A line of this most ordered chaos could not be thought up even in Hell, Donya mused. The redhead looked back over her shoulder once, right back at Donya, like she searched for her. It would be essential to recall details for Heldrig. Perhaps he would know what she was.

In the end, it didn't matter. Donya left the airport and wandered out into the snow. It felt wondrous—icy, and pure. Home, at last, the sunset blotted out by slate-colored clouds. She ran through the snow as only a troll can. Heavy and short, they were like bulldozers. She headed straight to a fir tree and broke off a branch. It would work better if she waited until sunset, but she wanted to be off. She ate the branch in one substantial bite. Said a few old words, then concentrated on Heldrig. His location welled up from the earth, her feet turned themselves, and she was off. Not caring that all of this drained the little strength she contained, the results would be worth it.

CHAPTER 3

# SCARLET

"So, my bag is where?" Scarlet said in what she hoped was an even tone.

"Maybe Sweden, maybe Russia?" The woman responded from behind the counter.

Another man from her flight waited beside Juan and Scarlet. He kept tapping on the counter and demanding something about his chocolate, which added to Scarlet's frustration and the clerk's.

"It is okay. No worries. I will make sure it goes to your hotel tomorrow. If not, the airline will buy you new clothes. Happy ending." The woman smiled but didn't look happy.

Scarlet looked down at her clothes. Was that an insult? Maybe, Scarlet thought her dark wash jeans and green blouse looked nice, but everyone in the Spanish airport looked tailored. It didn't matter. "Okay, thank you for all your help."

"Yes, muchas gracias, senorita," Juan added, this pleased the woman more than anything Scarlet had said.

Scarlet's feet dragged as they approached the taxi line. Juan led her on. He got them a cab and gave the hotel address. Then he made Spanish small talk with the cabbie. Warm rain splattered the cab windows as they moved through the streets.

The lack of sleep, the cold snowy north, and now the wet night air made Scarlet feel discombobulated. She understood Juan spoke about Mexico with the cabbie. She pulled out her phone. No service. Hadn't she told Everly to give her the international package for the workdays of this trip? She rolled her eyes and pinched the bridge of her nose—one more thing.

Thankfully besides the food and laptop in her backpack, it contained pajamas and a change of clothes. Everything was ok, nothing to worry about. She looked over at Juan, happily chatting away with the cabbie. If he was happy, then so was she. Making an effort, she relaxed her shoulders, moving them lower away from her ears.

Juan's black hair was tied back; it had grown long enough to pull into a low ponytail. His skin never lost its glow, even after all the hours on the plane. He leaned forward in his seat, happy to talk to this stranger. The cabbie asked him another question about Mexico, which made him gesture with his hands while speaking. Juan had spent all his teenage years there, although he was from California, born eighty miles away from Scarlet over in the central valley. She smiled and reached over to yank on his hair. He rubbed her knee and kept on talking.

She looked at her cell again. Juan wasn't paying attention. Opening her notes app. There was a note with all her passwords, a note for all the restaurants to eat at in Rome. And finally, down the list, a note called weird stuff.

She opened it and scrolled to the bottom—odd sightings since October. Her eyes moved to the bottom, nothing since the year before, and even that had been a slow year.

*Tahoe, green lights at night in trees, June*

*Seaside Home Depot parking lot. Angry growling winged lizards October*

She typed: *San Francisco to Stockholm troll on plane. March.*

She closed the app when they arrived in Malaga proper. They could have taken the airport train, but the department manager had said to take a cab and not risk getting lost. She felt thankful for that advice now. Her eyes burned after all the canned air and stress. The cab wound through the smaller streets, she rolled down her window, and the air smelled clean. Then the cabby pulled around a corner and stopped, waving his hands and talking to Juan.

"He says it's a couple blocks down on the left. He can't drive us there because technically, it's an alley," Juan said, opening his door. Juan handed the man an even twenty euros for the fifteen-euro ride. It was too big of a tip for the area, so the cabby started counting change. "No, no, gracias," Juan said, shaking his hand and then picking up the bag, "it is for you, amigo." The cabby smiled and hopped back in the driver's seat, waving.

"Are you excited?" Scarlet asked Juan. She knew the answer by the big smile plastered across his face.

"Yep, I felt drained at the airport, but being out is nice." He leaned over and kissed her on the cheek as they walked. Graceful, he could pull it off. He could also drink water and walk, something Scarlet seemed incapable of. "There it is!

"Look at the place next to it—it's called El Horno," she said with a smirk.

"Love, that means the oven."

"I mean, I know, but it's funny to me." She did not know. "We are gonna eat there tonight."

The next day started late for them. It was Sunday, so the whole city got a slow start. First, they wandered to the beachfront. There were palm trees everywhere. A broad strip of park ran along the waterfront. It showcased exotic plants and hundreds of Sago Palms—the biggest ones Juan and Scarlet had ever seen. The ancient palms leaned over on themselves. Branching side shoots pushed toward the light at odd angles. Juan bought some mango ice cream from a booth, and they sat on a bench under a large leafy tree.

Juan licked his ice cream cone. "Do you see those?" he asked, pointing with his left hand.

"It looks like some parakeets got away." Scarlet watched them. They played with some strange small spirits that tumbled around, red round inflated bodies against the bright green of the trees. She never knew parakeets could see spirits too. "They sure are noisy," she added, mainly to stop thinking about what she could see them playing with.

"Here, squawker squawker. You want a piece of cone?" Juan called, tossing a chunk of waffle cone in front of them. The parakeets didn't even notice him. The little red things did; they reminded Scarlet of day-old helium balloons. They made no move to come closer.

"Let's keep walking—we need to make it to that fortress," she got up and brushed off her skirt. Juan continued looking up at the birds. It was warm out, but he had worn a hoodie over his t-shirt. Looking around, she noticed they seemed to be some of the youngest people on the street. The plane down yesterday brimmed with older people too. She wondered if they were the European version of snowbirds in Arizona. Juan was slow to get up, but when he rose, she snatched his hand and pulled him along.

After seeing the spirits, she wondered if it was such a great idea to go wander around the eleventh century Moorish fortress. Europe is so different from home, she thought. There was more history and more clinging to that history. As they approached the Alcazaba, her eyes darted around, not because of the beautiful blooming citrus trees or towering stone walls, but to see if anything lurked on the ancient structure.

Only tourists lurked. How could there be this many in an offseason? It felt safe enough to her with all the other humans around. They bought their tickets and wandered in. First thing, they climbed on top of the walls to look out over the city. It was a picturesque day, big clouds rolling in from the sea. Oranges and white flowers hung from the trees lining the walkways in the fortress. Juan grabbed her hand and planted a quick kiss on her neck as she looked out over everything.

"Look, there's another one!" He twitched at the sight of another parakeet.

"Squawker," she muttered, looking at the lime-green bird. It was alone up in a palm tree, eating the fruit. "They can't be native. I wonder how they were introduced. How big is the population?"

"I bet there will be someone there at that conference on Tuesday, you can ask."

"They are mostly worried about marine invasive species. I'll Google it tonight."

"Smarty… now let's try to get it in our selfie," he said, pulling out his phone and turning around.

While he snapped photos, Scarlet felt the slightest cool breeze around her ankles, which, for whatever reason, reminded her of the troll from the plane. She looked down, but only cool stones lay under her feet. What a horrible way to start their trip. She recalled when she looked back that one time in the airport. Sure she'd lost the troll in the crowd, just to see its beady eyes focused on Juan. Maybe she would have to tell him. Tell him that she was not normal, and there existed a whole world of crazy stuff outside what he could see. She tried to picture how she would start. Hey babe, there is a creepy deflated balloon above your head you can't see.

Her mind rebelled. It wasn't necessary, and even if it was, she did not think she could convince him. If she didn't see these things, there was no way anyone would have convinced her. As a matter of fact, she would have taken such a person straight to a doctor and asked for a sedative or psychiatric evaluation.

"Look at those tiny canals set in the floor. What do you think they are for?" Juan asked, pulling her out of her thoughts.

"Maybe storm runoff. Let's follow one. This place is big–it will give us a direction."

"It is so perfect. If it's meant for storm runoff, then they sure liked to make things pretty."

They walked along the path into a courtyard with flowering jasmine climbing the pointed arches lining the walls. Scarlet snagged a flower off the plant and stuffed it in her jacket pocket to sniff later. At the top of the tiny channel stood a fountain carved out of smooth marble. It was unadorned and looked almost modern in its simplicity.

"I guess they did it for aesthetics," Scarlet said, studying the fountain. "It's all really, really beautiful." They kept walking into the fortress, admiring the mosaics. Most had been retouched, but some survived intact. The little blue tiles were Scarlet's favorite. They looked so refreshing and calming. It stayed warm here even in March—she tried to imagine what it would have felt like in the summer one thousand years ago. All the massive stone walls would have been good for shade, but they would have radiated heat once they got hot. Thank goodness she lived in a time with air conditioning.

The conference was on Tuesday, but the company had sent multiple teams to attend and booked a meeting room on Monday. It was a simultaneous team building and new product launch marketing brainstorming session. James arrived late Sunday night after touring Amsterdam the week before. This was the first time she would meet some colleagues in person from Asia. They brought the newly designed shrimp cans, except they were in a pouch, not a can. This reminded Scarlet of cat food, but she kept the comment to herself. The marine biologists were included more for a display item than to have input on product development.

Every hour she checked on Juan. He'd turned on "find friends" and shared his location. It only worked when both of them were connected to Wi-Fi. Neither of their company phones had service, and they didn't keep personal phones anymore. Every museum and café had Wi-Fi, so she could see where he'd been. His forays were short without her, coming back to the hotel around two. Her meetings ended at six. The group dinner started at seven; Juan and all the significant others were invited.

They met in the lobby of the hotel. Scarlet watched Danton's face, one of the big bosses, as she and Juan descended the stairs. He recognized Juan but probably couldn't place him. When they reached the bottom, he came up to shake his hand. "Hello, young man, I know you." His smile was genuine.

"Hello, Jefe. It's me, Juan, head of facility and fleet maintenance. We met last time you made it to California."

"Oh yes, yes, I remember you. You know Tom said you are the most valuable employee we have obtained in the last few years. I had no idea you would be at this conference," he said as if it was a failing on his part for ignorance.

"I am not here for the conference. I'm here on vacation. I came with Scarlet."

Scarlet wished she held a camera. Danton's eyebrows shot up into his bald scalp. He gave a short, kind laugh. Leave it to the French to never question a romantic involvement. "Very good, very good. I can still ask you a couple questions tonight about that new building schedule we have going, yes?"

"Ha, of course. I'll be on the tour Wednesday too, so we have lots of time."

"Well, I think that is everyone. James isn't coming, yes? We should get walking. You know, we are going to a Mexican restaurant. I will want your input on authenticity."

This got a giggle out of Scarlet, then she said, "if they can get the tortillas right, then that is half the battle. And yes, James is in his room, some sort of food poisoning from the plane down here."

With that, they stepped out into the night air. Orange trees in bloom lined their walk, perfuming the evening. Everything was still, even the alley cats watching from the shadows.

They arrived at the restaurant. Scarlet sat next to Dai, a new hire in the Asian subsidiary or sister company. Scarlet couldn't keep the company organization straight. Juan sat on her other side, with Danton on his right. Margo sat across from her; she was one of the heads of production, maybe the global head. Juan would know—he was better with names and titles. Scarlet never forgot a face. A waiter came to the table bearing wine almost immediately.

Dai showed her some pictures of his eight-month-old twins. They crawled around, smiling into the camera at their dad. She asked, "how is your wife doing with you being gone?"

"This is the first time I have been away. It is very hard. I worry all the time."

"Have you been calling home a lot?"

"Yes, just before we left the hotel. Look, here is a screenshot."

Scarlet looked at the picture. The babies pulled themselves up along a low table, fat stubby legs working hard to support them. It gave her a stab of homesickness, not that his home was anything like hers and Juan's. Their smallish apartment was inhabited by fish and a rescue cat. Juan came with the gray tabby cat, which he had found under a garbage bin when it was two or three days old. Scarlet liked to call her Trash Panda because she looked like a washed-out raccoon and of course the circumstances she was found under. Scarlet's parents would feed the fish and cat for the next two weeks, even though Juan's mother lived closer.

"I heard your new boss is sick. Will he come to any of the presentations tomorrow?" Dai asked.

"I don't know. It'll be a shame if he misses everything. We will get a lot of good information." She held back the jab that James sorely needed information.

"You have worked for the company for six or seven years," Dai started. He glanced a little to the side, then continued, "why didn't you get that position?"

Ah, a new employee worrying about upward mobility in the company. "I applied, but upper management worried I didn't have enough experience supervising. Maybe next time." Scarlet tried to keep her tone neutral. She did the job while it stood vacant. There were many reasons the company passed her over, some her fault, some unfair. She hadn't felt ready at the time either. Now having to deal with James, it was apparent she should have pushed harder for the promotion.

Dai nodded his head. Plates of sopes came to the table. They were very thick, with some red sauce on top and either cheese or white onion. She grabbed one, thankful that food could distract her from this awkward conversation.

Margo looked at her from across the table. "I lived in Arizona many years ago out of college. We had great Mexican food. This is not great."

Scarlet laughed. It was not good; the crust was so hard and thick that she had trouble biting into it. Also, the cheese tasted a little like parmesan. More food arrived; salads with oranges and avocado, stacked in a round cylinder, topped with a purple and yellow viola and some other flower she couldn't name. She took the flowers off just in case they were inedible. The oranges and avocado were good quality, but the combination was unusual to her palette.

Another round of food landed, some mussels in bowls. Everyone pushed theirs away. The smell coming from the crockeries was distinctly not fresh. Scarlet wanted to look in and maybe try to see the flesh, but any form of dissection would make the smell worse. Finally, some deconstructed nachos arrived. No one could mess up nachos. They were the best thing so far, tender beef and the cheese tasted right. It wasn't the main dish; four of the nacho platters arrived for the long table of maybe sixteen people. So far, no tortillas. Scarlet turned to Juan, who still picked at his salad. It looked like they would leave this place hungry.

Scarlet reached the last slide. Her hands were slick with sweat but her voice came out normal. She darted her eyes to her watch, still a couple of minutes in her time slot.

"In conclusion, of the five species sampled in the trawl, all numbers were up with *Cragon franciscorm* up nearly thirty percent," She finished and stiffly moved her body back toward the room. "Any questions," she stated instead of asking.

Some murmurs bounced around the room, but no one asked anything. Scarlet thanked her lucky stars. The presentation had gone well, but her knees felt weak, and she desperately wanted to sit. There were too many eyes on her, and it brought up bad memories. Picking up her note cards, she let the moderator take the stage, and a round of applause started, it made her cheeks burn. Thankfully the lights stayed low so no one could tell.

She returned to her seat. More presentations were to come. Hers was near the beginning of the day. Margo sat next to her; she patted her hand and passed her a glass. Scarlet took a sip instantly. It was wine, a tangy red. She looked over at her colleague, who grinned. "Great job."

Scarlet didn't feel great about it. No questions either meant no one understood or cared. Or maybe it meant they all hated her. Hopefully, the wine would help her relax either way.

## CHAPTER 4

# DONYA

Donya rode in the passenger seat of a shiny, fast black car. She approved of the leather seats and the speed. Her window was rolled down to help with Heldrig's overpowering smell: worm-eaten herbs, cheap human cologne, and the orange human concoction he used to cover his blue skin. He called it a fake tan. She did not know what that meant, but also wasn't sure she did want to know. Glancing at him from the corner of her eye she noticed that other than the tan, his looks had not changed. He kept his inky black hair long. It laid slicked back with a commercial product, not animal grease like the last time they met. His smell had definitely changed for the worse.

The road was bumpy and twisting, Heldrig concentrated on his driving. His eyes were sharper than hers. "Almost there. It is true I have not driven to this spot in many years, but I know the way. Honestly, going all the way to Warsaw was not such a waste because it brought us so close to this area."

She nodded. Her feelings were mixed about running on the fool's errand. Italy was the two humans' eventual destination. Heldrig's first simple casting showed Spain and Poland as their current locations. They tried the closer destination of Poland first. The humans were not there. Heldrig could not explain the mistake but wasted more time and magic to find an answer. A misplaced suitcase had thrown in the wrong location. At least they drove—Donya couldn't afford to spare any more energy running. She needed to feed soon.

They traveled south, into the mountains. It was the Tatras range. In the night she could see the snowy peaks all around them. The earth slept peacefully under the speeding car.

"Here we are." Heldrig came to a stop. There was nowhere to pull off. He left the car in the middle of the loose rock track.

Nothing seemed to be different in this part of the forest. There were snowy patches and some bare rock off the crushed shale road. Her legs felt chalky, but she followed her old acquaintance into the trees. A pinecone crunched under her foot. She scooped it up and chewed slowly on its decomposing fibers. The squirrels left her a few pine nuts. She savored their tang.

The smell of wet rock abated, overtaken by an animal rot and warm updraft. Donya's shoes stuck to the forest floor. In the moonlight, she could see it was black, not black from the low light conditions, but truly black. Heldrig stopped at what looked like standing stones in the center of the black clearing.

The earth under Donya no longer slept. Trolls can hear the earth, they could converse with individual stones and boulders. The sleeping earth should have a gentle hum, but here there was a scratching noise added to the deep rumble of the ground. It sounded to her like when she got a bone stuck in her craw. One of the small ones from a foot or a hand. This black substance irritated the very earth.

Closer, Donya could see the short pillars were not stones but large tree stumps. They oozed the black liquid, which from the smell was neither blood nor any oil she'd come across. Heldrig gathered a small amount, putting it in vials. He muttered incantations as he did. He filled nine vials.

"This is the place we make our oath," he said.

Donya felt no connection here. It was not a place she would have picked. Still, she needed Heldrig's power. And perhaps she hadn't been entirely honest with him. She had omitted her current weakened state when explaining the situation with the humans. There was no way to find the humans without him. She nodded her acceptance. A proper oath would require them to give a token to each other. She did not have much with her that would suffice, just a charm from her grandmother on a stone-beaded bracelet.

Heldrig used one of his long orange-blue fingers to scratch runes into the blackness around them. He remained occupied. This was one of his places of power. She slipped the little charm off her bracelet and placed it in her pocket. "Will you hold this as a symbol of our bond?" She held out the bracelet, it meant something to her, but not as much as the charm.

"We are to proceed in the olden way?" he asked, taking the jade jewelry from her. Smearing his forehead with the blackness, he moved forward and did the same to her.

She felt a little shocked. "Is there another way?"

"Yes, there is always another way. We will mix rituals as it were." He smiled and undid his tie, placing it in her hand. "Please, take this as my token. I Heldrig of Norflin will work with Donya, the troll, to find the human you seek. I will do no harm to Donya as long as we walk this path."

"When we find him, the split will be even, other than I keep the heart."

"You keep the heart, of course."

"I, Donya, child of Larwenhr and Stervrna, will stay with you and do you no harm as long as we walk this path." She made sure to emphasize her heritage; she was not only "the troll."

Psssss-pss hissed the runes cut into the ground. A breeze kicked up, stealing the sound away and bringing the smell of snow back to Donya. It was customary to take the offered tokens but not to keep them. Donya folded Heldrig's tie in on itself. Her hands quickly tied a diamond knot and then another. She placed the elaborate finished product on one of the oozing stumps.

Heldrig had watched her the whole time. When she placed the tie he laughed and shrugged—quickly snapping the bracelet. He piled up the beads around the tie. "That has turned out lovely. I am very pleased, yes very pleased." He said, placing one of the last beads down.

The two stood in silence for a moment.

"I thought you overly formal for suggesting an oath, but it feels nice to be in league with another. It has been too long. I've missed the company to talk to," he said, breaking the moment.

"Yes, I spoke sparingly during my time away," she said. He was right; it made her feel heavier in a pleasant way to have a partner.

"On to Italy then. You have to tell me of your travels. The new world, I never would have thought of you going there. Such a forward-thinker for a troll. Never in my wildest dreams, really." He still had one bead from her bracelet, he moved it between his fingers and he walked ahead of Donya.

They moved back to the car on a slightly different path than they ascended to their oath site. Donya picked up another pinecone and sniffed it before she ate, it had no trace of the black substance. Ahead of her Heldrig prattled on about their route to Italy. All this conversation would make it a long ride. Trolls were not much for speaking, perhaps Heldrig would be pleased if she listened, Donya thought as she dragged her feet. Heldrig had collected the black substance. But Donya did not like it. She especially didn't like it sticking to her shoes.

CHAPTER 5

# SCARLET

The boat was a little small for the number of people on it. There were not enough life vests Scarlet noted, as they motored along the coast. If the shore stayed in view, it wouldn't be anything to worry about. She was a strong swimmer. She had faith in her ability to drag herself and Juan back to land. Her lack of happiness and persistent dark thoughts annoyed her. All morning on the bus ride, people congratulated her on her presentation. If she thought about it too much, it made her neck and cheeks hot.

It was the group's last day together. Juan chatted with Donton again. Upper management seemed enamored with him. She smiled—he was enamoring, even warming her up. She stood at the front of the boat, not talking with anyone. Oddly enough, the fishing trawl had Wi-Fi. It seemed plush for a fishing trawl, but perhaps it was a party boat on the weekends. There were two chats on Messenger and six work emails for her to review. She decided fun first, then work—one message from her mom.

*"Hi, Sweetie. It's cold here, and I'm bored. What are you eating? You said the food hasn't been good. I hope it gets better."*

Her mother had started her food preoccupation. She penned a quick response.

*"The sun is out here. I think it might be warm today. Last night we ate paella. It was good. My favorite dish here has been the patatas bravas. The sauce is spicy."*

She added a selfie of her and Juan, then hit send.

The next message was from Lettie.

*"Hey, So my Mom and Bertha are feeling themselves. When you get a chance, could you send some pictures? I wish they would complain to Juan directly. Never mind... no, I don't, he would feel guilty."*

Poor Lettie. She was in the middle of her semester. Did they really call her to complain? Scarlet did another quick response.

*"Hey Lady, sure, sure. I'll send them more pics. You know I did already, right, those same ones I sent you? Here is an idea. When you graduate, you, me, and Juan move to a tropical island. You can be a vet for the parrots, and I'll give snorkel tours. Juan can cook for us, lol."*

She hit send but didn't open her photos app yet. Let the two busybodies wait a bit more.

Two emails were flagged as "Important." One from Vikki in the lab, subject line, *"Sam Quit."* That was annoying, as Sam only started two weeks ago and came highly recommended. Some people were not cut out for the smell of seafood all day, though. She read through it quickly. There wasn't much she could do from here anyway. They would have to hire someone new.

The second email was from James, a forwarded message, with a note from him saying, *"Let's talk about these numbers."*

The rest could wait. Where was James? She'd seen him on the bus. Scarlet made her way to the back of the boat, where James sat and brooded over his drink. They had a bar set up, and he indulged, strange for someone recovering from illness.

"Hey, just saw your message. And a message that said Sam quit, what a bummer."

"You should check your email in the morning. I sent that last night."

Scarlet felt her stomach sink. They hadn't worked together long, but she had already been caught in his moods before. She needed to figure out what triggered them. Then she could avoid it altogether or find a better way to deal with it. "It's the numbers again."

"Yes, I want you to run the test yourself. I wish you would have done that in the first place."

"I can do that when I get back, but our technicians know the equipment as well as I do."

"This vacation of yours was really poorly planned. It is busy at work; I shouldn't have approved it."

Scarlet couldn't respond. He took a vacation that left him unable to attend any company meetings and most of the conference, and if he thought the numbers were so important, why couldn't he run the experiment himself? He would be at work next Monday.

"Anyway," he continued, finally looking up at her, "I expect you to respond promptly. This vacation doesn't mean you are not an exempt employee. You have to get your work done, approved time or not."

They weren't alone on the back of the boat. Margo, Tran, and a few others had been visiting but fell silent. Scarlet felt her neck heat up.

"Sure, whatever you say. And we can get right on the hiring process when I get back."

"No, that I can handle. I want to change the job description anyway."

"Change what?"

"I think we need to increase the education requirement. A master's level should do."

"The pay will be increased too, then?" Scarlet asked, but she knew the answer.

"No, this is an excellent training opportunity. People will still fight for the job."

"True, but turnover will be awful. Our technicians do an amazing amount of work and take a lot of time to train. We need to be able to retain a few for more than a year."

"I'm sure it will work out."

I'm sure you are an asshole, and it won't, Scarlet thought so hard she felt like she said it. But she stayed silent and bit her lip. She looked up. The boat ride was over, they pulled into a different port, the one the restaurant was at. "Oh, looks like I better go get my stuff."

"One more thing. In the pictures of the trial packs, I noticed that the stickers were crooked."

Scarlet wasn't sure how to respond. She nodded.

"And that data from the bycatch report, the stuff on the server. The names are not capitalized. It doesn't look very professional."

Scarlet's mouth fell a bit open. "No one will see the rough data. The names are there for possible internal reference. It saves keystrokes the way they're entered."

"I think you should go back and change it." He stood up, not waiting for an answer. "See you inside." He stormed past. His face was red.

Scarlet took a few breaths. Letting him get ahead. Then she walked past the group. Margo met her eyes. Her sophisticated face looked pinched. Scarlet hoped that wasn't pity.

CHAPTER 6

# DONYA

Donya liked Florence more than she expected to. The cold wind whipped in off the river, and there was something run-down about the city. It felt like a wilted flower. There were also many bridges; she slept under a different one each day. Why hadn't she tried this city instead of taking her long trip to the new world? She ate well, and she took a man selling ugly art prints out of the back of a van. Heldrig kept a jar of blood, the liver, gonads, gallbladder, and the eyes. He did not eat people, but he needed the parts for spells. This man had one green eye and one blue eye. Nothing special for her, but Heldrig seemed pleased.

She waited for Heldrig now outside the Galleria dell'Accademia. It would not work to set a trap here, she decided. There was no reason for the humans to come here after dark when she could spring it. Otherwise, it would have been perfect, as there were many alleyways and dark corners. If only the Italians kept their museums open later.

She smelled Heldrig before she saw him. That chemical smell of the tanner might be the bane of her existence. She stepped out of her shadowed corner to meet him. He still looked strange to her with the orange tint; why couldn't he use a spell instead? He passed under a small light on the adjacent building, and his glassy black hair shone.

"This place will not work," Donya called.

"Yes, I can see that. It is fine. I have procured the last bit of paper I required. We will not need to wait and set a trap. We shall have them in hand this very night." His obsidian teeth gleamed in the distant light.

"A trap is safer. We will be sure to catch them that way."

"Small troll, I know your people love a good trap, but this will save us time. And as they say, time is money."

"You are talking nonsense again, Heldrig." She couldn't afford another hindrance. She must rein him in. During their car ride, she'd realized he'd changed in the century and a half since she saw him last, falling in with humans, using money, using beauty products. He had always been odd, as expected of the only lone Azish she knew of. However, she felt this was getting extreme. It was her fault. She knew she rushed into this bargain and would pay the price. She cracked open her mouth to speak again.

Heldrig spoke first. "I underestimated that redhead you spoke of, that is all. Perhaps I also overestimated your strength as well. You are exceedingly weak; you could not focus back in Uppsala." He looked down his long narrow nose at her.

Donya closed her mouth and looked back at him, her face a blank mask. He had her; she was weak. If she ate humans daily for a hundred years, she would not gain the strength she would get from eating this one young man. Humans were not a troll's favorite food. Rusted saxifrages seeds were, and they were more potent. She missed the harvest season this year, and they were difficult to find. All the seeds would be gone now.

"Fine, let us get to it," she said.

"Follow me, my tiny turnip-faced friend," Heldrig responded, with a smile that was cruel and cold.

They walked along the dark streets. Humans were everywhere, and many of the females took notice of Heldrig. He was tall, well-dressed, and walked with confidence. With his mouth closed, he looked almost entirely human. His movements were just a touch more graceful and a little fast. He never blinked, but one would need to stare to notice such behavior.

"Here we are, my abode for now," Heldrig said as they approached a dilapidated hotel.

Donya liked the look of this place. It stood solid, older than the buildings around it. She could feel its stones. They'd been transported here maybe four or five hundred years ago. Heldrig led her up the worn stairs—the centers lower from many feet passing over them through the years. He waited on the second floor.

"I found this tome in a local bookstore. It had been used to press flowers and forgotten. This spell works best for me with paper that has been against a flower. In most cases, I set this up myself. However, we lack time, and I did not pack appropriately when you found me and begged for my assistance," he chuckled to himself as they stepped inside his suite.

Donya was unsure what he found funny. She did not respond, watching as he lit a white candle and set down the book. He reached into his black bag set against a table. He held several small envelopes; she could smell them. Herbs. One was very distinctive, the woody stem of witch-hazel ground to fine dust. Then he brought out two vials, one of rancid oil and one of the black sludge from the clearing. She needed to ask him about that material—not now.

Heldrig leafed through his newly-acquired book. "Here it is. This page held a yellow petunia against it for many, many years, very powerful." He ripped out the sheet, opened his envelopes of powder, and scattered some on. "Now, I need you to concentrate with all the power of your tiny troll mind. You did not get their names but see them as clearly in your memory as you can. You said the woman felt strange, that she made you feel hot and driven away. Think of this phenomenon. Feel it all again. Keep doing this until we get where we need to go." He set down the paper, unstopped the oil, placed three drops on his left palm, turned over his hand, and slapped it on the paper. It stuck to him, clinging to the oil, and he held it all over the flame. The old paper caught fire quickly, the flame light blue. The second vial he opened, then imbibed in one shot.

She watched the blue flame as she let her mind fade into what he wanted. Donya thought back to both humans. They were middle height, skin still smooth as younger humans tended to possess, nothing sagged yet. The redhead appeared older than the man by a few years; she had less fat on her cheeks. His hair was black, and his skin a healthy brown. He had long enough hair to wear it tied back, a style not of this time, and he wore glasses that hid brown eyes. He smiled most of the time, his teeth very white. On the plane, he drank water. If Donya tried to think of his smell, trolls love smells, she thought he smelled like icy water or snow as it melted.

The woman had pale skin. She did not get enough light for a human. Her smell was of roasted grains and herbs, perhaps a touch of cacao. Pudgier than the average, she wore loose-fitting clothes to disguise the extra weight. It was harder to get her details because looking at her even made Donya's eyes feel hot. She used this to jump into the sensation emanating from that redhead—heat and revulsion—the level of both seemed to fluctuate. The revulsion Donya noticed as she approached them on the plane but it became overwhelmed by the magnetism of the boyfriend. Then when the redhead looked up, it hit her like a wall. That was when the heat started.

The room suddenly smelled damp. Donya felt space and time shift. She closed her eyes, continuing to concentrate, thinking of his high cheekbones and pure warm heart. They drew toward the humans. This was not just a locator spell; it really would pull them to where the humans were. Her vision faded—darkness ensued.

Something audibly snapped near her. Then Donya was all wet and gasping. Her vision came back. They stood in the same room. Everything around them dripped water, and the table was cracked in two. "What happened? We were almost there."

Heldrig's brow wrinkled. He looked angry and spent. "The Kraken happened. They are in Venice. She controls that city. We could not enter."

CHAPTER 7

# SCARLET

Scarlet thought Venice was amazing. They arrived at night, in the rain on the Ides of March, and got terribly lost. Only their smartphones saved them from never finding the hotel, which was warm, dry and cozy. The hotel was pleasingly appointed, and clean, with a lovely little osteria around the corner. Juan declared their first meal of gnocchi perfect. The soft dumplings were so tender they practically melted in one's mouth. To celebrate making it to Italy, they finished the meal with a lemon gelato for dessert, even though they were both full. It had limoncello poured over it. Juan loved it. Between that and the red wine they sipped, both left a bit drunk. Scarlet barely noticed something shimmering and squiggly in a puddle in front of a pizzeria two doors from the restaurant.

She added it to her list, though.

*San Francisco to Stockholm, troll on plane. March.*

*Malaga, sad red balloons in palm trees playing with monk parakeets. March*

*Venice, curly ribbon in a puddle, nighttime. March 15th.*

The next morning the sun shined bright. They looked up St. Mark's Square and what time a walking tour of Venice started. Offline Google maps of the city were uploaded to both their phones, and they felt confident. It took a while walking. The streets and canals were lined with so much to see—tiny, elaborate bridges, bobbing boats, and beautiful old buildings. They stopped a few times to take pictures. The walking tour began at three pm, and they had the whole morning open and time for lunch.

They approached St. Mark's on several occasions but their way was blocked by around six inches of water sloshing in the street. "I heard Venice was sinking, but I didn't think they were already underwater," Scarlet said to Juan as they came upon another small pond.

"We could buy those rubber booties we keep seeing for sale."

"The neon plastic galoshes? There's gotta be a dry way to get there. Those things are a waste of money."

They turned toward the lagoon; it looked blue and clean in the strong sunlight. Juan led the way with his exceptional sense of direction. "We need to turn left here."

"These streets are so twisty. It's amazing. You know they used to use it as a defense. Intruders would get lost, and they would ambush them with all kinds of horrible stuff thrown from the tall buildings," Scarlet explained as she looked at another store selling decorative carnival masks. "Should we buy masks today or tomorrow?"

"Save shopping for tomorrow—today's for exploring."

They passed a gelateria. Scarlet wondered if they should have gelato before lunch, eyeing the chocolate with cherries. She wanted to enjoy the food as much as possible on this trip, not caring if she gained more weight. Suddenly, the narrow passage opened onto St. Mark's Square. They came out on a corner. It was elevated about a foot above the square that was entirely flooded.

"What in the world!" Scarlet cried as she looked around. Her mind did not process what she saw. Raised platforms lead up to the basilica from the square's edge, and hundreds of people stood in line upon them. More people milled around along the side of the square; all the raised spaces were packed. "I guess we need to use the platforms," she finally stammered.

"Let's buy galoshes."

"They're cheap. They won't last, and then we will be all wet."

Juan looked out at the few dozen people shin-deep in the water wading around the square. They all wore galoshes over their shoes and pants. No one seemed to be complaining, and they appeared to be the happiest people in the whole area. "I'm going to go check how much they cost." He squeezed through the crowd to the nearest stand. The stand he chose was in the square inches off of the league. The bottom stood submerged in water. The merchandise all hung clear of the pool. "Signore, how much?" he asked, gesturing to the square packages of galoshes.

"Ten euros." The shopkeeper believed in his merchandise, he sported a pair of the bright galoshes.

"Let's get them," Juan said, looking back at Scarlet, who pushed through people to stay caught up to him. "It's gonna be flooded all over the place. We can use them a bunch, and who even knows how long this will last."

The vendor looked up. "It will be done in maybe… hour."

"Really? But there is so much water," Juan asked with a smile.

"It is the… the… ocean water."

"The tides?" Scarlet questioned.

"Yes, yes. Twice a day. You will hear alarm," the vendor said. He handed them two neon blue packages.

"We heard that this morning," Juan said.

It was true. As they finished their bread and apricot jam, a siren went off. Scarlet had wondered what it meant, but the hotel owner stepped away and she forgot to ask later.

Juan, still smiling, handed the man twenty euros. "Thank you. Have a nice day."

"Ughhhhh, I never heard about this at all," Scarlet whined as she found a shop doorway to huddle in, out of the way of the crowd. More people kept arriving, packing the edges of the square. The air started to feel warm from all the close bodies.

"It's cool," Juan said as he shimmied into the plastic. They both got large. The galoshes came with rubber bands that other people doubled up about mid-calf height. The tops were elastic but didn't make a faultless seal. "There!" Juan exclaimed, looking up at her. "Let me take your purse, my princess." He snatched away the purse while Scarlet struggled with the first galosh. After another minute of hassle, Scarlet had both over her shoes.

They walked up to the water, stepped off the ledge, departing from the landlocked crowd. The galoshes stayed dry on the inside. It felt amazing. The water pressed against the outside of the plastic was chilly and refreshing. The air smelled fresh out in the open space, the sky a pure blue, no clouds anywhere.

Of course, there stood the big church and bell tower at the front of the Square. But Juan scrutinized the water. Floating around inside of it were little pieces of pink, yellow, and blue confetti. "Look at all of this."

Scarlet watched him. She'd noticed the specks too. Some of the stone blocks of the square contained holes. Water bubbled up from some of them, and confetti went down other holes, she thought the tide was going out. But then as she inspected a different area the colored particles would float back up. "It must be from carnival," she said. Out of the corner of her eye she saw an older lady looking at them, holding up a camera in her hand.

"Excuse me, could ya get a picture of us?" the woman asked. She had blonde highlights in a pixie cut framing her round face.

"Yep, Juan, can you do it? You know I am terrible at taking pictures," Scarlet answered. Nine out of ten of her photos turned out blurry.

The lady traveled with two other women who could have been her sisters or old friends with merged styles. All of them wore short hair, dark-wash blue jeans, and brightly patterned blouses. They stood with their backs to the basilica, the two outer ones popping one leg back in a cute pose. Juan took about twenty pictures, half with a camera and half with their phones.

When they finished, Juan asked, "could you get a couple of us?"

"A course, a course, and thank ya much for getting all those of us!" the first lady said while scrolling through the pictures on her camera. When she finished Scarlet handed over her phone for the photos.

They posed with the same backdrop. Scarlet tried to pop her leg like the ladies had done. It made her forget to smile, though. They needed pictures with them in it, something to look back on when they were old and gray, but she was self-conscious about her appearance. Perhaps at least one photo would be good enough to send to their families and post online.

"Give him a hug, sweetie!" The lady yelled after a few poses. Scarlet obliged and put her arms around Juan.

Sloshing back up to the woman, Juan took back the phone. "Thank you," he said, then added, "this water is amazing."

"Isn't it? I planned this trip so we could see an *acqua alta*."

"Does it happen on a schedule?" Juan asked.

"Mmm-hmm October ta March. I lived in Italy for a whole year and never made it up here at the right time for it. The wind needs ta blow just right, and you need a good high tide. Today is perfect. Where're you kids from?"

"California," Juan answered.

"Us too, San Diego."

"Monterey," Juan said.

"We just moved there," Scarlet added. She watched the woman's mouth, not sure if her strange accent was because of where she hailed from or to do with her mouth shape.

"I've been there. It's so nice. Very romantic. You two enjoy yer getaway." She waved, and they were off, splashing across the piazza-sized pool.

Scarlet's eyes followed the trio, and when they reached about a dozen feet away, something moved in the water at their feet. Was it that same puddle ribbon from last night?

Scarlet focused on it. If it was this prevalent, it needed more study than one small note. Delicate and curling in the sunlight, it looked almost translucent. It contained black specks and confetti inside its body. Fern fiddleheads came to mind, but this was thinner, more fragile. What a strange little spirit, she thought. She felt calmer than usual when she noticed something like this. Maybe it was the perfect weather or the water. She did love water. Pondering it, she had never seen any spirits in water before. Until now, she did not think they existed. She scanned the square; this seemed to be the only one. Its long body emerged from out of the quarter-sized drains.

In an unusual move for her, she started to walk toward it. Juan still looked through the pictures on her phone. The small slender thing curled up and went under the stone floor. To lure it out, she fished around her jacket pocket. She came out with a few dried orange blossoms. Dropping them into the water, she whispered "Come out pretty ribbon." Nothing happened. The dried petals floated like boats on the surface.

Then she saw it, there, twenty feet away. It gradually unfurled around a family's legs. The leaves of the frond were minute. It seemed fragile. Scarlet moved towards it again, this time Juan catching up to her. She saw him aim the phone at her a few times, trying to catch some candid shots.

"What you lookin' at?"

"The confetti and the drains." She was happy something was interesting in the water to give her a cover story.

"Yeah, there's a lot over there. Maybe it is the main drain."

He could see the confetti in the tendril, but not the tendril. They were close now. The 'leaves' slowly gathered confetti. The tip of a tendril swayed against a child's foot. The girl smiled at the colorful water.

Scarlet decided it was harmless and turned her back on it, feeling a bit foolish at trying to use logic on a spirit. "What shall we do next? Gelato? Or the church?"

"We are close to the church, so let's go in there first."

There stood a small line of a dozen people waiting in the water by the platform to get into the church. The platform line stayed hundreds deep and growing. "Do we wait in the short line?" Scarlet asked, knowing it didn't seem fair.

"Don't know, let's ask one of the security guys that are everywhere," Juan answered, already making a beeline to the nearest uniformed man.

"Hello, excuse me, do we wait in that line to get in?" he said, pointing at the short line.

"Yes," the man standing in a power pose with big black rubber boots on responded in a tone that seemed to imply their stupidity for asking.

"Okay, thanks," Juan said, turning. He looked annoyed at the response but went to the back of the short line with Scarlet.

It took minutes, and they ascended the smooth marble steps. A few people still stood in front of them, but Juan and Scarlet's feet were out of the water. Scarlet turned back to the square to look out over all of it from this higher vantage point. The water glinted in the sunlight. The bell tower stood red and firm in the large shallow pool. Everywhere in the water, Scarlet could see hundreds of the tendrils extending, moving in the water, collecting its tiny bits of color and light. None were free-swimming. All stayed anchored in their drains. Scarlet realized they were all connected, like an enormous spirit tube worm. Someplace under the floors, down in the dark brackish water, there was a very large, very hungry main body.

CHAPTER 8

# DONYA

First, an errant bag then the Kraken, Donya thought the fates were against her. They needed to be more precise, she considered the variables in the plan hatched after their second failure. She walked through the train station. It was brightly lit after dark. It had a centrally-located seating area where she could wait all night, and to the left of it a stairwell where she would keep watch in the day. The staircase stood windowless, the walls lined with thin veneers of marble. They were newly placed but enough like a tomb that she felt at home.

Heldrig, depleted by the rebound off his casting, was irritable and acted even more peculiar. For this trap, one of the variables she hoped to eliminate was timing. She asked an especially bitter cornerstone in the Santa Maria Novella if what she sought would come to Florence via a train and what day. It responded "yes" but would not give up the day—stones often knew more than they let on. Instead, it began to tell the tale of how the façade stones were unwelcome interlopers. Donya needed to know the details of the human's arrival, but unlike the cornerstone, the future was not her forte. She also did not want to bring anyone else in.

Their plot consisted of Heldrig getting his act together enough to cast a good disguise spell. She would be a lost child and ask the young man for help. Meanwhile, Heldrig would wait, with a sleep spell in a blind spot. Donya would get at least the young man to follow her, and hopefully, both humans. Heldrig would drag them into sleep. In sleep, the redhead's power should be neutralized.

First, they needed to get the proper dates in line. Then they needed to get the spells worked out and gather any additional ingredients required. Pulling off a disguise spell on someone with the sight would be difficult.

Donya left the train station. Construction befuddled the streets, but she feared no cars. Hitting her would be like hitting a boulder. She followed the streets. Heldrig had moved to a room a few blocks from the train station. It was a necessity after the ruination of the last suite and the stench of foiled magic that hung around the place.

Heldrig's new stronghold was in a hotel, mid-range, with a piano in the reception area and a tired clerk behind the desk. He never even looked up at her as she passed. She knew the room number. The elevator up to the fourth floor labored under her weight. Outside the door, she smelled a mineral scent that reminded her of home. She knocked softly.

"Enter," Heldrig said from inside. He was barely audible.

Donya pushed the door open. The entire inside of the room was covered with paper, pages from books, old yellow pages, and new white shiny ones. Pages that held illustrations and pages marked only in black text. All the pages curled, still drying from the other night.

"The station. It is a good layout, not a lot of places for them to hide while waiting for a train. I believe we should work on finding out their schedule. Then grab him before their train departure."

"That only gives us the one chance." Heldrig glanced up from his reading. It was new. It had not been soddened by the Kraken.

Donya noticed his face was lined. His black hair looked oily at the crown of his head. "One well-arranged trap seems to be our best chance in this instance. We are both… not at our… strongest."

"Fool," he spat.

"We have an oath."

"I have pondered at length. I need to learn more about the, as you say, redhead. We should not ignore her; she could be worth something too."

"No, we agreed to what we would do," Donya thought for a moment. She did not want to give in to this.

"You need to appreciate the bigger picture. You cannot see the forest for the trees, or perhaps in your case, the pebbles for the canyon."

"You need to be less greedy," Donya used his phrasing, then added, "if you want to learn more about her, you can use their time in Florence. Follow her."

Heldrig narrowed his pinched eyes. "Fine. We stick to the plan. Now go find schedules—trains, planes, and automobiles. Be useful."

Had she not found things out every night? She so far was the only useful one in this pact. If she tended to oath break, she would leave him now and try to get the human on her own. Bells tolled outside, causing both Heldrig and Donya to flinch. The bells were a nuisance to them both. Finally, she said, "I have no aptitude as a seer."

"You have money?"

"Yes." She was unsure where this could be going.

"Go pay a fortune teller. I saw a good one in the tourist area the day we arrived. He is still around; I can feel him."

"Fine. How many questions can he answer?"

"Two queries with accuracy, but he might be able to get a third in. If you pay him extra, he can go into more detail. Also, he is human. You better hope he doesn't feel the need to protect others of his species."

"Humans always pick money over their species," Donya scoffed. She couldn't even believe she must say this out loud to Heldrig. He knew.

"Well, not humans who have an idea what is coming for them in the end," he said with a cough.

The seer was not hard to find. He did not try to cover his trail. Donya came to him with no ill will, even though she was sure he would make an excellent and hearty meal. His apartment lay on the outskirts of the town, over the river from the tourist section. A black dog sat tied up outside the building. It growled low in its throat as she approached. The night was icy and vibrant, the wind at her back.

The questions she decided to ask were, "what is the train and plane schedule of the one I seek?" And her other question would be, "what do I need to know now?" Both vague but structured. She brought three thousand Euros, a reasonable price for a true telling. She would ask him the third question, the one Heldrig wanted to be asked, "what stands in our way?" If they got an answer, they got one.

She was not sure why she gave her question more importance than Heldrig's. Perhaps it was that she lost confidence in him with each passing night. If the answers she got were decent, she had an extra thousand Euros to give to the seer.

The door was freshly painted. Donya could smell the chemicals leaking off it into the crisp air as she knocked. Her ears picked up movement inside. He expected her. The door opened and a mustached man, only a few inches taller than her, stood in the opening. He stepped to one side, so she walked in. She did not need a verbal invitation from anyone. The stone floors were covered with layers of threadbare carpet. The tones of the inside of the house were mostly browns and reds, the lights all old, no new bright LEDs. Donya liked it.

The man went and sat on the least worn carpet, a small potted plant next to him, some sort of grass, and a bowl of water directly behind him. He looked up at her, his eyes dark in the lighting. "Ask."

She finished examining the room. Children's shoes lay shoved against a couch. He had a family that lived here with him. They were out. He must have sent them out for tonight. Smart. She dug into her black purse, pulled out the first thousand Euros, and laid the money on a low coffee table.

"What is the train and plane schedule of the one I seek?" she asked, still standing in front of him.

He peered at the money on the table. He touched the blades of grass near their bright green tops, and a lemon scent filled the air. Donya, who'd never been to the tropics for obvious reasons, felt something like warm, humid air for the first time.

"There is a ticket to this city already purchased for Monday the nineteenth' arriving in daylight. No other train tickets have been purchased." He paused, eyes flickered to the money, then continued, "there is an idea to use the train to leave for Roma on Friday the twenty-third. They may use a train or bus on the twenty-first to go to Pisa. Finally, there is a plane ticket booked on Wednesday the twenty-eighth." At that, he turned around at an angle that must be uncomfortable to the human spine, and still seated, he reached for the water behind him. Put three fingers in and brought the hand to his forehead. He rested the moist fingertips on his third eye.

Donya blinked. That was precisely what she needed. She noticed his look at the payment. He needed this money. Pop, her tiny purse opened, and she pulled out the next thousand and piled it on top of the first. If he gave her this good of information, more Euros would come. She never lacked money. It was basically worthless to her, but she found it practical, so she kept what she came across. She inhaled the still-warm lemon-perfumed air. "What do I need to know?"

His eyes lingered on the money. This time he touched the blades of the grass in the middle. "Your partner was alone because he betrayed his whole clan. His clan is gone even from the troll history because of this action."

She felt her face flash cold. "Troll histories go back to before Asgard had a wall," she said with gravel in her voice.

"I am not finished. What you need and what you seek are two different things. Finally, your designs, as of this moment, will fail," he paused and continued, "a little piece of home can hold you down. This is true for humans and trolls." He once again reached around for the water and applied it to his forehead. "Ask again. This will be from the root. The dirt muddies the answer sometimes."

It took Donya a moment to make her mouth move, her jaw was locked shut. "What stands in Heldrig's and my way?"

He pressed hard at the whitish base of the grass. Donya heard the crisp sound of tender cellulose breaking. "You have angered the Kraken. It loves humans; they built it the city of Venice. They feed it with love and beauty. It tasted your plan within that casting. It will now endeavor to thwart you. Then there is a woman. She is a new bloodline with no training but plenty of willpower. If she embraced her gifts instead of shunning them, your current dreams would be dashed, and Heldrig would die."

Donya had not moved since she walked in. Now she reached up and pulled a lock of hair back behind her stubby ear. The warmth left the room. She watched as the man put his fingers in the water. She tossed more money on the pile. Then she turned and walked out the door. The dog growled and let out a bark as she stepped onto the cobblestones of the street. Heldrig needed to know about the first and third answers. She wasn't sure what to do with the second. Changing their scheme needed to be done. Leaving Heldrig in the dark would be best. Who told her Heldrig's clan died in battle; he was the sole survivor, saved by some witch from a slow death of a nasty wound? She held no recollection in her of where the information came from—none of it true. Who had she made a deal with?

CHAPTER 9

# SCARLET

Scarlet lay in bed next to Juan. The room was dark, it was after midnight, and she needed to use the restroom. Groggy from sleep, she knew the toilet lay down the hall, not attached to their room. They only had a sink inside the room, which had been great for washing up after they made love but couldn't help her now. She blinked into the darkness on the floor. Where were her pajama bottoms, she wondered? Standing up, she felt along the floor with her foot. Her toes contacted a shoe on the second swipe and encountered the pile of clothes she searched for after another couple of passes. She remembered wiggling out of the pajamas in an attempt to be seductive after her shower.

Making herself presentable, she walked out into the dimly lit hall. The hotel was immaculately clean but sadly cramped. The bathroom was a nice size, but the addition of the bidet made it hard to maneuver. Here in Italy, the bidet was a separate structure unconnected to the toilet.

Finishing her business in the bathroom, she headed back to the room, knowing she would never be able to fall back asleep. It was hard enough at home, where she memorized the floor plan and could stumble to the bathroom naked and mostly asleep. She kept quiet as she entered their room, not for Juan's sake—he slept like the just—not a worry or care, peaceful, except for the snoring. She stayed quiet for the sake of any other patrons, making sure the heavy wooden door closed with a soft click instead of the loud bang it tended towards.

Stopping by the edge of the bed, she opened a water bottle and took a drink; it annoyed her that when she woke up to pee she was also thirsty. It seemed a betrayal, her kidneys doing too good of a job. She left the bottle open for ease of drinking later. Laying back in the darkened room, she listened to Juan snore. The sound didn't bother her in the slightest, she even found it soothing. His profile remained visible to her in the darkened room. He always snored the loudest on his back, sporadically gasping. He needed to get his tonsils out or his deviated septum fixed—something like that.

Warm and safe in bed, she let her mind wander back over the day. The creature in the water had really been impressive. Checking the tide chart for tomorrow would be in order. She wanted to avoid that thing in the future, even though it didn't seem to do anyone any harm. Why take the risk? Especially with Juan. She loved him; lying there next to him, she was happy, perhaps happier than she'd ever been.

Before their tour that day, they stopped in a small shop and bought calzones, which made Juan laugh. Apparently, a calzone was a type of woman's underwear in Spanish. Not a sexy variety, more like a bloomer. The calzones were perfect. He got mushroom and speck, and she mushroom. His had been too big to finish, so he asked for a bag from the shop owner to take it with him. Afraid he was displeased with the food, the man asked what he thought and why he did not finish. Juan replied that the meal was simple and delicious. He just needed to finish it later.

The shop owner repeated simple and delicious, with such a look of gratitude on his face. Scarlet tried to understand the encounter. Juan naturally appreciated the little things, his daily life was filled with gratitude. If it had been her or most other tourists, the shop owner would have ended up insulted. Not with Juan. Juan, for lack of a better word, was different from other people. Maybe she could tell him about what she could see. Maybe he would think her unique, not a total freak. Perhaps it wouldn't matter to him.

She rolled over at the sound of another gasp, poked Juan in the side, and muttered, "babe turn over."

Juan did as he was told; she saw him blink a few times as he rolled. He reached up with the arm he'd rolled on and patted his side, a signal to her to cuddle closer. Scarlet scooched up, pressing against his back and wrapping her arm around him. He grabbed her hand and cradled it against him, "what's wrong?"

"Nothing—got up to pee and now can't fall back asleep."

"Mmmmm." He kissed her hand. "Maybe if we do it again, you'll sleep."

"Maybe," she said, nuzzling into his neck. His hair tickled her nose. She was too tired to want to go for another round, but teasing him was fun. "Go back to sleep. I'll wake you back up if I really can't fall asleep."

"Okay," he mumbled, then moved her hand, "you know, I'm ready."

She kissed his shoulder, "I know, you're always ready."

He reached up and readjusted his pillow, then snuggled into the bedding. Scarlet waited; he snored again within a minute. How could anyone fall asleep that quickly? She wished silently that she knew his trick. She held him in the dark. Her chest felt tight. There was no way she could risk moments like this. It would be silly to tell him about her secret now. It didn't help or hurt anyone to say something.

Scarlet let her mind wander, needing to find another subject. A train of thought without an air of self-destruction. Seeing how huge that spirit was earlier reminded her of the last time she saw anything so big.

It was a dragon. This was one of the few times a spirit frightened her. She visited the hot springs with a couple of friends. Elyse, Dakato and she used to frequent the secluded spa. The spring was located about forty minutes into the hills. It was expensive but worth it. Her skin always glowed after a trip. The sulfur in the water calmed and rejuvenated it. Laying back in one of the tubs with water about half full and the perfect temperature, she felt euphoric and relaxed. A beautiful California spring day unfolded around them, blue sky, white puffy clouds rolling in from the west, then dissipating as they hit the warmer air. She watched the clouds. The dragon rolled in the exact same color, long and looping. There were several sets of wings along the body. Long tendrils also flowed out into the sky, giving the giant an appearance of a fancy kite. The only color it had other than the cloud white was its great green eyes. They spotted her as it came over the hill. At first, she hadn't felt afraid. At first, she hadn't really noticed its large size.

It came closer, right to her. Her friends in the tubs on either side of her were silent. They couldn't see it, of course. They read books and magazines, relaxing with their drinks. It wound through the air toward her, never looking away. As it approached, she understood its size, maybe three hundred feet long, its body the width of a great sequoia.

It stopped and hovered over her. She could easily fit in its mouth. It opened its jaws, but all it did was breathe out. Its breath was bracing as it whirled around Scarlet's head. Distantly, she heard her friends squeal as the wind tickled them. Scarlet didn't move, gazing back. She tried to reach down inside her emotions—feel angry, feel calm—feel anything that wasn't a sort of shaky panic. Do something in what could be her last moments that weren't screaming in terror. It was too large. Both the order she asked of her body and the dragon. She lay there staring up into its great green eye. Then it inhaled. It inhaled like a cat sniffing fresh food—tasting the air. Finally, the dragon blinked leisurely, its eyelashes the size of eagle feathers. It repositioned its large head, pointing back up to the sky, and glided away, still heading toward the east.

Scarlet preferred to ponder the future, not think about the past—the past was done. The dragon should have been a once-in-a-lifetime event. Clearly, there were more spirits here, some of them very big, like in the water. When they got back to California, life would go back to her version of normal. It would probably be decades before she saw any spirit larger than a crow back home.

They overslept that morning. Scarlet faintly heard the siren go off for the tide, then closed her eyes and fell back to sleep. They hadn't set the alarm because they were exhausted the night before. Her watch tracked their movements and said they walked 13,525 steps. She believed it too. Her feet throbbed when she took her shoes off.

Today was supposed to be their more relaxed day in Venice. Rain was in the forecast, so they bought a museum pass to tour the prison and old palaces. They brought their galoshes in case they needed them. The prison was depressing, as one expected. It was cold outside and wet, but the inside of the thick-walled structure felt like being inside a musty refrigerator. Yesterday the tour guide showed them the Bridge of Sighs from the outside. She explained, in an entirely too upbeat of a manner, that to be sentenced to stay in this prison for any length of time was basically a death sentence. It flooded in the winter, and everyone died from the cold and disease. Although originally, it had been built as a new, more humane place.

Scarlet wondered if she would see something in the prison. A human ghost would be new to her, and it seemed like a place where one could be. Nothing was there. She peeked into every cell. She descended a slippery stone staircase with Juan behind her, still, no ghosts.

"After this, we are going to go on a gondola, right?" Juan asked from the darkness. They hadn't spoken much during their inspection of the cold stone structure.

"A walk around the palace first," she reminded him. "I hope it will be warmer there. I get why people say they are chilled to the bone."

"Yeah, no, I meant after that. Do you want my hoodie?"

"Then you will freeze? Nah, I'll warm up when we get out of here." They came out into a courtyard, through a door most prisoners used to dread.

She took Juan's hand, and they headed into the Doge's Palace. Catching a bit from a guided English tour, they saw an archway with historic interest. At some point, much had been invested in it. Anyone entering the seat of power would be impressed. The colors were all gold and red. The repeating shapes were octagons and perfect circles. The images portrayed contained symbolic significance, a God holding a trident, a man taming beasts. It was lovely, and the symmetry and colors brought on the feeling of order and warmth. Juan and Scarlet stopped to take pictures and marvel at the sight.

Inside there were more inlaid paintings. There were even paintings that looked like sculptures. Scarlet craned her neck, trying to figure out a pattern. Fat winged babies, one of her favorite subjects, floated, and Kings and their crowns tumbled down. Silk-robed figures plucked at harps. In the middle was a bare-breasted woman with a large plume. She also had fat babies and a strange beast in the painting. What struck Scarlet was this painting's irregular shape, all done in grayscale, which made it far more interesting than the rest. She wondered at the animal. Was it a mythological beast? Or a lion? It had a tail and claws like a lion, but the face seemed more ape-like.

"Which one's your favorite?" Juan asked, breaking yet another long stretch of silence.

"Oh, the gray one right there."

"It's cool. It is almost all too much, huh?" He paused then pointed, "my favorite is the fake statue paintings in the corners. I think the color they used is just right, and I like how it looks a little like they are moving."

"Yep, I really like those ones too. I wonder if they made them that color to resemble bronze?"

"Maybe." He smiled at Scarlet. "When we are rich, I think I want a painting like that."

Scarlet giggled, "better buy a lotto ticket."

They kept walking through the grand room and made it to a weapon repository. All kinds of ancient spears, swords, and armor were in glass cases. Fewer people milled about here than in the main room. One woman with fawn-colored hair and a large pearl necklace stood close to them. She kept her hands clasped behind her back. Scarlet took a similar posture; everything looked pointy. In the second room, Juan walked up to a suit of armor, studied it for a moment, and said, "they put this pin in wrong."

"What, how could you know that?" Scarlet was getting hungry, and the question came out entirely too incredulous.

"See, it's upside down. It would work its way out while moving around. If you put it in the other way, gravity would help keep it in."

Inspecting it for a few more seconds, Scarlet conceded, "you're right. Maybe you should come work here and show these guys how to put a display together."

She watched him for a while after that, the old-timey machinery of war almost entirely lost on her. Juan was in his element. Naturally observant and mechanically inclined, he probably could spend hours more here. She needed to remember to take him to more museums in the States. Although she wasn't sure if they had anything like this in California. Maybe he would enjoy a museum back east, or a Civil War reenactment.

He bent over a golden helmet with a beautiful etched pattern, a matching halberd laying to the left. Scarlet gave it to the Italians; they certainly had style, even with their weaponry. She hated to interrupt him, but it was almost two, and all the good restaurants might close soon for their afternoon break. They needed to head out if they wanted to eat. So, she mock whispered, "Hey, love, you ready for pizza?"

He looked up at her with a perfect smile and puppy dog eyes. "Yes."

CHAPTER 10

# DONYA

"I'm going to need this jug filled with fresh human blood," Heldrig said to Donya, holding out a large, old terracotta jug. "Do not open it until you have fresh blood to pour in; I have a few fine papers in there. They need to be steeped." He looked back to his desk at a glass vial and then thought better of what he would say. "Slit some human's throat and drain the still live blood into here. Yes, that ought to give the best results."

"Why me? I have other things to do."

"Donya, Donya, Donya, you find the most perfect specimens. It is like you specifically know in your granite heart what will work best. And we need the best right now." He grabbed at a book bound in human leather and laid it open in front of her. "Furthermore, I have to be busy tonight with those last-minute changes you requested. I am doing my best to prepare. A daytime train, really, they picked the worst time for you. Not to mention, I came upon a tiny but strong spell which could help us immediately, or at least in the very near future, despite the Kraken."

"Fine, yet know that I have my own business, and this is a hindrance to me," Donya said, standing firm. She peered at the words, brown letters in a language she did not know. It became ever more evident Heldrig used her for his purpose and kept her out of the loop on all he planned.

Heldrig's brow furrowed. "Really, you have business? What could it be?"

She was prepared. "I met a stone here, red granite, brought up from Egypt two thousand years ago. It was a piece of an obelisk. I am going to try to help it find its missing sections."

"This far north? I thought all the obelisks were in Rome."

"This one has been missing for a very long time."

"Fine, by all means, help the rock," he paused and huffed, "but please, get the blood as well."

Donya was pleased. There was no obelisk, she had successfully lied to Heldrig.

Out in the night, she stalked the city. It was a Saturday, yet the streets were relatively empty. It was strange for her to be unsure of what she needed to do. Obviously, a pure virgin child would work best for the blood, but should she do what was best for Heldrig? Would it get her the young man's heart in the end? Why did she have all these thoughts and feelings? A troll should just be, like a stone, but able to move. She kicked a tiny pebble, which shrieked with glee at rolling.

Donya was not enough like other trolls. Not as still, not as strong. All the things she did to remedy this made it worse. When she'd been very young, she even thought humans were praiseworthy. They loved stones better than trolls, even better than dwarves. When she was young, she heard tales of humans moving great stones over thousands of miles to build their holy places. They decorated the stones, polished them, and moved them around until they were in the most perfect position. The loving treatment made the stones happy. Certain humans even seemed to hear the stones speak, which gave them something in common with trolls.

Her lie had brought her a bit of free time, and distance from Heldrig. What she needed to do now was find a good old stone and ask for advice. Maybe not any stone, one that could understand a crisis, one that dealt with humans. She turned to the left—she knew the place.

Arriving at Cartier, she called in through the glass to see if any crystals were awake. A light blue diamond spoke up, calling back a cheery but muffled, "Hello?" Donya asked the blocks in the wall, and they let her pass through with a little rearrangement.

"Good night to you shining one."

"Aaa goodm nigh oo you as wele."

"Here, allow me to help you; you have platinum in your mouth." Donya bent a prong out of the diamond's mouth.

"You are too kind. It bothered me for months. I had half a mind to wiggle loose the first chance I got. Fall into a river and be swept away!" She shimmied in her setting. It was beautifully done, the bright metal setting off her facets. "Now you have done me a favor, and I owe you three."

"For that, no. I came here to get something from you in any case. Please answer my questions, then we will be settled."

"You have something to talk about with me? How exciting. No one around here ever talks. I am ecstatic!"

Donya felt a little taken aback. Now that she was here, she was unsure what to say. "I need…" she trailed off, then started again. "I am unsure of…"

The diamond cut her off, "you have fallen in love and are unsure if you should run off together?"

"What… no… no, no!"

"Then what is it?"

"I don't know what to do with anything!" she said, her voice rising a bit.

"What to do with anything?" The diamond sounded puzzled.

"Let me explain," and so Donya did, and it took a while as she started with when she was a small troll and liked humans fine, then her eventual disenchantment, and ended with the last week coming back from the new world, running into the couple and then teaming up with Heldrig.

"My dear, you are in a pickle. Here's the thing, I was so excited when I was dug up from the ground. I wanted to be in the sun. I wanted what others whispered of—romance. I wanted a human to put me on another human's finger and then spend the rest of their life carrying me around. But that is not how existence worked out. I am very high quality. I was bought by an expensive store and put in this necklace. Wealthy people come in and inspect me; I will eventually be added to one of their collections, possibly put in a vault," the diamond sighed. "What I am saying is, you and I cannot predict what humans will do or are capable of. Best to stay away from them and go back to your mountain. As for Heldrig, I have not heard about his clan and the betrayal. It isn't something I would be interested in, so no one would even think to mention it to me. However, I do have an interesting bit about his social life. He is not as alone as you think. He has a son. Or some daughters. Or both." She shuffled around in her setting again. "With this, you are in a very sticky situation, my dear. You cannot walk away, can you?"

Donya shook her head.

"Who do you want to kill tonight? What works best for you? Stop trying to think and just be. But as soon as is possible, excuse yourself from the situation."

"You are very wise."

"Me? You are too wonderful, my dear."

"Would you like a ride? I can take you with me."

"That sounds nice, but I want to see this through to the end. I am resigned to my fate," she paused then added, "also, I am a little vain and want to see how much I will sell for."

"Thank you for the advice. You are beautiful. I am sure it will be in the millions." Donya gave a wave over her shoulder and asked the wall to let her pass again. Some limestone had listened in. It let her know that one of the security guards liked to look at pictures of little humans on his light box. "It is called a phone, silly," she said, patting the stone as she passed. "Thank you for the tip. He sounds perfect." The stone gave her the memory of his smell, and she was off.

She tumbled along the dark streets. It rained again, cold and clean. The roads were high in the center and lower on the sides and rutted from long-ago wagon tracks. She used the ruts. Sending up spray as she passed. The human she tracked was miles away. She crossed the river and went uphill. A troll in the night can move quite quickly, soon she was at her destination.

She stopped in front of a small storefront; he was in the building, on the second or third floor. She went around the back, pushed on a thick wooden door, and it splintered open. Up the stairs to the left was another wooden door. She could smell him through there. Shattering that door, she broke into the one-room apartment. The man lay on a mattress on the floor. He was just sitting up, startled from sleep. His smell had the addition of alcohol. His dark eyes were wide, the whites showing. He could not see her in this light, yet she saw him perfectly—flabby skin and hair too long on one side to comb over his balding head. He moved to get a small knife on a low table near the bed, knocking over a mostly empty bottle of wine.

Donya was on him in mere seconds—she broke the arm that held the knife and used his own weapon to slit his throat. He gurgled as she drained the blood into the container Heldrig provided. She saw a small reaction with the paper, a sizzle of smoke, sludge green in color. No, this had not been the right blood at all, which brought a smile to her colorless lips. When the bottle was almost full, she settled in to eat. Heldrig would only get the blood from this one.

CHAPTER 11

# SCARLET

"Did you message your mom before we left?" Scarlet asked Juan as they rounded the corner.

"Yep."

"Okay, cause we could be out a long time again today."

"I told her, but she will still worry anyway."

"You probably should have shown her how to track your location."

"Pffff she already is, in her way. That is why she started messaging you the second you got online last night."

"She waited like ten minutes, probably giving you time to write, but when you didn't, she reached out to me. You know, just in case you were dead and I for some reason didn't tell her." Scarlet felt a little guilty right after she said it. She peeked over at Juan as they walked, but his expression didn't change. That line hadn't been hers. Lettie used it the night before. Scarlet hadn't told Juan about those messages.

"I'm hoping this trip will prove to her she can relax."

It might be making her worse, Scarlet cringed to herself.

He led them back to the Square. The siren had gone off again, and he wanted to see the water today before they started shopping. He'd been adamant, so Scarlet caved. She worried about the thing in the water, but something about Venice soothed her. They left the hotel with their galoshes already on.

The plan was to finally buy Venetian masks after revisiting the Square. They shopped at a cart selling masks yesterday, but the man at the cart said for more selection, go to the store. The cart sold more tourist fare, mostly plastic with bright colors and glitter. But mixed in the tacky glitter there were a handful of nice leather masks and two metal ones. The store would have traditional masks made of ceramic, and what Juan was interested in—leather masks done in the old-style. Perhaps he would get the terrifying one with a long nose. Scarlet hoped not. She never liked that one.

They made it to the Square. Water came in, but it was not like the other day. The sun hid behind a blanket of clouds, and the water lay clear and cold. It also was not as strong of a tide, so there were a lot of large puddles, not a continuous pool. Men tossed crumbs between the puddles, offering to take pictures of tourists with the pigeons that landed for the food.

Juan looked a bit deflated; it wasn't as perfect as the first day. Scarlet had already known. She had gone through this before, traveling back to places where she'd experienced something wonderful. It is never as sweet and enjoyable again. It didn't matter. Tugging at his hand, she led him to one of the puddles, she knew what would cheer him right up. "I could go for some chocolate cherry gelato."

"Yeah?" he asked as he splashed into the puddle, maybe five inches deep at the center. He seemed happier already.

Scarlet was looking down, so she saw the tendril come out. Even with her standing right there, it went for Juan, slower but still moving steadily. She glanced up, and he smiled again. This is nice, she decided and stood still in the water up to her ankles.

The air was colder today, but the water felt about the same as before. Looking back down, she noticed another tendril was on her. She watched it snake around her rubber-covered boot. The last few days must have washed out the confetti—she only saw maybe two in their whole puddle. Glancing around, the tendrils were in other pools too. One wrapped around a dancing child, almost to his belly button. She thought perhaps this was a nice spirit, her great aunt had said they existed.

The tendrils seemed to pass right through people usually. She moved her foot to see what the tentacle would do. It caught on the boot. A handful of the delicate leaves opened and closed in a quick undulation. When Juan moved to her left, the tentacle passed right through him, letting him walk over to the gray and white pigeons out of the water. She made an attempt to follow, but the tendril constricted.

For a second, she recalled the orange trees in Spain, the smell, the warmer air. It was such a clear memory, then it was gone. She thought that with a bit of force, she could snap the tendril. Scarlet didn't want to do that. Perhaps it was the spirit's underlying beauty. Or maybe she always liked sea animals best, but whatever the reason, she stopped and waited until the creature finished. It started to unravel then, letting her go, but she saw something moving up its length to the tip. It was silvery and tiny. Maybe a coin? It could be a shard of candy wrapper catching the light. It got to the tendril's tip, which still held her right foot. The tendril flicked, phasing into her boot. She felt a dull pain on her pinky toe, and then the tendril retreated into the drainage hole.

What just happened? She felt slightly slow and silly for a second. A smell came to her; she blinked and saw the inside of the plane, smelled the dry air, and the horrid little troll. Blinking again, it was gone.

She hadn't expected the thing to do anything harmful with how happy it made everyone else. The feelings all passed quickly, and she seemed fine. Testing her foot, it stayed the same level of soreness it had been for days. The bones ached from all the walking, but there was nothing else.

"Let's get going," Juan said, checking his phone. "It's about a ten to fifteen-minute walk, and I'm sure we can find you your gelato on the way."

"Uh-huh," Scarlet replied, stretching out her hand.

"You okay, love?" he asked. "You look a little pink."

"Yeah, it's the cold on my cheeks, I think. Maybe we could sit inside to eat though, that would be nice." She moved her hand up to her face; it felt flushed.

They started walking and found an inviting gelateria after a few blocks. Inside they offered perhaps twenty flavors. Juan tended toward the fruit flavors, mango and banana being his usuals. Scarlet liked to get chocolate with either cherry or berry. Sometimes there was *amarena*, which was chocolate with cherry already mixed in. This counter had *fior di latte*, she loved that flavor too. It was a delicate sweet flavor that she couldn't put her finger on but was recognizable.

"Hello, I'll take two scoops," Juan said when they reached the counter. "*Ananas* and," he paused and walked two more steps, "*limone*."

"Sure," said the girl from behind the counter. The blankness of her face and slight slouch made her appear disinterested in the transaction.

Scarlet decided. "Umm, two scoops, the *fior di latte*, and, um, the *chocolate fone dent*." She knew she messed up the fondant pronunciation but again, the girl didn't seem to care and got her the dessert.

Scarlet perched on one of the tall stools by a window as it started to drizzle outside. She wiggled her foot around in her shoe. It felt fine, maybe a tad warm.

"Here, try it," Juan said, pulling away her focus on her foot.

She felt the slightest hint of hesitation, which was weird, then leaned forward and licked it. "Babe!! That is the pineapple side. I hate pineapple," she scolded, then stuck her tongue into the dark chocolate on her cone. "You know pineapple eats you back, right?"

"Ha-ha, sorry, I forgot. Here, this is the lemon," he said, turning the cone.

Scarlet took another lick. It was superb, tangy, and light, refreshing after the chocolate, which was almost too dark. She needed to remember to get the milk chocolate. "I can't believe you gave me the evil fruit first." She turned her cone to take licks of the *fior di latte*. Repositioning her foot under the stool, she noticed something. A pale yellow light glowed from inside her shoe and galosh. The light came from the spot the tendril had nipped her. The light shone even through the material, like a bright bulb through a lampshade.

CHAPTER 12

# DONYA

Donya sat under the bridge. Dawn approached on the eastern horizon. Two teenagers tagged the wall in front of her; they could not see her. The spray paint stung the morning air with stink. One of the teenagers was talented, his paint never dripping, and the color palette he used was excellent, bright orange, fuchsia, warm-toned purple, white for highlights, and a dark gray for contrast. The gray cement benefited from his work. The other boy used black and neon blue; he fidgeted looking over his shoulder too often. His paint dripped in six places despite his work's small stature. When done, they walked away, the fidgeter taking off his hood to display a bright shock of blue hair, a theme of his apparently.

Donya closed her eyes. It was time for rest.

Immediately her mind went to what she would be doing tomorrow. Their train would be coming in. Was she recovered enough? Heldrig would deal with the redhead, or at least he thought he would. She took stock of her body's condition.

Her legs still felt weak, not as fragile as a chunk of talc or powdery alabaster, more like fluorspar, which is brittle. She was not hungry, having eaten. Those men, the ones she ate, lacked substance or power. Her arms felt as weak as her legs. Like this, she could not survive a whole hour in sunlight. Her head buzzed, needing the sleep of this upcoming day.

What had the diamond told her? "Stop trying to think and just be." It seemed sound advice, but perhaps not something she could do constantly. Sleep would quiet her mind for today. Donya would meet Heldrig far into the night. Eyes still closed, she finally relaxed, settling in like a stone.

The drizzle of rain was unnatural. Donya felt it on her skin as the droplets struck. The water felt oily. Heldrig must have schemed it up, and she wondered, to what end. She lurked in the dark by a chain-link fence. The train station stood in front of her, full of bright lights and loud colors. Heldrig was there on the steps, barely out of the rain, waiting for her. Time to go in there and not overthink it. Their trap would work. After today she would be solid and strong—she would be like granite.

The moment she strode into the puddle of light, Heldrig turned toward her. His orange glow faded. His clothing was human casual, light-colored trousers, and a dark blue shirt with a collar. He wore tennis shoes with white soles and a backpack slung over his shoulders. It did not suit him. The look was disconnected. He had not enacted his disguise spell yet. When he enabled it, surely the girl would be fooled.

"There you are, my petulant pebble," he said as she mounted the steps. "You have truly made an effort these last few nights. You appear to be much better. Your hair is even laying back as a proper troll's hair is supposed to do."

Donya nodded. Then she held out her hand to the rain. "You have made an effort as well?"

"Correct, you noticed... How wonderful. I did this for you. I could not let the sun come out and do damage to you. It has been raining already, and I helped it along. No stray beam of light will get out today."

She tried not to bristle at the answer. A little sunlight would not have stopped her. She took a deep breath instead of responding. He was helpful. This was for the best. This gave them more options. Finally, she asked, "now what, we wait?"

"I have looked up the train times coming in from Venice. We have hours before the first one arrives. The enchantments will last around nine hours. But will be strongest, of course, in the first three. There is now a decision to make. Do we enact them in the moments prior to the arrival of the first train? Alternatively, do the two of us wait, do we attempt to spot the humans and then enact the spell? We could have you feel out if the redhead has arrived, then engage the spells?"

"Before the first train arrives." Donya could feel the sureness in her ribs. If they waited and the girl got a sight of her with those strange eyes... she wasn't certain what would happen, but it would not be a positive outcome for her.

Heldrig frowned. "We could be outside for three hours if they arrive on one of the later trains. Of course, the spell would be active the full nine hours. It should be alright, it is a fine spell."

Donya thought Heldrig leaned toward one of the other options from his frown. "It is better to be cautious. Can you strengthen the spell? Do I need to get you more blood?"

"Trolls are the better trap setters—thus, we will go with what you say. No need for extra blood. I could reinforce the spell a bit if need be." He fingered an object in his pocket as he said this.

"We will start with a walk of the building together then," Donya said. Heldrig smiled a little and got the door for her.

CHAPTER 13

# SCARLET

Juan fell asleep as they rolled out of the lagoon and continued to sleep the entire train ride, which was too bad. The scenery was worth more than the cost of the tickets. Rolling green hills and snow-capped mountains rose in the distance. The train stopped at a couple of small villages. Juan's eyes would flicker when the train came to a stop, but he always fell right back to sleep. The stylish woman who sat across the aisle from Juan exited, her orange scarf trailing behind her.

Besides admiring the beauty flashing past her outside the train, Scarlet read *Good Omens* to keep her occupied. She had thought she would get more reading done on this trip. In her head, she saw herself nightly unwinding with chianti, a soft-lit lamp on, and a book in her hand, while Juan slept next to her. So far, that didn't happen. But she was happy she grabbed this paperback off her shelf. It was funny, a gift from her sister.

Scarlet's alarm chimed, a few minutes until their stop. She felt sure this was a terminus, no need to rush, but still, Juan needed to wake up. Leaning forward, she touched his knee. He did not stir.

"Hey, it's time to get our stuff."

Juan's eyes opened, and he raised a hand to straighten his glasses. The outskirts of the city passed by the window. In this weather, it seemed gray and grimy. Scarlet stood up bracing her legs against the sway of the train. She grabbed her backpack and dislodged his as well. Taking another peek outside, she turned around to set her backpack down and get her scarf out of the top pocket. The forecast had been in the sixties, but it looked really dreary. There appeared to be a gray shroud covering the sky over Florence.

"Put your beanie on babe, it's ugly out," she said to her sleepy boyfriend. The train squealed to a stop, and more passengers stood up. She always hated this part of train travel. Everyone rushed to get out. If it wasn't a terminus, there were usually people pushing to get in at the same time. Then, on the platform, the air reeked of cigarette smoke. All the smokers either had to get one last puff before boarding or were lighting up the moment they stepped from the train. Walking the aisle, she could already smell the polluted air coming in the door. She quickly grabbed her suitcase from the cubby by the door and stepped over the gap. Her injured foot gave a deep throb of pain as she alighted—she let out a little noise of discomfort that no one heard.

Juan stayed right on her heels. She grabbed her phone from her pocket. Her next steps caused no pain, so she didn't bother favoring the foot. The GPS didn't work effectively with big metal awnings over the platforms. The station looked like it was solid stone from their vantage point, which wouldn't be great for reception. Once they were out on the street, her phone would guide them to the hotel a few blocks away. They'd splurged on an expensive room. Everyone at work raved about Florence, and she hoped for it to be the most romantic stretch of their trip. Although, it was hard for her to think of that now with her foot throbbing.

Her foot gave off another stab. What is wrong with the way I am stepping? Scarlet wondered.

They walked past a small convenience store when the burning started. It was her baby toe. It felt warm, then hot like a toaster cooked her foot. She glanced down. Her foot glowed a pale yellow through her boot again. She glanced at Juan. He smiled and took no notice of her strange foot. She tried to take lighter steps with it, but it was her right foot, her stronger side.

"Hey, you want water or something?" Juan pointed to the little shop.

"Nope, I want to get to the hotel."

The exit sign shone weakly in front of them. Church bells rang outside. It was two-thirty, but the light from outside looked dim, like nightfall.

"Oh," Scarlet exclaimed as a middle-aged man stepped into her path—causing her to come down hard on her foot. He wore khakis and a blue polo. He smiled, but his face seemed strained. Her foot throbbed, hot pulses with her heartbeat. She didn't have time for this guy selling crap.

"Scuzi miss, but would you,"

"No." Scarlet did not let him finish. She traveled enough to know how to handle this situation. Give them no hope if you knew you would buy nothing.

His smile faded, and a strange look washed over his features. Right then, a small girl popped up beside him—her shiny black hair in pigtails. The skin on her face was like peaches and cream. Petite tears still clung to long curled eyelashes. "Mammi," she whimpered.

Juan's face fell. Everything happened in a sort of slow motion for Scarlet. Her leg throbbed nonstop. Juan looked around for the girl's family. The girl reached for Juan's hand. Then Scarlet heard a pop. It wasn't loud or even startling. It almost sounded like when your ears clear driving over a mountain range.

Nothing in the tableau before Scarlet changed. But she smelled something, a rotten stink, she had smelled before. It was uniquely familiar, but she could not place it. She did not like it. The light shifted. Darkness drained away and sunlight hit the pavement a dozen feet in front of them.

Scarlet focused back on the child, who no longer reached for Juan but glared at her. The eyes that had been big and beautiful seconds before shrunk and squinted. The awkward man standing in the way watched Scarlet too. He looked at her leg. His pinched face was pained. His mouth hung open a bit, as if to say more, inside his teeth were black. Scarlet stomped her right foot. It hurt like a hot iron poking her, but it felt right, and time seemed to snap back.

"Are you lost?" Scarlet asked the little girl.

The child shook her head once.

"She might not be able to understand you," Juan said.

"I am sure this nice gentleman could ask her in Italian," Scarlet snapped.

The khaki man, still stunned, moved his hand out to the girl, then croaked, "it is fine, I know her."

Scarlet moved toward Juan; people streamed around them. She stepped into the crowd, pulling Juan with her. She wanted to turn back, but she was afraid of what she would see.

"That was super weird. What just happened?" he asked when they hit the fresh air.

"I don't know. Maybe he is a conman or pickpocket."

"If he is, he's really bad at it."

"He probably isn't used to someone saying no. He seemed pretty slick," she said as they walked past the chain-link fence that held the machinery for road work. Her foot still hurt with every step, but it was nothing compared to before. Maybe when she knocked it, she popped the blister. It appeared to be a blister on her toe when she inspected it the night before. If it hadn't been for the strange light and the fact the spirit bit that foot, she would think nothing of it even with the pain. Her feet hurt worse while she traveled in Japan one summer.

The wind hit her in the face. She stopped to look around. Florence was famous for its gelato, and there were three shops in front of her. Craning her neck, she could see the tip of the Duomo. They'd headed in the right direction. Their hotel was that way.

After the train station, nothing went smoothly. The hotel was cold. But not the whole hotel, only their room. They blasted the heater, but no warm air came out. An hour in, they complained. The man who came to fix it did not know what he was doing. Finally, Juan, seeing him messing around in the breaker box, stepped in and flipped a switch. After that, the heat worked, well, sort of. The room overlooked a stone courtyard, which was not as charming as the garden view in Venice.

At least they had their own bathroom with a large shower stall. But the lighting was poor, and pigeons cooed at the window all day long. One of the pigeons built a nest. The shrill squeaks and coos of an immature pigeon could be heard. It especially bothered Scarlet because she couldn't see the birds, just hear their calls and flapping wings.

It was time to head out to dinner, but Scarlet still didn't feel prepared to return to the outside world. She missed something at the train station. She thought she missed a lot of things. At work, she was competent, someone others sought out to answer the hard questions. Or at least they used to. Now they could ask James. But here, she felt like something stared her right in the face, and she was too dense to notice.

"Let me see your foot before we head out to dinner," Juan said out of the blue.

"What, why?"

"It's bothering you. I saw you check it last night. You get a blister from all the walkin'?"

"Yeah," Scarlet replied, twisting the soft bed covers under her fingers.

"Okay, I will drain it for you. You brought the sewing kit, right, and Band-Aids?"

"Not before dinner! God babe, I know it doesn't gross you out, but I don't like it one bit."

"Don't be a baby," Juan said, sitting next to her and grabbing her foot. Then he continued, "at least let me see. We can buy anything else we might need for it while we are out. Maybe rubbing alcohol."

"Fine." Scarlet yielded, relaxing her leg so Juan could manipulate her foot. She had no fear of him seeing anything other than a small blister.

"Gotta take care of my girl." He smiled up at her, then his head bowed to the task.

He slid her shoe off and peeled back the black sock, then started inspecting her foot. "Is that it?" he asked as he got to the little toe with the blister.

"Yep, that is all. I told you, it is small. It's in an awkward place."

The blister had grown, but it still was not even dime-sized. It nestled between the pinky and the next toe. It wasn't even significantly raised, merely a normal blister. Juan pressed the sole of her foot and wiggled her other toes. His eyebrows were still scrunched up over his glasses. Scarlet finally asked, "what is it?"

"I don't know, I mean, it looks like nothing, but your foot feels warm. Could it be infected? Nothing else I touched hurt, did it?"

Scarlet paused before she answered. Her heart felt squeezed in her chest. It was infected—magically infected. And now, whatever the thing in Venice had done altered her physiology. Her mouth felt dry. She couldn't explain it right now. She lied, "it can't be infected. It isn't off-colored, and the skin isn't broken or anything. I bet my feet feel hot 'cause your hands are still cold."

The concern on his face did not decrease at her logic. "Okay, but let's stop by the pharmacy on the way out and see what we can get for you."

Switching the subject was in order, she couldn't let him get too worried about something he could not fix. "I'm not gonna argue with that. Now, where should we eat?"

CHAPTER 14

# DONYA

"Did you see that? I must admit I believed you to be exaggerating, at least a very small amount. You were correct in your original assessment, though. How surprising, the woman is very impressive. What a find, what a find indeed!" Heldrig crowed. His eyes and mouth distorted under the wavering spell and orange pigment.

Donya was in the small stairwell, not recovered enough to talk. She was afraid if she moved her jaw, it would crumble off. The redhead again somehow scorched her. Her tongue stuck to the roof of her mouth; her throat closed in the drought-besieged desert of her body. She desperately wanted to know what Heldrig thought of the young man. Did Heldrig know what he could be? What made him so magnetic? Instead of asking, she slid down the wall and sat on a step.

Heldrig paced in front of Donya on a lower landing. He looked up and laughed. "The very first thing I need to do is have her followed. I will have to make another disguise, of course. You know, actually, I think I will call in my son to help. My daughter, furthermore, although she will hardly be any help. My son, his name is Mars, has a wonderful nose for these sorts of things. Also, he is a quarter human. He can pass easily. She won't suspect a thing." He stopped, then peered at Donya. The rickety spell wore thin—she could see his dark eyes and long hair again. Then he continued, "her name, I must find it out. It will give me many more options."

Did the searing heat bake Heldrig's brain, Donya wondered. He rambled. What about the other human? Donya worked her tongue around in her mouth and cleared her dust-caked throat. "The man, Heldrig, the man?"

Heldrig froze, one cheek crinkling up. Then he cackled, "yes, him, the one you were very fond of—keep him, my dear. Keep him. His heart, and his spleen, and all his fingers, both eyeballs even!"

"What?"

"I want that woman. Did you feel her power? Perfect for me, really. It was like a wave of lava out of Mount Vesuvius. It is inherent to her. She is not even casting, instead simply breathing in and out power. Then whatever is on that leg of hers… it amplified everything. She broke my cloud calling by doing nothing, nothing at all." He put his thumb in his mouth as he talked. His eyes showed the bluish whites all the way around.

Donya leaned back against the steps by her spine. If he wanted the woman and she wanted the man, all her misgivings were for nothing. This partnership would succeed. Great power, as well as strength, were within her reach. If he wanted to call in some family members, the more, the merrier. She felt more herself, more stable. She blinked a few times, still watching Heldrig. "Tell me more."

Heldrig's smile widened. He seemed pleased with this statement. "Let me see where to start. In the last hundred years, I have been experimenting with starting a family. As you know, I have been alone for nearly two millennia. My first child died. Although humans can successfully breed with most fae folk, this child was a bad mix. Died of a high fever very early on. The mother was from one of the last great families out of northern Europe. Next, I met a Naiad; with her, I begat Nerawen, who survived. She turned out to be a strange mix. I almost gave up. Her magics are nothing like mine, all elemental water, and binding. Her strengths would probably be more recognizable to you. She is of use, occasionally," Heldrig paused, running his hand through damp-looking hair. His energy seemed less manic now.

"You can tell me less," Donya managed, with a slight upturn of her mouth. Heldrig might have let slip something he hadn't intended. Donya tried not to dwell on that feeling.

Heldrig peered at her and nodded, "I do tend to be long of wind," he chuckled. "In any case, my son is more of what I wanted in an offspring. He is still very young, a child really, to anyone like us. He is nineteen, and very obedient. Like me, he uses blood magic. Very proficient for his few years of practicing. As I said, he is part human. So, he passes very easily. In the last few years, it has become apparent he should specialize in dream magic."

"Dreams and binding? Heldrig, you should have called them sooner." Donya watched him as she said this. He preened, taking in a big breath of air and moving his shoulder a fraction of an inch.

"I previously thought of bringing in Nera. Not to insult you, dear little troll, but as I mentioned, possible overstatement made me weary. Nera is hard to control, so I did not believe it was worth the trouble." He redirected his gaze to an upper corner as he said this.

"Fair enough." Donya noticed he shortened his daughter's name. Perhaps that explained the off feeling earlier. He gave away his child's true name. They were allies; he had nothing to worry about from her, although a part nymph was almost immortal, so having her name out could cause problems for her in ten thousand years.

"You are the most practical of creatures. I should have known better than to think you would inflate an encounter."

Donya noticed it wasn't an apology, although she did not require one. "We will construct a new trap, a better one, with the assistance of your children."

"This is the most excitement I have felt in a very long time; I will call them. They could be here quickly, perhaps by the end of this night."

"I will need to rest until they arrive."

"Yes, of course, I need rest too. One brief meeting has really taken it out of me. I now understand your weakness when you came to me. I feel it down to my spirit. I will leave you here then. The sun should set in a few more hours, and you can be on your stony way."

Donya nodded and closed her eyes again. She heard Heldrig's footfalls as he descended the stairs. The air in the small stairwell cleared with his departure. He smelled of musky cologne and old burned blood. Finally, something was going her way. She needed to sit back and relax.

Later in the cold, murky waters of the river, Donya practiced sitting quietly. She found a shallow spot under the open night sky. All the clouds cleared from earlier in the day. Now the sky winked with dim stars. The water swirled around her folded legs. Her chest and the tops of her knees cleared the water. Troll magic came from the earth and shadows. Night was the ultimate shadow. Donya could not gain any power from sitting in the darkness and river mud, but she could recover from that day's events a little.

She concentrated on the mud under her bottom and squished in her toes. It was cold and thick with a few small, smooth stones mixed in. The rocks made happy grunts whenever her toes touched one. She stayed here for most of the night. Still, her mind wanted to run. It kept replaying the earlier events in the train station. Heldrig appeared wild in the stairwell. She breathed in the scent of the silty water.

She opened her eyes. Her grandmother had been a river Henkie, so the water helped her take in the darkness better than if she sat under a bridge. The sky changed to navy blue in the east. Donya felt a powerful presence enter the river. It was upstream of her.

Donya stood, water tumbled from her, feet sunk deep into the mud. She was very heavy. She pushed forward. The mud and pebbles gave way as she slogged to the shore's concrete lip.

She stepped up out of the water. Mud clung to her pants. She would need a change of clothes tonight and maybe a shower in cleaner water. Staying presentable in the streets was essential. She walked toward the figure in the darkness.

It was a beautiful woman, tall and slender. Her black hair was cut to chin length. Strange, her father did not prefer this child as she looked like a stunning version of him. Her skin was a lighter shade of blue. It fell almost in the realm of human shades, white with a china blue tint. She had a high forehead decorated with a circlet that gleamed in the starlight. Her petite mouth formed a little mew right now as her face was directed at Donya. She even had her father's ebony teeth, a defining characteristic of her race. The old troll word for them meant black teeth, *Karshun*.

One thing was off. Her eyes were stitched shut. She wouldn't need to see near the stream. If her magic was tied to water, the stream would have told her Donya's location.

She walked up to Nera, who stood unmoving in the stream. Nera smiled in her direction. "Father told us to let you rest, but I could not wait. I am very pleased to make your acquaintance."

"You found me on your own?" Donya asked. She wasn't shocked by this, more by the sweet bell tones of the lady's voice.

"You are a troll; I thought you would be under a bridge, so I followed the river… I am already in love with this river."

Donya did not know how to respond. She stood feeling especially small. The silence felt heavy, as if both held back several questions they wanted to ask. Finally, Donya said, "I should get to my bridge."

Nera laughed, "I will see you tonight. Father says we are planning."

Donya coughed. There must have been a better way of saying they would be meeting later. The lack of eyes was striking.

Nera laughed again, "I really will be seeing you. Father has promised me a new set of eyes. He said I could have them later. These ones might last a whole month, well, if he doesn't get mad and take them away like before." Her mouth turned down.

"Until tonight, Lady Nera," Donya said with more composure.

Nera waved a hand back and forth in Donya's direction as she walked on toward her favorite bridge.

# CHAPTER 15
# SCARLET

Scarlet and Juan relaxed at a winery. Through the tall windows, yesterday's clouds had all but vanished. The day held the kind of clear skies that seemed to go on forever. Small birds sang in the cypress which ringed the property; they were slightly audible in the room through the glass windows.

Juan planned this day. And it turned out to be very relaxing and worth the high price of the food and wine tour.

The day would have been perfect if she could get the magical infected foot out of her mind. After the blister had been mostly drained, it did feel better. Also, there were no more light works. If it turned out to be a simple fix, Scarlet would be amazed. She'd worried late last night if she should call off this final part of their trip. It felt extreme, but between the weird encounters and the foot, she felt it safest. Although she couldn't explain any of that to Juan. He would think she was crazy to suddenly call off their trip because her foot hurt a little. Scarlet tried to keep these thoughts and feelings pushed down. The wine helped with that.

They had spent the morning trying different dried meats in Florence. Then they were picked up by a van to be shuttled out to the countryside for wine. Their guide, Lucia, was a slight woman with mounds of curly black hair. She wore jeans, comfortable shoes, an incredibly chic leather jacket, and a blue wool scarf. Leather is a historically important textile in Florence, and now helped rake in tourist dollars. There was a separate tour run by the company for leather in the city. Lucia pointed out the best place to buy a nice leather bag as they passed it.

Lucia expounded for hours on the ins and outs of wine and cheese. Scarlet tried to commit the wine information to memory, as at more than one company dinner, she'd been asked to pick the wine. California boasted great wines, visitors assumed locals would know about wine. So far, Scarlet remembered that after you select a bottle, the waiter should wait until you try it, then pour it for everyone. And that she needed to swirl the glass to open the aromas and sniff it. That was important.

Lucia glided across the room, holding another flight of wine for everyone. There were only two other couples on the tour since March was still the off-season. It made for a more intimate experience.

"Alright, everyone, for these next wines, we are going to work on developing your ability to find the finish." Lucia set the tray of three varieties in front of Juan. They were all reds. "Hold the goblet by the bowl for these."

Everyone picked up the first glass and swirled, sniffed, then took a sip. Scarlet looked into her glass as she did. The wine was cherry red.

"After your first sip, exhale through your nose. What do you notice?" Lucia asked.

A young blond man with an accent Scarlet couldn't place answered from the other table. "From the color and the lingering taste, this is a young wine. The taste stayed for a very long time. When I breathe out as you instructed, I taste pepper."

Lucia clapped her hands and exclaimed, "perfect, Franklin, a wonderful description. You will notice it is the brightest of the three in front of you. It is, in fact, the youngest. Just from last year. Maybe a bit too young to enjoy all it has to offer. Now everyone try the next sample."

Scarlet disobeyed and finished the first wine. There was still another nice-sized sip. She liked it. Besides the pepper, it tasted rather bright. She picked up the second glass and went through the procedure of sipping. This one was, in fact, even better. Again, she inspected the glass, the liquid appeared more red-orange. When she sipped, the first thing she thought as the wine hit her mouth was that it felt buttery. Nothing in the wine made her mouth pucker. Across the table Juan faced a sun-soaked window. He squinted at his glass and tilted it to the side, assessing the color. He caught her watching, shifted in his seat, and mouthed, "it's good."

Lucia caught the interaction. She stopped her wandering by Juan. "You like it, don't you?"

"Yes, very much," Juan responded.

"The estate owner will be very pleased. She is eighty-three years old this year. And every year, she picks a preferred batch. This was her favorite of 2014. It's a beautiful Chianti." She turned away from their table and projected to the other couples, "this particular wine comes from one vineyard on the estate; it has olive groves to one side. Tell me, can you taste the olive influence, the terroir in this wine?"

Scarlet sipped again and closed her eyes. Still, the only thing she could think of was that it was soft. Breathing out, she got no hint of olive. She wished for a full-sized glass. It was her favorite of the day.

"On to the next wine, everyone. It will be our last before dinner, notice the swirl on this last one," Lucia said, clapping her hands again.

Scarlet picked up this wine—stalling before tasting it. The last one still lingered in her mouth, warm in the back of her throat. She examined the wine. It had the same vermillion hue but was not as vibrant as the last. Swirling the drink caused it to stick to the side of the glass a bit more.

"This wine has something we like to call, serious leg, it is very sticky and tears down the glass slower than other wines."

Scarlet put the glass to her mouth and tasted, again, watching Juan. He didn't react much to this wine, although his shoulders were tense. It tasted similar to the last but with a mustier flavor at the end. It wasn't bad, but not fresh.

"As I said before, all the wines we are tasting are from this estate. Can you guess what field this wine is from?"

"A spot with flowers," said the lovely woman at the third table. She had a warm complexion and smooth black hair draped over her shoulder. Scarlet didn't get the sense of flowers at all from this wine.

"Close, it is by the stream you can see to the east. Look at that, here comes the cheese," Lucia answered. A heap of cheese on a small blue plate arrived, brought by the master of fields they had met earlier. There were shreds of sun-dried tomatoes on the side. "Is this the mozzarella?"

"Yes, fresh from the town over," he answered.

"Mozzarella is fairly quick to make. It is from a category called *pasta filata*, which are stretched or kneaded like you would a pasta dough. They take one day to make. However, this does not lessen the complexity of the flavors. I find it is the perfect way to start a meal after much wine tasting."

Juan reached for the plate first. It was supposed to be a food and wine tour but mostly concentrated on wine, which made the edges of the world a little fuzzy to Scarlet. He cut into the cheese and made several thin slices; his hand shook slightly, so the slices were not even. He caught her eye. "You take the first piece."

Scarlet smiled and used her fork for the first time, spearing the moist white slice. She placed it in her mouth. It was exactly as promised, perfect after the wine, clean, creamy, and cool in her mouth. It instantly brought a smile to her face. Juan grabbed his slice and nibbled it. She longed to try it hot. Mozzarella stretched out on pizza sounded amazing right now.

The master of fields was a weather-beaten short man, he cleared his throat and said, "the courses will be more simple than usual as it is winter. We use local products here, relying on preserved vegetables and mushrooms which are available now." Scarlet could not recall his name. She'd concentrated on not falling in the slippery vineyard when he was introduced.

"If by simple you mean rich," responded Lucia. "In winter, there will not be many fruits or vegetables, but there will be plenty of meat." As if by magic, someone emerged from the kitchen with a plate of salami for each table. Each slice lay folded in half. There was one Scarlet recognized, one crusted in pepper, and another larger slice.

What was bothering Juan? Scarlet hadn't paid close attention while the wine flowed, but now that food hit her bloodstream, she noticed he seemed more tense than usual. Was he worried about this tour? Or maybe her foot? She needed to talk to him. Unfortunately, there was no privacy on this tour, the group was too small. They all were wrapped up in everything that happened. She settled for watching him while chewing on a slice of the pepper-crusted salami.

Scarlet missed the whole salami spiel, and now a beautiful plate of hot pasta was set in front of her. The sauce was a rich brown, almost milk chocolate brown. It smelled heavenly. Wisps of steam came off the plate into her face. Across the table, Juan looked like his usual handsome self. Except for his tight jaw.

The plate of food tasted terrific. The pasta was delicate, and the meat sauce savory and balanced with an herbal flavor. Juan pushed it around on his plate. And he hardly touched the salami. Normally in their apartment, it was all she could do to keep the stuff stocked. He would often take a few slices from the fridge and eat them standing in the kitchen with the cat begging at his feet.

"Boar ragu, it is a regional specialty." Scarlet heard the snippet of Lucia's explanation as she tried to concentrate on Juan.

Lucia had her back turned, and the servers were out of the room, so Scarlet hazarded a whisper, "don't you like the food?"

Juan jumped in his seat; he'd been avoiding her gaze by looking out the window. He whispered back, "yeah, no, it's fine. I mean, it's great."

Scarlet cut him off, shaking her head. "Did the wine bother your heartburn?"

She saw Juan's shoulder drop a little at this. "Yep, that is it. It was the red wine." The side of his mouth quirked up.

That smile wasn't real, and that answer came too fast. Scarlet felt a shiver up her spine. Was he lying to her? Why in the world would he do that now? Like any of these people matter. Her hand gripped her fork harder. She scooped up a big pile of pasta and shoved it into her mouth.

"And now dessert! Sorbet, it is made with clementines, which are so popular here in the winter. Of course, they are not grown around here, but brought up from Sicily and Spain."

The courses were coming unusually fast. Part of this package was a sunset view of Florence from this estate's courtyard. Probably the staff wanted to pack them all out there soon, as the sun had moved off Juan's face and turned dark gold on the wall beside him.

Scarlet glanced at her sorbet. There was something on it. Juan's had dried flowers on top. Her flowers were scattered around the edge of the small serving glass. Something round sat on the top. She poked it with her spoon. It clinked. Juan stood up then and came to her side. "I guess you saw it."

She turned to him. He was kneeling. The pieces came together. That was a ring in the desert. Juan reached over and picked it off the top of the little melted knoll. "Scarlet Josephine Burke, will you marry me?"

Scarlet felt weak, and the room spun, she met his eyes for focus. Her lips smiled though her ears buzzed like a full beehive in her head. "Yep," she managed.

The whole room clapped. Everyone at the two tables and Lucia between them smiled. The server and the field master paused in the doorway, pleased as well.

Juan slipped the sticky ring over her finger. She looked down, the noise in the room receded, and now she could just hear her heartbeat. Don't faint. The ring fit perfectly, and she recognized it through the residue of dessert. It was a sapphire ring they'd seen on a trip to San Francisco. It was a solitary teardrop-shaped sapphire on top of two parallel bands. It had a low profile, but the eventual wedding ring would go in the space between the two bands.

The dark blue stone sparkled up at Scarlet in the light. Juan hugged her. She wasn't sure when she had stood up and faced the room.

"Thank you, everyone," Juan said, ending the embrace. His voice broke at the end of "one."

Lucia smiled and went back to directing the tour. "A very special moment, and to celebrate, we are all getting another glass of the fourteen you liked. Our hostess insisted when she heard of your plan. We will enjoy it out with the sunset before we head back to Florence."

Scarlet sat and took in the scene. Everyone smiled. The other guests politely inspected their orange desserts. The table was small; she leaned forward, Juan did too, and he gave her a light kiss. It was their first kiss as an engaged couple.

CHAPTER 16

# DONYA

The sun dipped below the horizon when Donya set off walking; she usually did not like traveling this early in the evening. After meeting Nera the night before, she felt it necessary that she see her and Heldrig. Time ran short. After all, their two humans would not be in Italy forever.

She arrived at Heldrig's door, knocked, and it opened immediately. A sullen teenager stood in front of her. As Heldrig said, he seemed quite human. But he did not smell the part, he smelled like old blood. Mouse brown hair shagged into his eyes. He suffered acne-pocked skin with a pinkish hue. He wore all black, though it did not seem to be of any style, a thick black sweatshirt and baggy jeans. His teeth were black, not shiny ebony as his sisters, more of a flat black. His lips remained parted. Donya wondered if she had missed hearing a greeting. He stepped aside to allow her access, then moved past her into the hall.

Heldrig sat at a desk in the room. "Good evening. Mars is only this minute stepping out for the night—my son attempted divination this afternoon but could not get a fix on any location. He will wander the streets searching. I gave him their descriptions and he is usually very lucky at such things. He has the Devil's luck, I like to say."

Donya looked around but didn't see Nera. Heldrig scrutinized her. "Yes, that other one. She is in the bathroom. Always loves to sit in water. Still, she is helping, I suppose. I have her attempting to detect anything and everything through the waters. It's the damn bells. There are numerous church bells, you are aware of I'm sure. They make more delicate maneuvers incredibly hard to do, always disrupting with their clangs."

"I've noticed them myself," Donya said. "I could never stay in this city long term. All day, the bells disrupt my sleep, even under the safety of a good stone bridge. Do you have any ideas for our next move?" She hadn't meant to say so much, but the words spilled out.

"I am creating a timeline, researching spells I might have access to that would work in the limited nights we have. Blood is probably what I will need to continue to use. It is always faster than oil. In any case, I am taking down notes now; you arrived very early. I need more time." Heldrig turned to lean over a pad of paper on it. He picked up a fountain pen and began scribbling.

Donya did not move. She closed her eyes. Binding. Nera's abilities were for binding. She wondered if she could create snares with her, a web of shadow that would tighten around and hold the human couple. They could lay traps all over the city, pull them into a magic void, or make them instantly fall into sleep. But if they set them in tourist areas, they would catch a lot of extra humans. It could draw unwanted attention. But it would be worth it, and once they obtained their prize, there would be no need to return to this place. She needed to discuss it. She needed to talk to Nera. Donya opened her eyes. Heldrig stayed bent to his work. "May I call on your daughter? Or would I disrupt her work?"

Heldrig flinched at her voice, "feel free, do what you would with my daughter."

What an odd thing to say. Donya felt herself shrug. She walked to the closed door in the room and knocked lightly.

"Come in," Nera sang out.

Donya pulled the door open to see Nera nude in the bath. Her one adornment was the delicate circlet she wore on her head. She watched Donya with her new eyes, one blue eye and one green eye. There were still tiny purple marks where her eyelids had been sewn shut. The tub was large, orange rose petals floated in the water. They were very striking against the vast expanse of light blue skin.

If Donya could blush, she would have. Although she felt chagrined at her surprise over seeing a naked half-nymph. Full nymphs never wore clothing, their hair plaited in attractive designs infrequently covering different parts of their body. Nera grinned at her.

"This is what you look like. I imagined a little taller."

Donya stepped inside the tiled room and closed the door behind her with a click. "Your father told you about me before last night?"

"Maybe," she said, then dipped under the water. It was an old long tub with clawed feet. She gracefully flipped over and popped up. Her short black hair glistened in the light from the lamp. Donya perched on the bidet by the tub. It was a well-appointed hotel. The tiles gleamed bright white, and everything smelled of flowery chemical cleaner.

Donya took her eyes off the half-nymph, which proved harder than she thought, and peered up at a small window. It lay open, letting the cold night air in. "I'm thinking you and I could work together to make snares."

"Snares?" Nera faced away from Donya but glanced back over her shoulder. Donya could see her from the corner of her eye.

"Yes, it is an idea I've newly formed. We would need many snares. We could set them up at tourist locations. It isn't the best plot, but we are running short on time, and our more elaborate trap did not work. Too many variables with these unknown humans." Donya knew this was the longest she had spoken in ages. It was uncomfortable, but not in a bad way.

"Father wouldn't like it. Relies much on me. Although I believe it could work." She sighed and sat up, getting to her knees in the tub. Water poured down her smooth back.

Donya's face scrunched up. What could she come up with next?

"Do not distress, for Father made a partial plan already. That is why my brother went out. He will find them, get the young gentleman's name at the very least. With the names, we can track them."

"Why not the woman's name?"

Nera flipped around, her eyes wide. She giggled loudly and said, "silly, I don't know that." All while coming up closer to Donya. She put her hand on Donya's shoulder and raised out of the water, quickly whispering, "he is afraid."

Donya responded to the first comment quickly attempting to cover Nera's whispered comment. "We must start somewhere, I suppose. Works for me in any case."

Nera moved back but still sat on her knees, gazing into Donya's eyes, with the eyes that Donya procured for her. "I like the way you look. You are my rock."

"Ummm, I like the way you look too."

"Pervert!" she said with mock ire, splashing a sprinkle of water at Donya. A few droplets hit her face.

Donya smiled, enjoying the encounter. A new idea coalesced in her mind. "Love! That is how we will trap them!"

"What?" Nera appeared shocked, and a bit of the blue ran out of her face. As if she could get even paler.

Donya popped to a standing position in her excitement, "I have it. We only need to trap one of them. Probably the man. Then we can use him as a lure to catch the girl." She paused working at the details. "This works if the girl can sense where he is."

"Of course, she can."

"I am unsure. When we were at the train station, it didn't seem like she knew what occurred or the danger. In the plane as well, she was almost oblivious." Donya wondered what if that redhead had no idea of her abilities.

"She possesses the sight, even if she was not taught by an elder. Finding a teacher would have been of utmost importance to her."

"Have you ever been to the new world? It is wanting of spirits. I existed in a city of millions, and I felt nothing significant while there. I am not at my best, but would have been able to sense a witch or a seer." What was it about Nera that made her babble on? The seer, in her secret question, the part she had not told Heldrig… She knew the redhead had no training.

"No, I have never been to the new world, but you have given me an idea. Could you fall asleep right now?"

"No."

"Do you trust me to bind you? And then read your dreams?"

Donya started a little where she stood, then went very still. Her stomach seemed to be buzzing. "For what purpose?"

"I will see the new world; also, if I can push your dream to both, I will see the humans."

She swirled the water in the tub. The rose petals danced around her legs. "It will allow me to know you better. I promise not to bite."

"You would break your pretty teeth on me anyway," Donya said with a laugh in her voice. Nera smiled widely. Donya relaxed. This was her ally. It would help them, but underneath the buzzing sensation, she got the nagging feeling she'd forgotten something. Then she added, "I trust you. How do we begin?"

"Get in the water with me." Nera's smile lingered from Donya's joke.

Donya slipped off her large boots and stepped in fully clothed. She liked the smell of wet cotton. The tub was slightly overfull when she sat—water and petals sloshed out over the brim.

"Turn away from me and lean back into my arms," Nera said while she pushed a leg on either side of Donya. Donya stretched out her legs to accommodate her, then leaned back into surprisingly warm arms. The water felt cool, she expected Nera to be closer to the same temperature.

Nera murmured, warm lips close to Donya's ear, strong arms wound around her, pulling her down into the water.

CHAPTER 17

# SCARLET

The night air became too frigid to get gelato and continue walking outside. Scarlet and Juan found refuge in a gelateria with chairs facing a large glass wall to the street. Scarlet felt like her whole body glowed, not merely her foot. It was the first evening of their engagement. Duel urges warred within her, to get back to the room and celebrate with Juan or stay out having fun all night.

"When did you buy this?" The faultless sapphire winked at Scarlet under the fluorescent lights. She kept stretching out her fingers to admire the ring.

"Right after you saw it last year."

Her scalp tingled. That was such a long time. Curiosity clanked around in her head; she had many questions for him. Seizing the first one she asked, "where did you keep it this whole time?"

Juan reached up pushing at hair that escaped his hat, he hadn't stopped smiling since she'd said yes. "They needed to special order the stone. It didn't arrive right after I bought it. I know how you feel about mining, so I got you a lab-created sapphire. And I wanted a perfect one. It took the jeweler a couple weeks to find just the right stone. I think the whole process took like two months. And then, after that, I kept it in my truck." He sped through the last sentence.

"What?"

"I know it was stupid. But I kept thinking I would find the perfect time to propose. I would take it with me when we walked on the beach at night. And I had it with me those couple of days in Tahoe."

"Did you almost propose when we went to see the magician?" Scarlet suppressed a laugh. She would have hated that.

"That could have been elaborate, and I watched a lot of YouTube videos to get ideas. I really wanted to do it in Venice, that first day in the water. But you know how I am." He poked at his gelato with his spoon. He ate fruit flavors again, berry and banana.

Scarlet swayed in her seat, bumping him in the shoulder, "you thought a small crowd would be just right so you wouldn't chicken out."

"No, yeah. Although I almost chickened out again. I know we talked about taking the next step after this trip, kind of having this trip as proof of our stable relationship."

"I think this is good. Maybe we both worry too much. And it is only a ring. If stuff goes wrong, we can always call off the engagement." She paused and inspected the ring on her finger. She didn't like talking about negative situations on a happy night. She changed course and continued, "I want a long one, we'll have plenty of time. Fiancé is one of my favorite words, and I want to get full use out of it."

"Pragmatic princess," he said and smiled. He draped his arm over her shoulder.

They were one street away from their hotel. Juan insisted on buying wine for their room. And a few snacks. One of the snacks was digestive cookies, which Scarlet found delicious despite their name. They picked up another Chianti. It wouldn't be like the one from earlier, which they had a bottle of, but it should be saved for home.

Someone followed them, a teenage kid. How long he'd been there, she didn't know. She moved her crossbody bag up on her torso, so it didn't hang low on her hip. The bag was a pretty light blue, not the best for traveling, between dirt and pickpockets. It caught the eye. But the design seemed sound. Usually, Scarlet wasn't this paranoid. He probably walked behind them by coincidence. If they hadn't made a bunch of turns on these old streets, he would have gone unnoticed.

They got to their hotel's front entrance and went in. The ground floor stood empty except for the elevator door, which she always took up to the lobby on level one to be easy on her foot. She turned and watched through the glass doors. The boy stopped outside and peered in. A lot of hair flopped over his forehead, even dangling into his eyes. He seemed sickly. His mouth parted, and his teeth looked wrong. The elevator chimed, and the doors opened. Scarlet turned to board, then stopped when she realized the boy stared at her feet.

She glanced down. Her foot glowed in her boot again—no pain though, only a glow. The boy, he could see it. He could see it too. Scarlet felt the urge to run out to him. She could ask him what he saw. If he knew what it could be. She could ask him a thousand questions. No wonder he followed her.

Juan held the door next to her. She stared at the boy's unremarkable face. She memorized it. Then she stepped towards him. That step did hurt. She had to try. Hopefully, he spoke a little English as she spoke no Italian.

The second step hurt worse. The teenager saw her movement, pivoted on his foot, and bolted. He dashed around the corner within a couple of seconds.

"Babe?" Juan asked from behind her.

Scarlet didn't respond right away, her stomach feeling queasy, "I thought he needed me to get the door for him or ..." she trailed off.

"Weird."

"Yeah." Scarlet felt foolish and bewildered by the pain. She got into the elevator feeling cold and woozy. This lightheadedness felt nothing like the pleasant tipsiness of earlier in the day.

"Big day tomorrow. We need to get you cleaned up and straight to bed, young lady."

Juan's tone brought her out of the funk. She dropped her voice and responded, "yes, I am feeling desperately tired. I'll be out when my head hits the pillow."

"But before that. I thought the shower is pretty big. I'm gonna help get you all clean, you know, scrub your back," he said, leaning against her.

The doors popped open in the lobby. Scarlet could feel her cheeks flush pink. They walked past the silent piano and up to the clerk. "Room five," Scarlet said. The man handed her the heavy key on a leather strap.

"Thank you, have a good night," Juan said to the clerk as they rounded the corner.

Once they were out of eyeshot, he rested his hand on her bottom and gave a small squeeze. "You are tense. I think after the shower I'll have to give you a massage. You know, to help you rest better."

"A butt massage. You really know how to butter a girl up. Is there something else you are going to spring on me?" Scarlet mock whispered as they drove the key home.

"A full body massage," he took a moment to laugh then continued, "I guess I am so relieved I asked, and you said yes. I'm feeling extra frisky."

"You are always extra frisky. Have you been upgraded to super frisky?"

"Yes, that is what I am now. Isn't there a song about that?"

"She's a super freak," Scarlet sang, then added, "not super frisk, but it's close enough." They stepped in and closed the door with a bang.

# CHAPTER 18
# DONYA

Water surrounded Donya, a feeling she was used to. Donya also felt like she was floating, a feeling she was not used to. No troll in the history of all the worlds had ever felt like they were floating. Donya got to be the first.

Her eyes opened. She could see the bulb shining far above her, light rippling through the thin layer of water. A warm body moved under her. Slippery skin next to her arm. How long had she been under?

She sat up, sputtering water from her mouth and nose. An unpleasant haze clouded her mind. She held no recollection of what happened. One minute she got in the tub, the next, submerged and awakening.

The woman beneath her moved and then exhaled water. It murmured beautifully like a bubbling brook, which made sense with Nera's lineage. Donya peered over her shoulder at Nera. Although the water was cold, a soft flush spread to

Nera's cerulean cheeks, and the different colored eyes sparkled behind the long-wet lashes.

Donya's hair stuck to the side of her face; she wiped at it and cleared her throat. Despite the disorientation, she felt better than before coming into the room, heavier and more substantial. She wanted to start another conversation. Seconds ticked by, and she decided to ask the most obvious question. "What did you see in my dreams?"

Nera wrapped her hand around Donya's mouth. "No talking from you yet," she cooed. Her hand slowly slipped away, but her arm continued to dangle over Donya's shoulder.

How was Nera able to see her dreams? That was her brother's power, not hers. She should have only been able to bind her. Unless the water told her what existed in the mind of those bound. That seemed an unlikely concurrence, but water and all its creatures tended to stick together.

Nera moved closer to Donya, draping herself over the little troll sitting in the front of the tub. Her breasts pressed against Donya's upper back, her arms dangled on either side. She brought her hands around in front of Donya and put them barely a few inches apart. In the center, a shadow formed. It coalesced taking form, first a rough sphere, then two pointy ears popped up and a tiny round tail. It was the shape of a bunny. "Am I doing it right?" Nera asked, her chin on Donya's right shoulder.

That was Donya's magic. She could control shadow when she stayed healthy enough to really do a fair bit of magic. Earth and shadow, that was what she contained. "You stole my power?" Donya shot out of the water spinning around, clenched her hands, though she wasn't sure what she would do with her fists.

Nera was fast, probably faster than a troll, but Donya's head bumped her chin when she sprang up. Nera's delicate hand rested on her face now. "No, oh no. I borrowed it. I can borrow."

Heldrig called from the other room, "keep it down in there; I'm trying to work!" He rapped on the wall for good measure.

"Sorry, Father," Nera called back. She leveled her gaze at Donya. Then casting her voice very low and she continued, "I understand. I should not have played around with you so." Her lip jutted out in a pout.

Donya felt the tension go out of her. She had judged her ally too quickly. Perhaps suspicion grew like a weed as even Nera's own father found his child untrustworthy, or maybe it was that lingering feeling of unease. Donya shook her head. "I have overreacted. Please explain. I want to… understand."

Nera's smile returned, and she said, "it is this, you see." She placed her hands on the circlet she wore. "My father won this many years ago. It allows one to take on another's talents, only one at a time."

"An interesting prize. I have never seen Heldrig use it himself."

"He cannot. It is a prize and a trick! He was promised it, and then it turned out to be a woman's tool." She laughed in merriment at this. All past hurt feelings were forgotten.

"He saved it for a daughter to use. Prudent."

"He tried for many hundreds of years to alter it first."

"Would you like to try more shadow magic?"

"No, I am not good at things I have not practiced with much, and I hate being bad at things. When Mars returns, I will take back his dream magic unless my father needs my help with something. Then I will take on his elements of oil or blood." She paused and sighed. "I hate oil the most."

"Because you are naturally of water?"

"Yes, you are brilliant, and oil and water do not mix!" This got her laughing again. She scooped a few rose petals out of the water and began stacking them on the side of the tub.

"Alright, now tell me what you saw in my dreams." Donya felt she needed to be direct, or working with Nera would take all night.

"I saw lots of things. I preferred to stay in the parts about the new world. I want to go there one day. I will start in your San Francisco. Maybe take a lover or two and work my way up that big estuary." She leaned out of the water, grabbed a towel hanging from a hook, and handed it to Donya, who waved it away. "I saw the two humans. They are younger than I thought. Both are very beautiful in your memory. I will not like to kill either of them. I am forced to do many things I don't like." She stood, pressed the towel to her face, and made gentle circular motions to dry off.

Donya watched as she moved the towel down over her arms and along her torso. "After this, maybe you can take your trip. Once your father has the woman, he might let you run free."

Nera snorted, "he will probably need me to bind her all the time at first." She put a foot up on the side of the tub and dried her leg. Donya sat back on the toilet and put her shoes back on. "In your head, she is mighty. I suppose Father is right to go after her. The young man is special. Are you sure you want to eat him?" She wrapped herself in a dress that tied at the waist and came to her knees.

"Look at me. I am sure."

Nera turned and studied her, "I see you. It depleted my strength to bind you willingly. I will need help if I am ever to do it again."

They heard voices from the other room. Nera stepped past Donya and opened the bathroom door.

"She spotted me, and that thing on her foot glowed like a tiny star. But I know the hotel and tomorrow I will go back when they are out. I spent many hours outside the hotel after they went up. I know their energy properly and can locate them from a distance. If either of them slept while I stood there, I could not tell, which is odd," Mars spoke rapidly but without emotion. He didn't gesticulate, purely reporting to his father.

"Wonderful. I will go with you. It will be a family adventure," Heldrig said.

"Will you be going into their room?" Donya asked.

"Yes, I think it best. We can get their names off paperwork or luggage and collect other effects additionally," Heldrig answered without moving crouching over his work.

"Get me hair. I think I have an idea of how to trap the redhead," Donya said.

"Yes, of course. Do you care to elaborate on this plan you have formed?" Heldrig asked.

"Not yet. It is a new idea. I'll need to think about it. It would hinge on Nera," Donya said.

"Nera, Nera, Nera. Everything always ends up wrapped up around my darling daughter," Heldrig said, tapping his fingers on a stack of papers.

"If that is the case, I should go with you. We can talk while we walk to your bridge," Nera added brightly, ignoring her father's annoyed tone.

Heldrig waved a hand dismissively. "Go on then you two, we can reconvene at dusk tonight. Mars and I will come to you then. Do not go anywhere else, Nera."

Nera nodded and they were on their way.

Donya slowed her pace for Nera to keep up. Nera drifted around the street, stopping to inspect anything she thought might be interesting. Like a stream flowing over boulders, she never moved in a straight line.

Donya realized she had been bound for many hours. The sun would be up again soon. Still, they were not far from the river. A small outcropping of grass that grew between cobblestones held Nera's attention. Donya needed to get a better handle on her binding power if she was going to plan. Instead, she felt incredibly interested in what Nera glimpsed in her dream, in what Nera glimpsed in her.

"In my dream, you got to see the streets of San Francisco?" Donya blurted.

Nera stopped gazing at the grass. "Oh yes, it stayed dark because you see almost everything in the dark. Can you not go out in the sun more?"

"I can go in it more than many others. Female trolls are not as delicate as males. When I was young, it hardly bothered me. I am not sure what is changing. Now I can take a half hour, or less. It drains me." And it needed to be weaker sunlight, the hour before sunset was best, hazy skies worked as well.

"I think I know what it is."

"From one dream about the New World and my flight here?"

"I did not merely see that."

Of course, she didn't. She wouldn't stop prancing around the street, peeking at every little thing. How far back did she go? "What else did you see through my eyes in the dream? And what do you think about my sunlight intolerance?"

"I went back to the day your parents turned to stone. It could be I am wrong—dreams are not accurate. I think it is because you trolls get lazy."

"I am a lot of things, but I am not lazy." Donya felt tense again right between her shoulders. Who cared what this trite half-nymph thought?

"Yes, you are. You all are. It is easy to eat humans, so that is what you do, even though other food would make you happier. Eating humans is what makes you less tolerant of sunlight. I'm not sure why. But I saw it in the dreams. All the trolls you knew who have been taken by sunlight ate a lot of humans. How many people have you been eating?"

Donya remained quiet. It wasn't her fault the glaciers receded. The warm weather, even up in the mountains, did not allow trolls' favorite plants to bloom and set seed properly. And the situation worsened in the last few hundred years. She blamed circumstances, not laziness.

"Wait, look!" Nera jumped forward; a broken shard of blue glass lay in the street. She grabbed it up, holding it to a streetlight.

Donya remembered she didn't often have eyes—thus, an ordinary object must be more fascinating. Maybe her lack of permanent eyes gave her clearer vision. Donya considered if she could be correct about the humans. If that was the case, all she did made her more vulnerable to the day. She opened her mouth to ask for more clarification on the human hypothesis when Nera flicked the glass into the air to watch it come clinking down to the ground. When it hit, she twirled and grabbed Donya's hand.

"Let us go. Come on, we only have all day in the water." Nera pulled Donya now, finally, quickening her pace.

"We need to talk about your binding magic. We need to talk about a lot of things."

"Talk, talk, talk. You are like Father all of a sudden. Effusive. We will. I want to give you as good a chance as I can."

Donya didn't follow Nera's words. Except for the part where she talked too much, which she felt was true. Shame crept around on the back of her neck. Nera sure brought something out in her. She just wasn't sure what.

# CHAPTER 19
# SCARLET

"Lean a little more over the grass," Juan called with the phone held up.

She leaned over the perfectly manicured lawn a bit more. The lawn was roped off, it was not meant to be walked upon, it looked amazing in the pictures. The bright green set off the leaning tower. Scarlet kept the smile plastered on her face while she tilted forward. The picture would probably turn out better if she took her sunglasses off. Still, it was bright out, and she didn't think she could keep from squinting while smiling and pretending to hold up the tower—too many things for her mind to force her body to do.

"Perfect. Come see," Juan called her back as another group of tourists meandered into the square.

"Do you want to go to the Cathedral? Maybe we could take pictures in front of it. I think it's free to go in," Scarlet said, not enthused about the idea. They'd already taken so many photos here, but she knew what made him happy.

"It is kind of a nice day, not as cold as Florence. I think I'd rather stay outside."

Scarlet looked up at the sky. Clouds covered it, but today they felt like a wooly blanket, holding the slight warmth in. There was no wind. Occasionally the sun would peek out. Pisa did feel nicer than Florence, more open, despite the large number of people. "We can go see the botanical garden. It's on our way back to the train station."

"Great, but first, we need lunch."

"Do you want lunch or gelato?" Scarlet only half-joked. Juan normally liked ice cream back home, but he'd eaten gelato one or two times a day here in Italy, not that she complained. She loved it too.

"Both. I want both."

They walked through the botanical garden. Scarlet loved to find gardens when she could. One of her favorites had been in Edinburgh, found during an after-college trip with several friends. Its walls were filled with rhododendrons in bloom. When the group made it up to Loch Ness, Scarlet waited for something supernatural. Nothing happened. She rode around on the black water in the warm comfy boat and looked at the scattered old buildings along the water's edge with everyone else. That was very uneventful compared to this trip.

This garden promised peace. She wasn't sure if it was associated with the University of Pisa, known for the sciences, which Galileo attended. The grounds were large, but they arrived there too early in the season for most blooms. The trees along the garden wall were massive. Several stood there for hundreds of years. In one corner towered an immense camphor tree. With a white trunk and dark green leaves, it was taller than the surrounding buildings. The paths were filled with pea gravel, which bothered Scarlet's foot through her shoe.

She could see an old round fountain ahead, next to a giant bamboo grove. Instead of flowing water at the center stood a large rock, covered in maidenhair fern. Moss clung to the outside of the fountain, and a large magnolia tree grew beside it.

"I'm going to rest on that," Scarlet let Juan know as they approached the fountain.

Scarlet picked the least mossy spot and sat. It wasn't designed for sitting. The edge was rounded, and the whole thing hung low to the ground. There were not any benches around either.

"I don't like it," Scarlet whined to Juan with a mock frown.

"There's a retaining wall. Do you think it will be more comfortable?"

The low wall lay in deep shade along a raised bed. "It'll work." Scarlet reached up a hand, and Juan grabbed it to help her up.

"They don't have benches, but they have a lot of lawn. I bet most people sit on that."

"It's too mucky to do today. Maybe our next trip here should be in summer." Scarlet said it without thinking. After several strange encounters, she wasn't sure it was safe for Juan to travel to historical places.

"I hoped you would say that. I love it here. I know I am a fraidy cat when it comes to travel. But I really want to do more of it," Juan said. He smiled and gripped Scarlet's hand as they walked to the stone edge of the garden.

"Maybe we could go to Hawaii for our honeymoon. And you haven't seen a lot of the other states. We can do an East Coast tour."

"Hawaii sounds amazing, but you went to Asia, and you said you loved Japan. I want to go to Japan with you."

Scarlet plopped down on the stone wall. Japan for Juan was a terrible idea. Even with her abilities, she had been approached by a spirit dog in Kyoto. The large white dog wore a rope leash. Scarlet walked back to the hotel from a bathhouse, tipsy on sake and warm water. She couldn't remember why she was alone—her friends might have headed to a bar. There was a 7-Eleven on her way and she wanted snacks. The dog appeared normal, maybe a bit too fluffy. Afraid it would be hit by a car on the street, she picked up the end of its leash. The dog yelped, and she felt a zing. The contact lasted a second. But as near as she could tell she'd moved—teleported to a block that didn't have a 7-Eleven on it. The dog didn't seem malicious. But if anyone else would have grabbed that rope, well she wasn't sure where they would have ended up.

To Juan, she managed to say, "of course, dear. We can plan it all when we get home."

Juan smiled and leaned over to kiss her on the head. "Okay, I'm gonna check out that bamboo, then I'll come back."

"Good idea. It's amazing even from here, but all those stems poking up won't work with my sore foot." And she needed to look at her work email. The gardens had free Wi-Fi throughout.

"When I get back, let's go into the greenhouse with all the cactus," he said, walking to the tall bamboo. It could have been something from a Hollywood set, the green was vibrant and the stems waved pleasingly in the slightest of breezes.

Alone, Scarlet thought about what she needed to do. Juan's new desire was it, the final straw. She had a magically infected foot, and now her future husband, a spirit magnet, wanted to travel the world. She must do something. She couldn't keep ignoring the supernatural world she could see.

The scene she sat in seemed serene. The water, the magnolia, and a line of blooming camellias started a few feet to her left. But on the inside, she could feel bubbling energy. Turmoil and acceptance zinged around in her head.

She hadn't noticed it, but the sound of dripping water surrounded her. It didn't come from the fountain, but down the wall, water dripped. And there were other water fetchers scattered in the garden, ponds with sunk-in boxes containing water lilies and lotus.

Scarlet admired the magnolia blossoms. Then she floated in a memory. It was a hot sunny day. She visited her grandmother's ranch. Her young self sat on the ground in the shade of the eucalyptus which held her treehouse. Her grandfather built it before he died. It was not pretty, just plywood, but stable—kittens played all around her. A black cat had wandered onto the property that spring. Her grandmother kept it around to mouse. But she didn't spay her, leading to five equally black kittens, which delighted Scarlet. One came out fluffy, which seemed extravagant in a barn cat.

The mama cat stayed skittish, but the kittens were easily lured with food and the promise of playing with a string on a stick. Scarlet made the toy herself. She swung it back and forth in front of her—the kittens tumbled and ran to and fro. Occasionally she would grab one, spin it around, and hold it like a baby. The kittens did not tolerate that. But they stuck around, continuing with the game.

Child Scarlet heard the car coming up the dirt drive and turned. Auntie Lou drove an olive-green bug. She always visited when Scarlet spent two weeks with her grandma. Scarlet preferred her great aunt to her grandmother any day. She wished she could spend the two weeks with Lou instead, but that wasn't the way her mother designed her summers.

Lou stepped out of the car and rushed right over to Scarlet and the kittens. "Hey there, sweetpea, whatever are you doing?"

"Playing with my kittens," Scarlet said.

"Your kittens? All of them?"

Little Scarlet pouted, "I asked, and I get to keep one for at home. Grandma says she will keep the mama and all the boys cause they are cheap to fix. Oh, and the long-haired one 'cause it's pretty."

"How many are left after that?"

"Two, this runt girl here." Grabbing a smaller kitten and displaying it, "then this girl here." She held up the final kitten.

"Which one do you want more?"

"I love the runt the most. I already picked her. I can't decide if I want to name her Pepper or Midnight."

"I will take the other girl then. But you know, black cats are special. Every time they cross your path, the fates take a look at you."

"You mean like this?" Young Scarlet waggled the stick in front of her. All five kittens ran back and forth. The mama cat watched from a short distance away then decided to come over too. She wasn't that old of a cat and still had play in her.

"My dear, yes. You have been playing this game a lot."

"About a hundred times this week."

Auntie Lou laughed. "That will make your life interesting. How about you name your kitten Pepper and mine Midnight."

The sound changed bringing Scarlet back to the present. The water didn't drip or trickle but rushed. Scarlet opened her eyes, not recalling when she closed them. She felt as warm as she had the day of her childhood memory. Her mind felt clear and relaxed. She could recall that memory easily. But right now, it was more like reliving the day, like a vision. Sucking in a breath of air, she felt surprised it was not warm and dry.

Her eyes rested on her foot. The glow was back, coming through her boot, now through her pant leg. It spread, but there was no pain. If anything, she felt a sense of calm and strength coming from her foot, if that was possible. Perhaps that thing in Venice hadn't meant to hurt her.

Tonight, when she got back to the hotel, she would start Google researching. It would be hard to know where to start, magical bites, mythical monsters, but she would start. It wasn't an ideal research method, but better than her usual nothing. Juan popped his head out of the bamboo and motioned for her to come to him. With a small sigh, she got up, no email checking for her.

CHAPTER 20

# DONYA

Donya felt the day went by too fast. The first few hours after sunrise, she and Nera spoke of everything—what made the best bindings, such as combining items of the past, present, and future or the four elements. Nera was thrilled they shared a connection to the water. She never seemed genuinely surprised, though, about anything Donya revealed.

Nera did not care about giving away secrets to Donya. That simple childlike trust made Donya trust Nera back. It occurred to Donya this was not the best idea as nymphs were known to be fickle. Although elves tended to be steadfast in their loyalties, except Heldrig, perhaps. Because she was half of each, Donya wondered if she could be loyal and fickle.

Nera disclosed that her father did indeed have a long-term plan to grow his clan again. However, no Azish woman would have him; thus, he settled on humans or others. He changed this narrative. He'd not been jilted by his own kind. Rather, he chose to work with others to make stronger children. Nera was wise enough to know he deluded himself.

When the sun got higher, Donya finally gave in to sleep. She was too weak to stay up through a full day. She thought Nera would leave, but instead, Nera sat on the bank of the Arno River, dangling her feet in the water. Donya chose to sleep in the flowing water in the shadow of the bridge.

Near dusk, Donya awoke. Nera basked in the thin sunlight on the far shore. She stood very still with her head tilted back, gazing up at the sky. Her expression appeared sad in the distance. Perhaps the nymph yearned for attention, she thought. Donya uncurled slowly, but Nera sensed the movement, quickly diving into the water and streaking across the bottom of the murky river, popping up not five feet from Donya. The dirty water spilled from her milky blue skin and her dress.

"You are up early," she said flatly. "Father came by a few hours ago. He said he would be here at full dark to talk."

"You don't sound happy about any of that. Including me waking up early."

Her small mouth popped open. She flicked water at Donya, saying, "don't you tease me. I am very happy you woke up early. It gives us a chance to run away together. Let us go to your mountain."

Donya stood stiffly. "Why would you say that?"

Nera didn't move. She studied Donya and perhaps found her wanting. "It doesn't matter. Father would find us. The path would go wrong. The water will fix everything, it already told me."

"Nera, what is going on? I would say you are speaking in riddles, but that is not even a riddle."

"I have to hope she is not angry at you. But why would she be when you are so cute?" Nera said. Twilight painted the sky bright pink. Her mismatched eyes took in the colors above as she and went on, "why can you not be more like father and fail to listen to me?"

Donya got the hint to drop the subject. Maybe she could get the answers later. She realized with a pang that she wanted to spend more time with Nera. She wanted this little adventure to take the whole time the humans were in Italy. What had that seer said? It will end in Rome on March twenty-eighth. Only one week left. Not even, really. The silence went on too long, and Nera's eyes strayed to the water. "Why doesn't your father listen to you?" Donya asked. "Why does he seem to prefer your brother?"

Nera stepped closer to Donya, her mismatched eyes sparkled with energy but her lips were pressed tight, like someone holding in a scream, "I hate him, always have. I ran away many times, starting when I was knee-high. That was what got my sight removed, then I hated him doubly." She reached out a hand. Looking Donya in the eyes, she put her fingers in the troll's spiky hair. "He would not let me go; he needed me to use the circlet. Also, I beget girl children. He wants his new family to be more men for fighting. I am such a disappointment."

"He took your eyes," Donya didn't question it. She stated it. That action sounded like something he would do. It sounded like he did more, but she didn't know how to ask that.

"To be fair, he warned me if I ran away again, he would do it. I ran away, and he found me, and he did. I was young and impulsive. I thought I could swim fast enough, but blood calls to blood, and I have half his."

"And now he is the only one who can give you back your eyes, so you must stay with him." Donya could appreciate the trap aspect of it. He held all the power.

"He always takes the best things away from me," she said with a pout and a tug of Donya's hair.

"What else did he take?" Donya asked.

Nera pulled her hand back, winding her fingers together and twisting her hands. "My mother. He kept using her blood. She died when I was not much more than a babe. I can still remember her songs though."

"Do you think getting the redhead will help? Have I brought you something that will ease your burden? Or have I made it worse?"

"You will ease my burden," she said with a real smile and a hand moving to Donya's forearm. "Now come, we must be off this subject. It is almost full dark. Tell me important information. Tell me a truth I can use." The hand moved down Donya's arm.

Donya did not know what to say. She tried to be herself, following the diamond's advice, but every second she felt pressure, hidden beneath her other warmer feelings but recognizable. It seemed like a trap, a trap for who or what, she wasn't sure. But Nera couldn't possibly mean her any harm. "I think we need to capture the young man and then use him as a lure for the redhead," Donya blurted out. That must be important, right? "We can do it in Rome. Wait 'til they get there. Steal him one night, then with our magic combined, call her out through shadows and bind her."

Nera puckered out her bottom lip. "A perfect plan, but not what I meant." Nera squeezed Donya's hand.

Donya tried to think quickly. What could she mean? What was more important than capturing those two humans?

"Hurry, hurry, your information. Stop asking about me. I need to know about you."

Donya thought of something. She located it in her pocket. "I always carry this." She held it up. It was a small piece of metalwork bent and folded around a single grain of sand from her grandmother's river. The detail was very fine. In it a minute troll stood under a rainbow. The colors of the rainbow were done in gold. It had an enchantment, so it never tarnished. It was a lucky charm, although Donya never felt lucky.

Nera clapped her hands. She leaned forward and clutched the charm. Quickly placing it on her tongue and closing her mouth around it. She kissed Donya on the cheek. "I knew you could do it."

Donya wanted to protest. That charm was one of the few things she always kept. It had been on the bracelet she used to form the oath with Heldrig.

"There you two are, up on land. Nera, get back in the water. I told you to be at full strength tonight," Heldrig called as he descended the stairs to the riverbank. Mars followed behind him, eyes cast down at the stairs.

Donya nodded to the two of them. She could smell magic in the air. Let Nera hold the charm for now. Maybe it would be luckier with her.

"Here, catch, you tiny bit of trouble," Heldrig said as he tossed something at Donya. She reached up, snatching it out of the air.

A wad of human hair from the young man landed softly in her hand. She relaxed as some of the creeping anxiety about her situation lightened. The trap they would set was for the humans. Nera couldn't help being contrary and dramatic.

Without prompting, Heldrig began talking, "their names are Juan Giovanni Nieves and Scarlet Josephine Burke. He has passports from both Mexico and the USA. She has a US passport and her California driver's license. He didn't have a license, which is too bad. It has height and weight and the date of birth—so much valuable information. We learned their home address. That means should our efforts fail here, we can follow them back to California, sunny California."

Donya studied the hairball while he spoke. The hairs mostly came from the young man, Juan, with a few of the redhead's hairs tangled in the cleanings from his brush. She set to picking out nine strands of his hair, the longest she could find, with the little ball of skin at the end. These would be the best connection. His name was Juan. Her name was Scarlet. She cemented that information in her mind.

Nera floated out into the middle of the river. She used her strong legs to keep alongside them even through the powerful current. Donya watched her for a moment. It was wonderful. They had much more time now. The advantage was theirs with all this information. Not only that, should plans go wrong or feel off, they could follow them back to California. Nera said she wanted to go there. Donya would not mind going back to that blasted place now.

"Now you get in the water too," Heldrig told Donya.

This struck her as strange. They had all this information. They needed to get to planning. She wanted to ask why, but Heldrig stepped forward and made shooing motions with his hands. It was fine. Everything would fall into place. She felt a little lightheaded with her hope for the future. He got her exactly what she asked for, so she obliged. She stepped in; mud squished up past her knees.

Nera swam up behind her, wrapping her arms around Donya. Donya felt a flutter in her gut.

"For me?" Nera asked, opening her hands in front of Donya's face.

"Yes, of course, there is a trinket for you." Heldrig took a small heavy object from Mars and tossed it to Nera.

The smell of Donya's mountain wafted past her nose—home. She looked down. A simple rock screamed up to her, "move move move!" It was hard to understand as a single strand of her hair partially gagged it.

Donya did move, but not fast enough, though. Nera's hand closed over the rock. A rock from Donya's home range of mountains. Then the fist came to Donya's chest. It felt like being bound before but worse. She was conscious. Fully awake, but her body did not respond. Nera fell back into the water, kicking hard to drag her deeper. Was this what standing stones suffered? Did that just happen? Donya couldn't even move her eyes. She couldn't look down to see her body. Only straight ahead. Nera pulled her into the deeper water. The night sky sparkled above them full of stars.

CHAPTER 21

# SCARLET

Scarlet sat at the little desk in their Florence room, scrolling through the hundreds of pictures on her phone—pictures of gelato, their lunch, the leaning tower, and a bunch of plants in the garden. Trinkets and souvenirs spread out across on the desk. There were also dried flowers and seeds, she had taken seeds from every pod she came across. It was a bad habit of hers picked up from her mother who loved to garden. As a child, Scarlet had been sent after seed pods from other people's yards or even cuttings. No one said anything if a mostly well-mannered child took a twig off of some plant. People were happy the child stayed quiet. The ones laid out were not even all of the seeds, a few stayed jammed deep in pockets of jeans packed in her luggage.

She needed to put photos on Facebook or Twitter to prove to their families they were safe and having fun. Apparently, proposals were not enough to assure them. She selected three good photos of Juan and sent them to the messenger group of his family. Then she picked a favorite of the two of them with the tower in the background and sent it to her mother. Posting to the public could wait. Captioning took too much time. At the last minute, she sent a photo of a pink camellia with a yellow calyx to Lettie. It was nice to have a soon-to-be sister-in-law who liked her.

Before closing the app, Scarlet inspected one photo more closely. One that she hadn't sent to anyone, but she saved it to her favorites. Juan didn't smile at the camera in it. His head was turned. He smiled at her.

Once Juan fell asleep, she needed to start googling the supernatural. She wasn't sure where to start though. What would be a reliable source? Should she look up old books? Or maybe reread original versions of fairytales? Harry Potter? Could that be a source?

Scarlet sighed. Her body felt tired, and her logical mind saw no place to start. Maybe she could Google psychics. Some of them had to be real if she was in fact real, and could see what she saw, right?

"Do you think I should get the skip-the-line pass for the David tomorrow?" Juan asked, breaking Scarlet out of her train of thought and picture-scrolling.

"Nah, we'll go early like we said. It's the off season, the line shouldn't be long."

"It could mean less standing on that bad foot of yours."

"If we're not standing waiting for one big statue, we'll be standing around in another museum looking at smaller statues or walking someplace else."

"True. After we see that I want to go buy more stuff at the leather market."

"Okay," Scarlet said, then went on. "I think we should get to sleep. My foot isn't even that sore. It's all my other muscles." Stretching as she rose, Scarlet wondered if she should have checked her work email.

Juan leaned over and clicked the lamp off by him. "We've been walking a lot. It's my shin bones bothering me, they ache like I've been playing soccer." He put his phone away, but Scarlet kept hers out. "Hey, you said we need to sleep." Juan swatted at the phone.

"Okay, okay." She turned off her phone and set it next to her on the bed. She never put it far away in case she needed the flashlight in the middle of the night. Also, she knew the moment he started snoring she would pull it out and get to work.

It approached midnight and Scarlet googled in circles. Multiple websites agreed on never thanking any spirit or fairy—this seemed ungrateful to her. Most other information was all over the place. She searched for trolls. She couldn't put her finger on it but that little troll on the plane had felt like trouble. Trolls existed in several different traditions. Sizes varied from giants to smallish stature, temperament from bloodthirsty to harmless forest spirit.

Turning her search to location. "Supernatural Venice" got her a reference to an old TV show from the Seventies. Also, a couple ghost stories. There was a short invite to a colloquium to discuss witchcraft in early Venice, where witches were persecuted between fifteen and sixteen hundred, but none were convicted. Not a single conviction seemed strange, it could mean a possible lead. She bookmarked the page.

None of it explained the tendrils Scarlet saw under the water back in Venice. The thing bit her and now her foot glowed. Searching sea monsters was next, which led her to Wikipedia. She wanted to see what the most popular sea monsters were. One of the oldest accounts came from Pliny the Elder about a giant octopus. That seemed promising, but she continued through the list. There was Leviathan and Cecaelias, the Sea Monk, and a section called various sea serpents. Finally, she clicked another tab: Currently reported specific sea monsters. She saw Nessie, Nigen, and a shell monster specified.

Scrolling further, the Kraken was listed. That word popped, it even almost wiggled. Scarlet took a deep breath and clicked.

The Kraken was from Sweden and lived in the North Sea. It had a long history going back more than eight hundred years. But the area was all wrong. Still, the name felt right. This wasn't science. The Kraken must be close. It had tentacles after all, and that feeling when she saw the name. Scarlet turned off her phone. It was very late and every day would be long until they got home. They had a lot more sites to see, and her foot slowed her down but she would get through whatever this was. She had to.

With the light of her phone off, the room was not dark. She lifted her head a tad, peering at her foot. It glowed dully through the sheet and blanket. The glow was strong; not bright, but it cut through everything. It turned on at the oddest times. Sometimes it throbbed with pain and then there were times like now. It felt warm, there was no pain.

She would have to Google supernatural bites tomorrow night. Probably she would just get info on vampires. Her eyelids grew heavy. "What did you do to me, Kraken?" She mumbled around a yawn.

"My name, finally," came the faintest whisper of a voice, seemingly from Scarlet's water cup. This worried her, but she couldn't seem to stay awake to finish the path of that worry. The last thing she saw was the clock on the wall strike midnight.

CHAPTER 22

# DONYA

Donya could not move. But she could hear and see. Nera kept her bound under the center of the bridge now. At first, Donya faced downstream. Now, Nera laid Donya on the riverbed. Nera continued to hold her but not from behind. She sat astride her, her arms pressed on the stone over Donya's heart. Donya could see her face.

Heldrig worked on top of the bridge, she could hear him occasionally call commands to his children. Mars hung from the edge of the bridge to draw a circle on the underside. Donya could just make out what he did through the turbid water. He worked from the outside-in, drawing a large oblong circle with two triangles inside. It was a yenters circle. Yenters were off-balance, they did not use all four elements. Donya could see this one was advanced, as it focused on water and earth, then called out to fire.

Mars worked steadily. It took him a handful of hours. Donya lay sentinel of it all, a captive audience, hoping he would make an error and fall, knocking Nera from her perch. That never happened. Now it was finished. It was very dark, but she knew the time. Witching hour. It was midnight.

Heldrig came to the upstream side of the bridge, a light flickered into being, he burned something then it went out. He poured blood into the water. In the quick current, it moved slowly, creeping to form a sphere under the circle, clouding around Nera and Donya. Her nose recognized this blood. She obtained it for Heldrig days ago. He had always planned on trapping her. Nera was in on it—she always had been.

In the first hour, she mentally pleaded with Nera. If she let Donya go, she would do everything in her power to make Nera happy. Forever. She would give an oath of fealty. Anything Nera wanted. In her heart, she felt certain Nera could hear these surface thoughts; they were deeply connected. In the cross-flow of magic and power, she got flickers of Nera's emotions, mostly despair and hardship.

As time wore on, as Mars worked on the circle above them, Donya's feelings and pleadings changed. She turned to anger and menace. She thought if she did not get free that moment, she would never speak to Nera again.

During her insignificant threat, it occurred to Donya that if she did not get free soon, she would not speak to Nera because she would be dead. The strength had drained out of her during the binding. She wondered what would happen once that magic circle activated.

Blood hit the water and gathered around them, and she knew. She was not meant to last even the night. The trickle of strength leaving her became a torrent, surprising in its potency. Strange to know you have something because you are losing it.

The energy that left her funneled through Nera and up to the circle. It did not glow with light. It pulsed with shadow, like her magic, like what Nera borrowed from her the night in the bath. The connection between them was stronger while this magic flowed. Donya tried pleading again, yelling to be let go. Screaming internally. Nera buckled under the spell's pressure and mental strain, her face crumbled into sobs.

It wasn't much but Donya must keep going. She thought of Nera as she'd seen her in the last light of the sun. Donya let herself feel the beauty of the scene all over again. Then she imagined Nera dead. Like the man whose blood surrounded them. Throat slit. Blood pouring out.

Nera's hand fluttered, only a tremble but it was the hand over Donya's heart. Donya tried to move with this. She used everything left, pulling and straining. Trolls were one of the strongest of all beings in any realm. She believed with all her heart she could break free. Much to Donya's disappointment, her body did not obey, but she thought she managed a blink.

The water got darker with shadow as the spell continued to build with time. Donya did not give up, but her strength was almost entirely spent. She threw the most venomous thoughts possible at Nera, who weathered them better than at first. All were empty threats. Mostly they involved tearing Nera to pieces. Donya tried to throw in a few of killing Heldrig or Mars. But in the bit of her mind that received some magical feedback, she knew Nera didn't care about those two. She might have even felt a thrill at the idea of Donya pulling off all Heldrig's fingers.

It was ironic to Donya that a few days ago she felt weak, dry, and chalk-like. Now she felt waterlogged, her limbs soggy like wet clay. Maybe that was the consistency of her body at this point. She did not know, as she could not look down or move any part of herself to see.

She had an hour of life left. Maybe a little over. She would not make it to dawn. It was a trap. Heldrig must have spent the day finding out the woman's power type. Fire of course. What was the name again, Scarlet? Now that Donya was exhausted and giving up the fight she could wonder at such things.

With a fixed stare she focused on the dark lines of the magic circle. Details were hard to make out. She examined the left side of the circle, where a good trap would be built. The fire rune repeated, surrounded by water runes. Heldrig designed it to play into everyone's strengths, water for Nera, blood for himself, and shadow for Donya. Shadow powered the circle. Donya was being used as the power source instead of the blood and other elements contributing equally.

She appreciated the complexity. She never could have won. Heldrig was too far ahead of her for too long. She felt sorry for herself, just a little though. Had she not been warned about Heldrig? Several times, by the seer and the diamond.

The self-pity finally affected Nera. She leaned forward a bit, whispering in Donya's ear, "stop being dramatic."

Donya wanted to laugh. She would die at any minute. She felt like that was the one thing she had the right to be dramatic about.

# CHAPTER 23

# SCARLET

Scarlet woke up standing in the dark with one leg in her jeans. The blazing pain in her foot and leg brought her around to consciousness. Hot lava would have been more comfortable. She hissed through her teeth.

Juan snored in their warm bed. Why was she standing getting dressed?

'You were being called. I did my best to wake you,' came the small voice again. It was less even than a whisper.

Where did it come from? In her head? Scarlet wondered then waited, expecting clarification or at least a hysterical laughing fit to escape from her mouth. Nothing happened. Her leg pulsated with pain that made her want to whimper. Instead, she bit back the sad sound and stumbled to the bathroom. She was sweating, even in the cold air.

She had a shirt on she didn't recall going to bed with. She tugged it off over her head and started the water in the shower.

A shower would rinse the sweat off but probably not make her sane again.

"Perfect." There it was again. The voice came from the shower spray.

Scarlet gave in to her initial impulse to be clean. Being sweaty was not something she could stand. She stepped into the tiny but spotless glass box. When the water hit her, the pain in her foot vanished too quickly to be natural. The sudden soothing happened before too. Was the last time her pain completely faded in the shower as well? She couldn't recall.

"Please please please go away," Scarlet whispered under her breath.

All of this was too much. She wanted to be normal, or, at least go back to her version of normal. Newly engaged, this should be the happiest time of her life on a romantic trip. She put her hair under the water to try and rinse out all the babbling.

"Good, breathe and calm down. Panic has never aided any living thing."

"What are you? Where are you?" Scarlet whispered, water dripping around her mouth and off her chin.

"You know, you found me earlier. I am the Kraken. I reside in the most glorious city in the world, Venezia. Now things are very complicated."

"Please explain," Scarlet barely whispered. She was getting shrill.

"Be glad I have always liked humans. You gave me a gift in addition to this. I will explain soon. Now you need to go into the river. I will lead you to the spot needed. We will not be able to commune much until you arrive at the water."

Scarlet was not liking any of this. But she felt the power of this Kraken before and had seen how large and beautiful it was. She knew she needed to act, but stalled for a few more questions. She tried to lower her voice and slow down, but she rushed out, "okay I'll do what you want, but I need to know, can you read my mind? And why are you helping me?"

"I have only responded to things you say. I help you because of a compliment and a transgression. We will see if it helps anyone else. Now go. You have 'til daybreak."

Scarlet had more questions. All she seemed to be was a quivering mass of questions. Her anger showed up for her. Irritated that she could not ask everything she wanted. However, following directions seemed prudent. She stepped out of the shower and toweled off. Leaving the light on in the bathroom, she walked out into the room using the light from the open doorway to navigate silently, grabbing the sweater she wore that day and the pants she had been stepping into. It was cold out, maybe freezing. She wanted to grab her jacket. But something about getting into the Arno River stuck in her mind. How the hell was she supposed to do that? She swam regularly but an icy river in the dead of night seemed a bit much for her skill level. Her mind kept reeling. Wasn't the Kraken known for drowning sailors? If the Kraken wanted to drown her or Juan it had plenty of time to do it in Venice though. She shoved her hair into a quick bun and put a wool beanie on top of it.

She stopped and took in Juan. He lay on his side, curled toward her side of the bed. I'll be back as soon as I can be, she promised silently. Scarlet wanted to whisper that, but her throat wouldn't let her. When she returned, she could be his little spoon, warm and safe again. She kissed him on the forehead. He didn't like it when she did that if he was awake. He thought his forehead was too big. She thought it looked noble. Tears stung her eyes. If something happened to her he would never know what went wrong.

Grabbing the cheap hotel pen and notepad which sat at the tiny desk, she scribbled, "I love you." with a heart, then pulled on her tennis shoes and headed out the door. She held the door till it closed with a slight click.

She rushed through the lobby past the distracted night clerk and down the stairs two at a time. She felt the pull of the river and the ticking of the clock. When she hit the street, the cold felt like a slap to the face. Every part of her would be numb soon. She almost went back for her jacket. She didn't even have her cellphone. What if she got lost on her way back to the hotel? What am I doing? She screamed internally.

Part of her wanted to run but she kept herself to a brisk walk, this close to the city center. The voice called to her from puddles, guiding her on. The night was brightly lit. Without looking around too much, she noted as many landmarks as she could, to make her way back to the hotel.

A twenty-minute speed walk and three right turns later she stopped at a spot on the river.

"Here stop here," came the voice from the water.

The water rushed past below her feet. She hoped the spot she would step into was shallow. There was no way to tell. Everything was dark, the water was black. She took off her socks and shoes leaving them on the concrete ledge.

"Please help get me back here and back home," she said out loud, dangling a foot into the water.

Frigid water and the current pulled at her foot. She leaned over and felt no bottom. She'd put the glowing foot in first. But at this moment it did not glow. Way to poop out on her in the moment of need.

"Jump in. I will get you where you need to go. And keep your voice low or they will hear you," the Kraken said from the water.

The voice sounded clearer than ever. Scarlet looked around. What "they" was it talking about? She saw no one. It was pitch black by the water. "Fine," she responded.

She tore her hat off and tossed it by her shoes. The air bit into her skin with cold—she jumped in. She expected to be swept away but didn't feel movement. She also expected to be very cold, but the water temperature felt neither warm nor cold. Suspended in the water, she bobbed, which managed to be more disconcerting than if she had been tumbled over by the water as expected. She opened her eyes. A sphere of clarity formed around her. The water glowed teal compared to the blackness seen from above. She moved her arms and moved forward.

"Good. Be prepared to grab on. You need to grab both of the women."

"Sure," Scarlet said or tried to say. Water flooded into her mouth when she opened it. Magic was all around her, but she could not breathe or talk underwater. This better go quick; she could hold her breath for a lap pool length swimming hard, but that was all.

There was no time to think about it. She moved rapidly through the water. Kicking her legs, she swam but it didn't seem like she controlled the direction. It felt a little like being a missile, moving at speed through the dark water.

Then she saw them. It was only a split second. One lay on the river bottom, and another woman held her down. She reached out immediately. Her hand grabbed the one on top by the arm, which stopped her forward motion. Her other hand stretched for the prone figure. She felt cloth and a hard arm and clung on.

Water erupted all around them with a boom and it moved away in a wall. Her suspension system was gone, blown away. She plopped on the riverbed by the two women, still holding on to them, her butt in the mud. The three of them were the eye of the explosion. Water and strips of dark material peeled away.

Scarlet looked up and around. For all the sound, she felt unharmed. The river water was held away from them, they were in a big bubble, open to the surface. There was writing on the underside of the bridge. The edges smoldered. Then it caught and blazed for a moment. It went out and whatever forced the water away collapsed in.

It was not a very complex thought or a romantic one but as the wall of water crashed on Scarlet, she managed to say, "shit."

CHAPTER 24

# DONYA

Donya could not believe her eyes. One minute everything seemed to be going Heldrig's way, and the next, destruction rained upon him. She felt so much happiness, she wanted to holler and laugh, maybe dance a mad jig.

Scarlet, the redhead, appeared very suddenly and grabbed Nera, then her. She stopped the spell. Then an explosive reaction took place, the backlash of power implausible. Donya would not have believed it if she had not been there. The circle burst into flame. Heldrig and Mars were sadly out of her line of sight, but she was sure they had gotten a little flame treatment. It is possible she heard a scream, but it was hard to know with the roar of water and power.

The sphere that materialized around them felt strange, possibly a shock wave of magic, but maybe something altogether different. It pushed away magics. But there was no time to ponder. As the water crashed back, she had enough strength left to shove at Nera.

She shoved her while the water fell in on them. She expected chaos. Instead, a pale glow enveloped them. It reminded her of the light through a thin piece of jade. When it subsided, Scarlet and Donya held hands on the other side of the veil. They still sat in a river, a shallow slow-moving warm river.

It was rare to get pulled to another realm easily. Donya wasn't sure which one this could be—probably one of the fey Queendoms from the hum in the air. She still held the redhead's wet hand, her body felt slow and weak. Perhaps it is enough to lie down in this river and die.

"What happened, where are we?" Scarlet asked, swiveling her head around to see Donya.

Donya waited to answer. Scarlet's face took on the same intensity it held on the plane. She let go of Donya's squishy hand and scrambled to her feet.

"You!" Scarlet yelled, pointing at her.

Donya prepared to explain but two men at arms knelt on the river's edge. Both bore obsidian swords at their sides. One held a flute in his hand, the other a small string instrument she did not recognize. Donya was not much for music—no troll really is.

"Yes, me. Now pay attention. We are not alone." Donya's words sounded strange in her ears. The men-at-arms were fish folk, seaweed folk was more like it. They had a distinctly kelp-like appearance and smell, both a yellow-brown with wavy fetchers. They looked damp.

Scarlet spun around. She saw the men and took a step away from them, back toward Donya.

"Ladies, you will be honored to know her magnificence, the Kraken of Venezia has requested your presence," the two men said in unison.

Scarlet looked down into the water around her feet and said, "a little help here. What is going on?"

"I said to pay attention to them, not me," Donya responded.

"I'm not talking to you. I'm talking to the Kraken," Scarlet snapped.

One of the men interjected, "the lady will not be able to communicate with you here as she did in the human world."

"This makes no sense at all," Scarlet said, turning in a small circle.

"Let us go with them for answers," Donya said and tried to rise. It took a lot. Her legs felt heavy. Her arms bent uncomfortably when she leaned on one while getting up. The material status of her very being was questionable. She hoped they did not need to travel far.

The men stood and walked in front of them. "Follow us."

They wore red clothing with rich gold embroidery. The style was ancient, with tight pants and long jackets. The man on the left did not have symmetrical legs. One leg fell shorter than the other, which gave him a strange gait. Donya focused on that as she walked. It made her feel more dignified by comparison.

The Kraken was tremendously powerful. Donya wondered what she could want with them. Perhaps the human knew. She'd apparently been in communication with the Kraken. If

Heldrig knew that, perhaps he would have given up, as he had in Venice because of the Kraken's interference.

"You work for the Kraken?" Donya asked over her shoulder. The human brought up the rear of their troop.

"No, I think it bit me in Venice."

"Bit you? At the train station, on your foot, you had something you did not have before," Donya said.

The man on the right interrupted, "our lady does not bite, it was a kiss."

"It did not feel like any kiss I have ever received," Scarlet said too quickly.

Donya at some point in the river with Nera sitting astride her, feeling betrayed and on death's door, started rooting for Scarlet. She wanted her not to be taken by the trap. Those feelings had not dissipated entirely, causing her to say. "Be mindful. Those stone blades at their sides are not for show."

Scarlet's eyes swept the men. She caught up with Donya and met her eyes. "How are you here? And you said the train station? I saw you on the plane"

"You are slower than expected. I have been following you. All of this is probably my fault," Donya said with a scowl—*so* much truth in that last statement. Getting out of the trap put her in a great mood, but the truth brought her more to herself, her weak, and wrong self. Too weak to stand the sun, she continued with a question for the men, "how long 'til sun-up?"

The one with the strange gait answered, "hours but only a few. I know she plans to have the human back by then. You, I am not sure of."

Donya shrugged. Great, out of a horrible elf scheme and into whatever this old sea monster brewed.

Donya expected they would meet the Kraken in a palace. Instead, they were led into a tranquil wood. In the center of this wood lay a beautiful deep pool. Old marble stones lined it all the way around—perfect smooth stones. There were seven steps dipping into the water. The water started at the base of the third step and then went down, far down from the looks of it.

On the third step reclined the Kraken. She had no legs to speak of, instead hundreds of featherlike appendages spread out in the water. It bloomed like the bottom of a frilled dress. Most hung at the same length, but a small number stretched deep into the water. A few shorter ones floated on the surface in the dappled moonlight. Her top half had a torso and face. Delicate features and a distinct grace were apparent despite her lack of true arms. In place of arms hung tentacles with grasping cups and long curved black hooks at the end. Her salty smell hung in the forest air.

While Donya studied her, the Kraken studied the two of them. Scarlet had the good sense to not speak. Perhaps she took in the sight too. Finally, after a handful of minutes, the Kraken raised her right tentacle. The water shimmered, and a voice emanated from it, not a single voice but a chorus of voices murmuring like water tumbling over rocks, "ladies, it is a pleasure."

Donya dropped to one knee. She was unsure how to do any of this, but it seemed best to go with what felt right. "Your splendor lady Kraken, I apologize sincerely for any irritation my previous actions may have caused you. I would endeavor to redeem myself."

"Yes, you do need much redeeming," the Kraken responded, pinning Donya with a dark gaze.

Donya saw Scarlet shift on her feet. Scarlet's fist clenched and unclenched next to Donya's head.

"Could I maybe ask some questions before I get rushed off again?" Scarlet asked.

"You will get rushed again, soon even, my dear. Now wait. Knowing what happened before will help you as much as knowing what you need to do in the present and future," the Kraken answered from the water.

Perhaps the Kraken would help them, or at least the human, Donya mused.

Then the Kraken continued, "where in the world is Nerawen?" She paused, either for dramatic effect or because the strange way she spoke required it. "Scarlet, I told you to grab both of them."

"I did. I held on to them as hard as I could. But it felt like being in a tornado. I'm not that strong," Scarlet responded.

Donya remembered what happened. She was the reason Nera didn't come through. It felt like the wave crashed on Donya again. That whole time, Nera planned on saving Donya. She sank even farther, bowing her head. "It was me. I pushed her away."

She couldn't see what happened, but she heard the water splash like a tentacle arm smacked it. The night fell silent. She raised her eyes.

The Kraken still sat in the same position. Her color changed, her skin pale like moonlight before, and now she flashed a crimson red. Her eyes fixed on Donya. "You." Again, she paused. "Have the same luck as poor Nera. None whatsoever."

Donya could have told her that. "She did not betray me then? We were to escape?" Her questions came out quiet. All her earlier joy drained. A feeling she had never experienced took joy's place.

"Obviously. Now you sit there in your shame. Think about what you left her with." Her color faded back to pink and violet. She continued, "we ladies need to stick together. I have kept to that dictum for the last fourteen hundred years. My grandmother who dwelled in Carthage would not have died so unceremoniously if she kept that in mind." The Kraken stopped, and turned to the men. "Husbands, go get Donya nourishment, I will show them."

Donya moved her head to make eye contact with Scarlet, then said, "I can take food here but whatever you do, eat nothing."

Scarlet bobbed her head to agree. Donya couldn't do anything about the situation she left behind, but she could help this human out a little.

The Kraken observed this, nodding her head, then gestured to the pool.

CHAPTER 25

# SCARLET

Scarlet kept the scream that wanted to rip through her lips contained at the back of her throat. She was both naturally impatient and inquisitive about the world around her. There were no answers, instead only more questions.

The troll next to her knew what was going on. What was the name she used on the plane? The little troll looked disheveled. In junior high, Scarlet made a pinch pot that looked similar, all lopsided, and the clay pooled at the base.

Then there was the Kraken in front of her, part fantastic sea creature, part humanoid, beautiful and terrifying. All her colors changed like she contained chromatophores. To be sure of any of it, Scarlet would need to get much closer and have better lighting. Several torches stood around the pool and tiny lights came on in the trees, then winked out again, like fireflies but larger. None of that made sense.

Under the water, the Kraken worked. Her feathery appendages moved in a rhythm, and for the first time, sound came from her mouth, a singing—soft, no words just tones. The top of the pool remained mirror smooth, undisturbed by the movements. This breaks the laws of physics, Scarlet thought.

An image formed on the water—Venice but long ago. There were horses in the streets and no electric lines. Carnival at sunset, everything painted in shades of orange. Women and men danced all around. Several women sat at the edge of a cistern—all of them beautiful, with long black hair and dark dresses. Masks shrouded their faces. The Kraken ceased her singing, and her eerie voice came again from the water, "*mi cerchia di risate*, they were all mine. I loved to work with them in my youth. They met for over a millennium. My weakness is disease. It would come to the city, killing them along with many others. There was little I could do."

She began the song again.

A woman floating in the water with her eyes sewn shut appeared in the water mirror. The image said, "he called, as you said it would be. He wants to use the troll. I will trap her."

The troll next to Scarlet whispered, "Nera."

Then this image changed. It was Nera in a bathtub. A horrid-looking man stood over her saying, "listen, you useless trifle. Go to the river and meet with Donya. It is very hard to get on the good side of a troll but endeavor to do so."

"Father, is there not another way? We can do what she asks. You will still be able to take the woman as a wife."

His mouth straightened into a thin line. He sat on the rim of the tub and reached out to Nera's face. He touched below her eye and said "If this all goes well, I will have more children.

I won't need you with me anymore. You can be free. We only need to cooperate together for a few more days"

"Yes, Father."

Scarlet shuddered as the image faded out. Nera in the bath appeared so vulnerable, naked, and helpless. That man she called father looked like a predator out of a Guillermo del Toro movie. She wrapped her arms around herself.

The Kraken stopped her singing again. She gazed at Donya first, then toward Scarlet. "You, Scarlet, are the one he intends to wed."

Scarlet's stomach twisted. "I've never seen that guy before! And I would never! The only one I would ever marry is Juan!" Scarlet shouted. Her right hand squeezed her ring, pinching the stone.

The husbands appeared on the other side of the troll with a platter of old vegetation. Scarlet moved away from the troll and the men. She wanted to be alone. Her mind reeled, she thought she should run away from here. Instead, she took another step and plopped on her butt, rocking back and forth a bit.

"Do not fret, I have no intention of letting him at you. Heldrig is very ugly and he ruins beautiful things," the Kraken said.

Scarlet wanted to calm down, but her heart pounded in her ears. Those words were probably quite kind from such an ancient being as the Kraken. She glanced at the troll who shoveled cattails into her mouth, and other seed pods too. She chomped a cattail in half and the fluffy seeds scattered into the air, hitting a warm breeze off the water, and floating up and away.

The Kraken gestured to her pool.

Another image formed; it was the dragon Scarlet had seen in the sky above the hot springs. The memory was not from her point of view. She could see herself sitting in her blue one-piece and the great beast breathed on her. "Did anything change after this day?"

Scarlet thought about it. "Changed? No, I never saw anything that big, but it didn't eat me and nothing else strange happened," Scarlet answered. The dragon seemed even bigger than she remembered.

"Is that the Western Sky Wyvern?" Donya asked, slowing the rate of her cattail intake.

"Yes, have you seen the Northern one?" The Kraken responded.

Donya nodded. "We call her Burl, she drank from the pond at the base of my mountain. She drank it all in one sitting."

"You are very lucky you did not run into the Western Wyvern. He eats earth and rocks."

Scarlet understood the implication of the Kraken's words. That troll next to her could be confused with a pile of rocky rubble, or at least mud and rubble.

"Was it going to eat me?" Scarlet asked the two monsters.

The Kraken shook her head. "He inspected you. When I saw this memory in you, I thought perhaps he enhanced you. The breath did seem to be a blessing." She halted, tilting her head as if a new thought occurred to her. "In your memories, you always seem to come out of situations with the best possible luck." She lowered her gaze to the water again. The image changed and it was an eight-year-old Scarlet with a black kitten in her lap.

"Midnight," Scarlet said.

"You picked the black kitten with green eyes, best for increasing power." The image shifted and she aged to a teen, midnight slept on the bed next to her. "And you slept with her every night. You should have cultivated your talents. However, then none of this would have happened. I am quite pleased it is unfolding though."

"The past is interesting, but what about now? What can I do now to go back to how things used to be?" Scarlet tried to keep the notes of begging out of her voice.

"Humans, you always want to go back. Onwards ever. We shift focus to Donya, then we can get on with the future," said the Kraken, her colors shifting as she spoke.

Scarlet noted she recalled both of those memories recently. The Kraken had rooted around in her head for a few days. She would not have remembered those incidents otherwise.

In the water, a nightscape hill appeared. A small version of Donya sat by a river, with a very hairy something by her side. A crone staggered up to her holding out a bundle. "Ewww, Nana, that tastes terrible, I can't ever eat it," the young version of Donya said. Scarlet could not actually understand the words as English, but she knew their meaning.

"Riken?" Nana asked.

"Me either," The hairball answered.

"A shame. This here is thrice-soaked cow hair. All Henkies eat it. As you have Henkie blood, I hoped it would be as tasty to you as it is to your old Nana. But no, stick to your seeds. Listen, don't start eating them people. They taste good but are troublesome. And they keep my cows safe, I like 'em."

"Yes Nana," both troll children said in unison.

The image faded and the Kraken watched Donya who looked sorrier by the moment. Scarlet thought the food would help her, but even if her body solidified, she seemed bowed under a weight.

"You should have listened," The Kraken said. The water changed and Donya stalked a hiker. A young healthy hiker, in bright red pants and a down jacket, '70s style that glowed in the twilight. He walked along a trail. The trail lay precariously along, but from the vantage point of the memory, you could see the trap he walked toward. A weak spot on the trail. He took a step and fell, screaming, his arms pinwheeling. He landed on sharp rocks, dying instantly. Still, the last few seconds of his life made Scarlet shudder violently.

"There were no saxifrage seeds. I replanted them the year before, the seedlings which emerged produced almost no flowers. There was not enough snow!" Donya explained. She had vigor in her for the last sentence but otherwise seemed like a piece of putty.

"I know," The Kraken replied. "You are especially easy to extract memories from when you sleep in the water."

"Saxifrages?" Scarlet asked. She thought that sounded familiar. What seeds had she plucked from the walled garden? Scarlet fished around in her pocket. "Are any of these seeds the same kind?" She held out her hand. The seeds were all wet. A few of the specimens had pointy seed pods and others bore fluff for floating on the wind. It was all a moist clump now. She poked at it with her finger. "You can have them all, I shouldn't have taken them anyway."

Donya stared at Scarlet's hand in a way that a man lost in the desert gaped at a gallon of water. "Really?"

Feeling uneasy about that look, Scarlet leaned closer, grabbed Donya's hand up, and plopped the whole mess into it. She watched the troll sniff the pile, then sort out two seeds from the rest. She gingerly picked one up and placed it in her mouth. Scarlet watched in discomfort as the troll started to cry.

CHAPTER 26

# DONYA

Donya was mortified as the tears slipped down her face. Troll tears, who would have thought there was such a thing? Blinking hard against more tears and sniffing at the tangled mess of seeds, she wondered why tears came from gratitude when she thought they were supposed to come from sadness. The seed in her mouth, she held onto the sweet flavor. She crunched it between her back molars. For all the other seeds she had eaten, this did infinitely more good. Her form took on a solid feel instantly.

Placing another seed in her mouth, she tasted cold winter twilight. The smell of night fallen snow was almost there in her nose. Two seeds and it felt like the events of the last night never happened. She pushed back at her hair and it stood up. By the torchlight Donya noticed the redhead avert her eyes, her gaze flickered back and forth between the Kraken and the two men the Kraken called husbands. If Donya defined her, she would use high-strung.

The Kraken gazed back at them. A small smile showed on her face. Donya knew what came next. "Freely given," she sighed.

"What will be the payment?" the Kraken asked.

Would asking her what she wanted serve her best, or would it be better to decide for her? Donya was surely unlucky, making the worst possible choices. This human could decide for herself. Safer that way. "What do you need?"

"Answers, a lot of answers," Scarlet replied. She didn't even blink.

Donya felt something shift inside of her. It seemed fair. Two seeds she needed for knowledge. From this point on she would have to answer Scarlet's questions.

"We all would like answers. Scarlet, I have been in many of your memories. They do not show who you are," The Kraken said. There was never inflection in the rush of voices, but you could tell the tones by watching the colors of the Kraken.

"Wait, wait, who am I, who are you two?" Scarlet asked.

"Donya will answer for you later. Time is running short. As long as you are here, I must find out about you," The Kraken answered, then went on. "If you survive the next week, we will have your whole lifetime to answer."

"Survive?" Scarlet said.

Donya watched as Scarlet squeezed the ring on her left hand again. It had not been there before. It must be important to her, Donya thought. When she squeezed it the stone in the ring babbled. Donya could not understand it. It giggled and squealed like a newborn. Was everything about this woman bizarre?

"Could you give me a condensed version of what is happening?" Scarlet asked.

The Kraken fashioned something in the water. Donya could see a spell swirling beneath the surface. Donya spoke up, "an old acquaintance, Heldrig who you saw standing by the bath, and I planned on taking you and your boyfriend. Heldrig angered the Kraken here. She decided to help you. He angered me, now I will help you."

"Maybe slightly more than that…" Scarlet trailed off.

Inside the Kraken's pool, a ball of light began to glow. The Kraken's voice sounded pleased when she said, "memory can flow to and fro. Forward is not my specialty. Get in and let us see what we can do."

Donya stood up. Her legs felt strong, about as strong as the marble stones around the pool. Pinned below Nera she came to know the amount of strength she possessed. She would not take it for granted again.

Donya walked into the glowing pool. The water was warmer than the night air. Pushing off the stone steps, she moved toward the ball of light. It was good she had Henkie in her, or she would have dropped like a stone. Scarlet hit the water with a splash above her, Donya entered the light.

In the light, she waited. Scarlet swam in. Then the Kraken's tendrils encircled the light. They crept in and brought Donya and Scarlet's hands together. The light began to concentrate. It condensed from a shining ball into a beam between the two women. Donya could not see the human through the burning white beam. The light shrunk. As it decreased in size, it increased in intensity. No sound reached Donya's ears. It was silent, like snow as it falls on a lonely mountain at night.

The light winked out. In its place stood a solid object, a blade. It looked very similar in shape to the swords the husbands carried. But the color was the opposite. This stone sword was made from opal. It flashed even under the water, red, yellow, and purple.

Not very practical, too soft a stone. Donya slid her hand along the blade; not sharp either. But it was beautiful. And this type of magic could be traced back to the beginning of tools. The sword would contain a pact, a bond that did not even need to be spoken out loud. As it formed from their natures, it could not be broken, like an oath.

The Kraken descended. She pulled the short sword from between them, then spoke. The sound came from everywhere. "This is lovely. Opal is the fire stone. I wonder what you contributed to it."

"Opal has water in it," Donya responded. She would always have a connection to water.

"Now sink to the bottom. Plunge it into the earth."

"Is this not for use?" Donya felt perplexed. Had they not formed this weapon to fight Heldrig?

"Not yet. For the next three days, it will help you both in other ways. Now hurry. The sun, it rises."

Perhaps this Kraken likes drama, Donya thought. Scarlet floated in the water in front of her. Donya grabbed the sword by the hilt with one hand and grabbed Scarlet with the other. Once her lungs ran out of air, she couldn't speak anymore underwater. She needed to plan her next words carefully.

With a few quick kicks, they landed on the sandy bottom. Donya could still see even in the near pitch black. She was surprised Scarlet did not struggle. The human could not see at all. She would need to fix that in the next few days. Such weakness was a problem in your companion.

She took Scarlet's hand in hers and wrapped it around the hilt. Then, they drove it down together. The sword lit up again, not brilliantly like before. In its place, a soft violet glow.

She looked across at the human. Buoyant with an open face. It was strange she seemed completely unafraid. Donya spoke her words, "tonight, be ready for answers." Then leaned forward, grabbed Scarlet by the waist, and pushed her up.

The human got the point, swimming away. Donya watched as she disappeared into the light near the surface. They would see each other, and soon. Everything would be different. Everything would be different for the rest of both of their lives. Donya hoped that it would be a long time, but even with all this help, she couldn't be sure the rest of their lives wouldn't be six days.

## CHAPTER 27

# SCARLET

Scarlet swam upwards. She took in another lung full of water. Apparently in this magic place, in this magic pool, she could breathe the magic water. It was a childhood wish come true. On land, she felt uneasy and burning with questions. The pool seemed to cool her off. She hadn't tried talking but she thought she would when she got back to the Kraken.

The Kraken hovered near the surface, tendrils hanging down, curling gently. At last, Scarlet got the mental image she had been trying to put her finger on. The Kraken looked like a very elegant, very colorful antique feather duster. Scarlet smiled at the thought.

"I have two answers now." An image of fire danced in the water. "That is your strength," the Kraken's voice rumbled around her. "Therefore, water is your weakness."

There was so much to take in and understand. Strengths and weaknesses, what did it mean? The part about water made no sense to her. Opening her mouth, water came out but no sound. She loved being under the water. How could it be bad for her? She kicked to the surface to speak.

Wiping water from her eyes, she coughed out the water in her lungs. It didn't burn. The Kraken floated in front of her, eyes out of the water while all else stayed submerged. Scarlet spoke when she could, "that can't be right, I love the water."

"Love does not make you strong against an element," the Kraken's voices came from the water. "You are more complex than fire. Now descend. I must send you home."

Scarlet was torn. Desperation to be with Juan again, to see him safe in bed, warred with her yearning for answers. What if she never made it back to this place? She had more questions for the Kraken. Knowing there were answers she could not have would be even worse than the blind stumbling she'd done before.

The promise she made before she ducked out of the hotel room flitted across her mind. She saw the Kraken smile under the surface of the water.

The urge to escape home hit her with a vengeance, the ultimate urge. She could stop all this by buying two tickets home and running. Ignore the problem. It was what she had always done.

"We can leave! Hop on the next plane home!"

The Kraken's appendages turned a brick-red under the water, but it did not reach her face. "They know where you live," she said in what seemed like fewer voices.

Was the Kraken breaking something to her lightly? Her eyes stung. Understanding hit her. The bad guy, that evil-looking thing, knew where she lived, in California. There was no escape.

She stopped kicking, sinking back into the calming water. She took deep breaths of the water—submerged hyperventilating.

The Kraken wrapped around her. Enveloping her in feathery tendrils. Scarlet's heart banged against her ribs.

When did I go back under? Scarlet felt confused again but totally calm. She watched the Kraken's tendrils as they moved around her.

"You must go home. Your beloved will wake soon. Take this." The Kraken held something small in her tentacle.

Scarlet took it. Her mind filled with the image of Juan smiling at her in that one special photo. A falling sensation followed, like the first second of an elevator ride. Then she was sitting on the riverbank, by her shoes and hat. Dawn broke in the east, dove gray and the lightest pink.

When she opened her now dry hand, she held fifty Euros neatly folded up.

Scarlet walked into the hotel room with a breeze. She was cold but she wasn't wet anywhere. Juan opened his eyes, looking sleepy and warm.

"Where did you go?" he asked in a groggy, slow tone.

"To get breakfast," she answered, throwing a bag of pastries at him. She pushed the lie. "Remember, I told you I wanted to try these."

"Oh yeah." He opened the bag. Cannoli stuffed the bag.

The fifty Euros was enough for a cab ride and an excuse. Scarlet felt exhausted. She should have bought coffee too, but honestly preferred tea which wasn't easy to come by in Italy.

"I'm gonna hit the shower, I just wanted to grab these before I got my hair wet."

"Didn't you take one last night?" Juan asked around a mouthful of sweets.

"Yep, but it makes my sore feet feel better."

"Bet you can't wait for a bath when we get home."

"You have no idea," Scarlet said a little more darkly than she meant to.

They went to see the David that day; a small spirit fluttered around the gallery which made Scarlet want to cry. Then they climbed a hill up to a palace to see the city from above. There was a porcelain museum up there that they spent probably too much time in. But it was a warm place and contained many beautiful objects.

Scarlet pushed hard to get them back to the hotel before dark. The number of times she yawned during the day concerned Juan. They found a wonderful tiny eatery with the creamiest sauce poured over fresh springy noodles. Scarlet endeavored to enjoy the meal as she had endeavored all day to live in the moment and not fret about what was coming for them. It was not easy, but the exhaustion seemed to help, slowing her mind.

Juan pushed a bowl of green olives toward her. Scarlet picked one up and popped it into her mouth. It tasted salty and refreshing after the gorgonzola sauce. She finished getting the meat off the pit and spit out the hard seed. "I wonder if this will grow?"

"It has been in salt water for a long time, so probably not," Juan answered.

"I don't know, can't coconuts survive seawater for a long time?" Scarlet said, setting the pit on the plate next to the bowl. She wondered if she should put it in her pocket for Donya later.

"Coconuts are prepared for that. They have all that fluffy stuff on the outside and are full of juice."

"Huh, I hadn't thought of that. You're so smart babe," she said, smiling sleepily at him.

"You look really tired. Did your foot bother you that much last night?"

"Oh, it wasn't just that. You know how I get." She waved her hand and grabbed her water glass. No wine for her tonight. She needed all her senses.

Juan nodded.

Scarlet was never a good sleeper and had fits of real insomnia. Normally on trips, she slept better, but normally they didn't have traveling monsters stalking them. Scarlet sighed.

"You'll sleep better tonight. Maybe you should have gotten a little alcohol to knock you out."

"Maybe I should get a little gelato. It might not help with the sleep, but it will make me feel better."

"Same shop as last night?" Juan smiled, picking up the two last olives in the bowl. He leaned across the table and pressed one to Scarlet's lips.

She opened her mouth and took the small gift. He was always thoughtful. She cleaned the flesh off the pit again. This time when she spit the seed into her hand, she stuffed it into her pocket.

## CHAPTER 28

# DONYA

Donya woke as the sun set above the pool. Slowly walking along the bottom, she checked the stubby blade driven into the silt. It rested, dull in the evening light. She looked up into the water column. Nothing was there. She could see all the way to the sky. Kicking a few times she moved quickly through the water—her physical strength completely returned. She broke the surface. The torches burned out around the pool. No one waited for her. The only company she had was another pile of cattails and the hum of this place.

She sat down at her breakfast and ate. It would be rude to waste these, although she felt they did nothing for her. Perhaps made her feel a bit less hungry, but not nourished. How was she going to get back to her realm? Moving between the realms was not something a troll did. They found a place and they stayed.

Worrying a seed head, she replayed last night's events. Much had transpired. Even at the end. Scarlet's power was fire, the opposite of hers. Nothing is farther from darkness and earth than fire. Then when Scarlet panicked, the Kraken used a memory spell on her, wiping out several moments. What a terrifying power.

There was much to be done. She spread her jaw and shoveled the last seeds in. She got up, legs solid under her, and set off.

The forest thicket was not large, turning into a woodland with open spaces between the trees before she got to the river. The open spaces allowed her to see the approaching husband, just one, the one with the uneven gait.

Donya stopped at the sight of him. Perhaps she was meant to wait by the pool.

When he made it to her, lumbering up slowly but surely, he held a cylindrical object out to her, and said, "a scroll of introduction from my lady wife."

"Introduction?" Without the human with her, she felt like her silent old self.

"In Rome, there are the seven Wolf Kings. You will request their aid."

Donya nodded and took the scroll. She kept her doubts about their help to herself. The kings were known to her, but not known well. They were the spirits of the dead human kings who ruled the city. They haunted the city for several millennia but not much was said of them, which meant they did not interact with the world. Perhaps they would be moved to help the human, for they had all been human once, albeit long ago.

The man turned on his heel and began walking again. She followed. He said nothing more.

The walk took less time than it had the night before. She had been weak and slow. They approached the shallow river at the spot where she and Scarlet came through, where Nera should have come with them. The second husband sat on the bank, relaxed.

Her new role started, and she needed to gather information so she would be able to inform Scarlet. How to go about asking the question without offending her benefactors though? She spoke quietly and slowly, "the mark your lady left on the human… why did she do it?"

His hobbling didn't slow as he answered. "Our lady would probably prefer to answer herself. You will be speaking to her in two nights."

"My duty to the human must be upheld. She will want answers in a few hours. I need to provide them. I mean no disrespect." Donya thought maybe she should have led with that. Eventually, she would learn tact.

"You have seen our ladyship kept humans in the past. We believe she saw Scarlet, thus getting the idea to do it once more." He paused, digging in a sack for several vials, then proceeded, "she would rarely give so lucky a kiss this quickly. It is reserved for the most powerful and loyal."

They made it to the river, joining the other husband. He held a flute.

"Not to presume her intentions, but mayhap she holds hope in the future of the human, that she will live up to those qualities." Donya watched them. They seemed pleased. These two husbands possibly did not know everything their lady wife intended. Then Donya asked, "what will the mark do to the human?"

"Wrong question," responded the short one. His seaweed face appeared closed off now.

Donya thought of her misstep. "Ahhh, I see it is a gift. What will it do for her? I did not mean to imply it would cause her harm."

"Our lady can give her additional power and communicate with her more easily. It would be more effective if Scarlet's talents did not lie in fire," the taller husband answered. He did not seem as edgy as the shorter one. "Now it is time," he continued, then gestured toward the low, slow river.

Donya stepped in. The two men started adding herbs to the water. One opened a book saying something in a sea language she knew from childhood. The spell used sand. It was slow.

She decided to change the subject. "What realm is this?" Donya asked, as the taller husband poured a vial of pure white sand into the river and raised his flute.

"One of the intermediate. It has no name."

The other husband spoke up as the taller one began his tune. "This is the same realm the Wolf Kings inhabit. It runs alongside this sea, ending where the dark sea and large sea begin," he paused, adding in a harsher tone, "we will not bring you back again, we cannot do everything for you."

Donya did not think she liked either of these two. But they were helpful. The magic built. It was not strong, being only their magic. The Kraken did not lend anything to this spell. She had one last thing to ask, one thing that swam around inside of her, but she kept forestalling. "What about Nera, any word from her?"

"No."

The magic came up like an egg around her, cream-colored and shifting. She smelled salt in the air. The answer still rang in her ears, and then she stood on the bridge, the same one she had been under with Nera.

The bridge was almost empty. She could see the mess last night's magic left. Mud was tossed up on the cobblestones—dark mud from the river bottom. Scorch marks marred the stone blocks. She took a big inhale of air. The smell was reminiscent of the night they first met the Kraken—spoiled magic. Another scent clung in the air this time though, charred, and bitter.

"Is anyone awake? Could someone tell me what happened here?" Donya asked the stones of the bridge. She wanted details.

"You know full well what happened here young troll," responded a block from her left in a low timbre.

"I know my part, not the rest," she said, turning to it as a car rolled down the center of the wide bridge.

The block was positioned neither on the top of the bridge nor under it. It stuck out on one of the supports, a good vantage point from which to observe.

Another stone on the walkway spoke up. She was red and a perfect square. "I heard everything. I lay awake the whole time. Nothing that exciting happened for my whole life."

"Because you came after the bombs dropped," responded the stone from the edge.

"Please tell me," Donya finally said. Rocks were often hard to keep on topic, but the open-ended request might lead to the information she forgot to ask more specifically.

"First, all day that beautiful nymph lazed around. She came to the top of the bridge and sat on the handrail above me. Traffic stopped because all the men gaped at her. A lot of them even tried to speak with her," The red square spoke excitedly about Nera.

Donya got a small pressure in her chest. She didn't need to know about the day, but she found she wanted to know.

"She sang a lovely song at the water's edge. The birds joined her," added the block.

"Do you remember the words in the song?"

"Yes, but we cannot speak them," responded the red square.

"I could for a price," said the block.

Donya couldn't afford to pay any more prices right now, but she asked anyway. "How much?"

"Your left leg for the song."

"I need both my legs for at least the next few weeks," Donya sighed. A high price meant important information. Although not for her current purposes. Both stones were silent at that, so she went on, "what about after the tall man and his son arrived when I was trapped?"

"I don't know a lot about magic. This is the third time I have seen it in action, a mean spell" the red square spoke up.

"You could not even see most of the spell," said the block. "You could right, trolly?"

"Under the water and my eyes were fixed, but yes I could see the circle," Donya said.

"It was a wordless blood magic casting," the block added.

"Yes, he didn't use words," said the red square. "But he explained a lot to the son. He is teaching that boy all his bad habits. Probably too late to do anything for him. Chip came right off the block."

"What happened when the spell broke?" Donya asked.

"New even to me, it was. You could feel the spell pulling. It worked. It sputtered and spun in the air and water. The target got close. Right when that crook looked smug and excited, the magic collapsed. In a split second, the river bellowed and reared up. The center opened. You were there, under the nymph, and the victim of the spell was there too."

"But when did the fire start? I saw the fire. Tell it in the correct order, you gray old dolt," red square interjected.

"The fire did not start, it erupted at the same moment the water parted. A force from below passed by us all. When it hit the scoundrel the fire sprang into being."

Donya recalled what it was like to be around Scarlet. The wave of heat she first felt on the plane. Was the woman strong enough to manifest actual physical fire? "Did it feel hot to both of you, this force which passed through you but caught Heldrig aflame?"

"No," said the block.

"I recall heat but not from below, from the feet moving around by me. The son stood near me. He did not burn but he smoldered and groaned in pain," said the red square.

"How badly was the father burned?" Donya asked with a hint of glee in her voice.

"When you and the human vanished, the source of the combustion vanished. The flesh on his face turned black as his teeth," said the block.

"He laid on the ground and did not move until the nymph came up to him," added the red square. Then went on, "she wasn't harmed but seemed very tired. They all went away together. They all went far away."

Donya waited at the last phrase. Stones always knew more than you thought they would. "You followed up on them?"

"Of course we did!" shouted the block, then went on in a more normal tone, "you don't get a show like that every century. They left the city, outside the last stone before dawn."

"The son stole a car!" came from not the first red square, but her twin sister next to her.

All the red squares woke up. She could hear the far ones whispering little things about being stepped on three times by the son, or Heldrig standing on them for more than a few minutes. At least ten stones were starting a chant, "go south, go south, go south."

"They went south?" Donya asked, knowing the answer. They headed to Rome.

"Yes," practically every block and square paving stone said in unison on the bridge. It was loud for the night. Several humans stopped walking on the street. They looked around, not being able to hear the stones, but they felt the vibration. Good thing Italy has earthquakes. No one would suspect.

CHAPTER 29

# SCARLET

"Time to awaken."

Scarlet heard the voice—she'd slept soundly at first, but as it got later into the night and Donya did not come for her, she became restless. Outfitted with a long sleeve shirt, underwear, and thick socks—it looked akin to what she might normally sleep in but was meant for easily slipping outside.

She grabbed the pants she had left out and put on her shoes and coat. Leaving clothes out was not suspicious, as they traveled to Rome mid-morning, their bags already packed with all unessential items.

She ducked into the bathroom, turned on the tap, and spoke to the running water. "Where do I go?"

"The lobby."

Convenient, Scarlet thought. She pocketed her key and money just in case.

In the lobby, Donya waited for her. She was still short and gray, but she seemed different, all her clothing new, a navy-blue long-sleeved tunic, and close-cut chocolate brown trousers. Her feet were covered by a pair of navy ankle boots with thick teal soles. A tote, also chocolate brown canvas completed her ensemble. Scarlet felt underdressed.

Donya motioned to the chairs at the front of the lobby, far away from the woman at the desk who appeared to be sleeping on the job. Scarlet obeyed and came forward, dropping into the chair with a bit of a flounce. She was not sure how to act. She still didn't like being near the troll.

"Could you please turn it down?" Donya said in a quiet but strained voice.

Scarlet had no idea what the troll talked about, which annoyed her. "Listen, I would if I could, but I have no idea what is going on or how to do anything." A little burden lifted with her honesty. She wasn't used to helplessness but at least it was out in the open.

"I'll do my best to explain," Donya started. Crossing her arms, she continued, "I do not usually talk much. Continue to ask until you are satisfied." Donya paused again, taking a deep breath.

Donya started by explaining how much trouble she brought on Scarlet when she saw her on the plane. With some asides on magic use, she emphasized knowing what elements were and one's strengths and one's weaknesses, and how to stop expelling magic out like a blow torch.

Several hours later Scarlet felt tired but still curious. "Let me get this straight. You bought all those new clothes so Heldrig would have a harder time knowing you're around?" Scarlet asked.

"Yes. Over time, your essence seeps into everything you own. It happens faster with materials you are used to. Therefore, this bag is of the substance upcycled, instead of the leather I would prefer. Also, I realize I said his name once, but try not to."

"I won't do it again." Scarlet shuddered. She hated him. "Upcycled isn't the material name; it means it's made from recycled cotton or plastic. Should I get more clothes?"

"You do not need to purchase new clothing. Let them track you when you are not with me. Take these for when we are together." Donya handed over a thick wool sweater in cream, a silk blouse, and khakis trousers from her bag. "Let me see your foot. I will bring shoes tomorrow."

Scarlet brought her foot up, her right foot, the one the Kraken had kissed. Donya hesitated to touch it.

"Maybe the other foot."

Scarlet brought up her other foot while she stroked the silk blouse. Donya softly handled the light blue Adidas, comfortably broken in. Scarlet wondered if it would be ungrateful to ask for another comfortable pair of shoes. She held in the urge. After the lesson, she knew about the importance of politeness to spirits. Uncomfortable feelings or not, she needed Donya.

"I must leave now. I will meet you in Rome at the same time tomorrow night."

"Can you come earlier? Juan might wake up around now."

Donya cocked her head to the side. "He rises early?"

"He's a deep sleeper, but usually he goes to work very early. If I get up when he has first gone to bed, there is almost no probability he will notice."

Donya nodded. "Midnight then."

"Our new hotel will be the—"

"I'll find you." Donya cut her off. "After we made that sword, I can find you."

"See you tomorrow." Scarlet stood feeling awkward. She fought her natural urge to be tense, that this would cause discomfort for any spirit in her area. Although Donya could not explain why entirely.

Donya stood and walked out.

At some point, the clerk woke. She set out dishes for the breakfast they served every morning, starting at six. Scarlet and Juan needed to grab the quick easy food. Their train left at nine am. She was happy to be leaving Florence. She wished Juan hadn't proposed to her there—it felt cursed now, or at least very unlucky.

They arrived in Rome with the sun shining overhead. Their hotel sat right on the subway line, which should have meant it was easy to get to. An unexpected subway strike changed that. Scarlet hadn't looked up bus routes. Even if she'd thought to, it wouldn't have helped with how complicated the routes were.

Juan stared up at the map in the terminal. "I think we take number twenty-two to nine, then it will be a short walk."

"Ugh, stupid phones not having data plans!" Scarlet was easily flustered in the best of times.

"Or there is that," Juan said, pointing to the taxi line outside the train station. It stood a hundred people deep and growing.

"We can walk to the hotel faster than we could get a cab."

"Not with your foot," Juan said.

Scarlet had not told him it didn't bother her as much anymore, well, at least not now. The pain was a side effect of the Kraken trying to protect and help her. She poured her energy into Scarlet through the bite, as Donya explained, but because Scarlet's magic was fire and the Kraken's water, a negative reaction occurred. That reaction caused her pain, more than there would have been otherwise. Donya thought strong magics shunting into her would cause discomfort anyway. Help from spirits and the fey came at a cost. If a little pain was her price, that would be more than fair.

The troll couldn't be sure her discomfort would be the only price though, which worried Scarlet, but not more than being kidnapped or dying did. Hopefully, this was not a Rumpelstiltskin situation.

They got in line for bus twenty-two. The terminal was not as nice as the train station, but it was a beautiful, if chilly, day. Nowhere to purchase a ticket could be found and no one worked in the bus terminal to ask, at least, no one they could see. It was very large and not set up in a way easy for tourists to figure out. People waited at all the terminals.

Scarlet wore out—she probably got six hours of sleep in the last two nights combined. She napped on the train ride. I wish I could sleep on my feet, she thought. Leaning her head against Juan's warm shoulder, she closed her eyes.

Perhaps she did doze, either that or their bus arrived right after she closed her eyes. Juan held a wad of Euros in his hand, unsure of how much to pay. A dozen people waiting with them in a loose line. Most everyone had a suitcase in tow. As they boarded, the driver waved them on. Juan stopped to try to pay, but the man shook his hand and shooed him away.

Apparently, they were all getting on for free. The bus was fairly full, but there were several open seats. Scarlet made a beeline for two in the back. They sat by the exit doors and open space, making it easy to hold their bags in front of them. She plopped down, and Juan took the seat next to her. She stared out the window. Maybe their luck would turn around after all.

The bus bumped along, and Juan kept count of the stops. They needed to get off after fourteen. It seemed like people rang the button between stops, though. Or maybe half the other passengers were also confused.

When the time came for them to get off, he hit the red button on the wall next to them. When the bus pulled to the stop, they stood and exited the middle of the bus. Several other people departed, all carrying luggage. They scrambled into the two available taxis. This stop seemed to be a small transportation terminal. Juan studied the list of buses that would be coming by and their timetables.

Scarlet had become good at reading Juan. His shoulders crept up toward his ears, and the corners of his mouth turned down. "Just say it," she said as mildly as possible.

"We got off at the wrong stop. There is no line nine here."

Scarlet really didn't care about this tiny inconvenience. It struck her as charming, such an ordinary problem to have. She smiled at her fiancé. "We can walk from here. I mean, we are closer than before."

"But your foot. We could at least wait for a taxi."

Scarlet pulled out her phone. She had a map of Rome pre-downloaded on Google Maps. It wouldn't give directions without data, but at least they could track their progress. She tapped at the screen, pulling up the pin with their hotel. It didn't look far, and most of it would be through a big park. "Done, let's go."

"One last chance to wait for another cab."

"We can see more of the city this way. It's fine, really."

"Okay, but I got your suitcase." Juan snatched her rolling suitcase away from her.

Google lied to her. They walked for at least forty minutes and still were in the very large park. It had been fun at first, but the sun shined brightly, and now Scarlet felt sweaty. There still stood some very steep hills in Rome. And nothing was friendly to wheeling the suitcases. The paths in the park were irregularly filled with pea gravel. Juan dragged both of their suitcases for the whole walk. They probably should have gotten a cab. It was too late now.

It couldn't be much farther. They neared the edge of the park. Scarlet could see the tree line. She could also see a long, possibly seamless, railing.

They kept going when they hit the railing. The city opened before them. A family posed for a picture, and young lovers stared out, entranced by the skyline. They found a point of interest without even trying. The ancient skyline was far more interesting than any of the other cities. Dark green cypress poked out between sienna buildings. Open piazzas created space. Domes lay majestically against all other shapes. The city felt almost organic, as if it sprang up from the ground—as if it belonged.

She needed to investigate this park when they got to the hotel. They passed the zoo and several signposts pointing at attractions. Maybe they would want to come back.

'Squawk,' sounded from behind them. Juan instantly smiled. He spotted it first. Up in the tree, a parakeet. "Look, they are here too!"

"They followed us," Scarlet said as a joke but then frowned, realizing she wished they were the only things following them.

"It's not the same, though, right?"

"No, it is smaller, I think. The ones in Spain were supposed to be monk parakeets."

"When we get home, I want to see if they invaded anywhere in California."

"San Francisco, saw them once. Maybe we should get a bird—I've always loved birds. I mean, we keep noticing them instead of the ancient history all around us."

"There are only so many old buildings and art pieces we can look at," Juan said, waving his hand.

It was true. At some point it got overwhelming. Although this was not as bad as Paris, where the buildings were even more opulent and went on forever. They started walking again, heading away from their hotel along the railing. Old stone steps led to a street through an opening in the railing. They let out on a slanting street which was not the safest walkway, but they took it.

They passed through the Piazza del Popolo, with its wide-open space and central obelisk. The open space after all the trees disoriented Scarlet. Men tried to sell bottles of water, cheap toys, and candy. The piazza was large, and people milled about—no cars though, which made walking through it pleasant.

They used an arch for a landmark. A piazza this size was easy to get turned around in when tired, and Scarlet felt exhausted. They could come to explore once their heavy baggage was dropped off. Their hotel stood across from the archway, in what she guessed used to be outside a city wall.

Among the shops that lined the streets stood a very large wooden door. Next to it hung a plaque with business names on it. Their hotel listing sat next to a number three. Juan pushed the door open.

Inside the building lay a central courtyard. It had old bones but seemed industrialized now, with several cars parked inside and a few lanky potted plants. Juan turned right when they came in the door despite the lack of additional signage. They came to an elevator fashioned completely out of old wrought iron. It suggested a beautiful birdcage, black with golden accents. They pushed a modern button, and it moved with a squeal.

Juan paused a moment before opening the door after the lift stopped moving in case it needed to settle. Then they both got in. Juan said, "this thing is pretty cool."

"And small," Scarlet responded. It barely fit the two of them and their luggage. It was heavy and well-made. She wondered if this was all real iron. Donya said many spirits were sensitive to metal, iron, and silver in particular. In a pinch, could she and Juan hide in this elevator?

They got off on the third floor. The first door in front of them was for the Porta Hotel. They opened the door to a tiny, spotlessly clean lobby. Scarlet liked the artful decorations immediately. All the pieces were eclectic but fit together; wood, stone, and bright colors. A smiling woman greeted them. She appeared bright-eyed and bushy-tailed, which strangely discomforted Scarlet. How would Donya sneak in tonight when there wasn't a gaping lobby and sleepy clerk?

# CHAPTER 30

# DONYA

Donya enjoyed the train ride to Rome, the night landscape rushing by her. If she survived the next week, she would take more trains. Midnight rides during the spring thaw sounded wonderful. Perhaps she could even ride in the cargo to avoid the artificial air coming from tiny dust-scented vents.

Disembarking, she made her way out into the night. The easiest way for her to get to that entwined realm again was through the catacombs. Places of so much death would be easy enough to pierce through. She also wanted to collect ingredients. Scarlet needed to be as prepared as she could be in a short amount of time. Darksight could be obtained easily enough.

Stopping to ask for directions a few times, she traveled outside the old city walls. She stopped at a church with bolted doors. They were beautiful, weathered, and solid, so she did not harm them, instead moving along the wall. "Let me by," she said, and the stones rearranged themselves for her. She walked into the space with the wooden pews. She could smell the cold draft coming up from behind a wall. Rounding the corner, she came to another door. It was not locked. Stairs led to a dirty stone floor.

An old column stuck up from the ground. Part of the church's foundation rested on it. She walked on and found more descending stairs, which ended in water. An old cistern, her first impulse was to walk right into the water. However, this would have spoiled her new clothing. She disrobed, placing her new things inside her tote. The tote could sit safely by the water's edge. No human would come this way soon.

The water was ice cold and crystal clear. She walked along the bottom, stirring up silt. The space was small. She did not walk long before seeing more stairs on the opposite side. Ascending them, she came back up out of the water into a stone room. This one was not made from blocks. This room had been carved out of the stone. She passed through an opening to her left. It was crudely worked.

Donya dragged her hand as she walked along the wall. Crumbs of rock came off as she did. She had never seen tufa before. It was a soft, lava-formed rock, very light and fragile.

Then the catacombs started. Human-sized cavities had been carved out of the wall. Some were occupied, some were not. She scanned the ceiling and floor. Nothing living came this way in maybe one thousand years. This would be the perfect spot for her.

"Hello," she said to the rock, then took a seat.

Nothing responded. She waited. Normally she would be willing to wait all night and even a few days more, but now time was of the essence.

"I have a very good story for you if you wake up and listen."

Still nothing, Donya breathed in and out. The air smelled stale with a sulfurous tang, maybe methane. If the stones were this slow, maybe the bones would be quicker.

"Do you think a human could survive this passage?"

Rattling from her right meant something. Bones are stone as well. They are simply new compared to most. She walked over to a cavity in the wall. It was the highest one. The crypts were stacked three high. It was not a large space, maybe four feet long, meant for a child's skeleton. Donya could not see up into it, so she pushed her fingers into the tufa below it and pulled herself up, resting her feet on the lowest crypt in the wall.

"What are you?" The femur of an ancient skeleton asked. It was pale brown in the absolute darkness.

"I'm a troll. Have you ever met another like me before?"

"No, only people and no one has been here in so long. I thought the world ended, and I was left behind."

"The world is still there, full of humans. This passageway is blocked by water."

"Good. I want to go to heaven."

Donya didn't respond. Bones were young compared to other rocks and stones. This one held the high voice of a child. It might speak in the voice of the child that once formed and contained it. She went on carefully, "is it alright with you if I stay here for a while? As you are the lone one awake, I think I can assume you can decide for all here."

"I do not know. No one has ever spoken to me before. But I think…" the bone trailed off, waiting.

Donya waited too. Nothing spoke, although it did feel like the rock walls around them listened. She pushed, "if I can come back, I will bring a human friend. Although I am not sure, she can breathe this air."

"A living human? Really? I would love that."

"Yes, we have much to do. We need to go see the Wolf Kings."

A slight murmur went through the surrounding stone. The tufa was large but soft. It didn't speak outright. Donya decided it best to offer more information, perhaps impress all these bones and rock. "I have been given a letter of introduction from the Kraken of Venezia herself."

The murmur coalesced into a delicate voice, raspy and pure, "The Wolf Kings of Rome help no one, not even humans begging to be saved from vandals."

"They surely will not help if I do not bring myself before them. Could they perhaps even become insulted at my presence in their city without an introduction?" Magical creatures who had once been human, such as the Wolf Kings, kept a bad habit of bringing human rules with them.

"They will not even notice you. They notice little," the tufa said.

"Trolls are used to being unnoticed."

"Is that why we all like you?" asked the bone.

Donya looked over at the bone. "It goes back to when the realms first formed. Rocks, trolls, and dwarves sprung from or were carved out of the same section of Ymir."

"There is more," replied the tufa

"There is always more. I have never been a storyteller. When I go back to the surface, please explain it to the young. I will return, and you will still be telling the tale."

"Mmmmm, this is not wrong," the tufa sounded pleased at the idea.

"Tufa, do you know if a human can breathe this air?"

"They can be found in the tunnels around here. There is an opening to the surface you did not pass through. It lets in the air and water."

Donya stood. Midnight approached, and she had a promise to keep. She reached up and grabbed the bone. "Lead the way."

"I get to come? This is the most wonderful thing that has ever happened to me."

Donya nodded. She walked through the maze while the tufa droned directions to her. It was not long before she could smell the fresher air. The opening lay past a stack of bones. They were primarily femurs and skulls piled in a complex web to make a wall. Near the end of the wall, there had been a cave-in. Soil fell in, disheveling the bones.

Donya could see the opening. There lay a leaf-clogged grate over the hole. She set down the bone with the others. They started chattering instantly. Word spread of her arrival through the catacombs.

One skull clattered its teeth at her. "It leads to a private garden."

Donya pushed up through the mud and algae. She pushed on the metal grate. It was old but sturdy. Leaves fell into her face and on her bare shoulders. "Do you know if the landowners know about this entrance?"

"Yes, but the old woman who lives there is bitter with age. She has not come here or tended anything in years."

Donya pushed again, and the layer of soil around the metal gave way before the old, rusted spots broke. She heaved it to the side, pulling her feet from the sucking mud and emerging in the misty air.

An overgrown citrus tree grew by the hole. When she surveyed the courtyard, she realized all the plants were overgrown, nothing pruned. Donya preferred a tangled garden, deeper shadows to stay in. It remained winter; the long canes of the rose bushes lay bare, and the new spring grass barely poked up through the browned weeds.

Donya approached the first level of the home. The windows stood dark. When she put her hand to the stone of the wall, it felt frigid, like nothing lived there at all. She wondered if the matron was dead and undiscovered, a path to explore another night. Now she needed to retrace her steps and get to Scarlet. They had a lot of work to do that night before the sun came up on them.

Scarlet was alert and prepared when Donya arrived, which gave her hope for the human. The situation deteriorated from there. The redhead spent too many years wildly using her magic. She was hard to train. Also, she required an explanation for everything. The few nights left to them made it impossible to adequately explain the workings of all the magical elements. Donya tried. She agreed to answer all of Scarlet's questions.

"Many non-magical creatures must pay for the use of magic, it is true," Donya explained.

"So, what am I paying?"

"Nothing I can see. The Kraken would not be interested in you if you were."

"How would I be classified then?" Scarlet asked, tapping her tea.

They'd found a busy all-night café. A few young human men looked at Scarlet. In the clothing Donya acquired for her, she shone like a new coin. Donya was not sure how to answer this. "You are probably a mage in the making, someone with the natural potential to be a mage. It runs in families closely related to witchling and witches. Do not merely accept this answer, though. It will take years of trial and error to know for sure without the help of other magic-using humans."

Donya could see Scarlet taking this in. She needed to keep her on task. "Did you do the exercises?"

She sighed and took a large sip of her tea. "Yeah, but I can't feel anything. Like I never knew where you were, and we are supposed to know, right? I think I am getting better at not being so repulsive," she said that last word louder than the rest.

"You are getting better at control. Keep doing the exercises. You will be able to sense me soon enough. And finish your tea. We need to work." Donya tapped the table.

She watched as Scarlet took a big sip of tea and stood. Donya walked outside. She studied Scarlet's kissed foot. The Kraken would be aware of most if not all of what went on. Scarlet lagged as they walked. She still clearly did not like Donya. It wasn't necessary to be liked at this point. It might not ever be that important. They just needed to work together.

Donya needed moonlight to get this spell started. They walked along an old lane and out into the open piazza. A grand obelisk stood in the center, which Donya was glad to see and would like to have a long chat with when this situation came to an end. She made her way to the running water in a fountain. “Sit here.”

Scarlet bobbed her head, doing as she was told. There were not a lot of other humans out and about. The ones hanging around all seemed suspicious, small groups of men laughing too loudly, and lone figures slumped in corners.

“Close your eyes and tilt your head to the moon,” Donya instructed.

“Do I have to close my eyes?”

Donya took a moment to respond. She would not have asked unless it needed to be done. “Yes.”

Scarlet did it. Clouds occasionally obscured the moonlight. Donya needed to time this right. She studied the sky. The clouds moved quickly through the sky, but there was a large gap coming.

The pot of dirt in her tote came readily to hand. She opened it and smudged the contents on Scarlet’s closed upturned eyes. Scarlet flinched.

Donya concentrated and pulled the shadows away from Scarlet’s eyes. She pulled the dirt, and it scattered down the redhead’s cheeks. Then she reached into the water with one hand. With the other, she used a single finger to put one drop in the outer corner of Scarlet’s eyes. This time she did not move. A little light flickered below Donya. The Kraken's mark gave a pulse of energy, perhaps her checking on what spell was cast.

"Finished," Donya said on an exhale. It wasn't a large spell, but she felt drained all the same. Perhaps it was her stamina that suffered the most in the last few years. If correct then she went about her life all wrong. Stamina differed from raw power.

Scarlet looked around the square. Her eyes were naturally wide. But they went wider still. "It's like daylight out here. I can see all the colors." She put a hand up to her face.

"It will not last forever, perhaps a few years a decade at most. It is useful when you are up against night stalkers."

Scarlet nodded again. "What do I need to practice with this?"

"Your eyes are exceptional to begin with. This dark sight is a small advantage. Try to notice the existences you missed before. Come."

She walked them to a lone cab parked not far away. She had noted the closest address to the entrance of the catacombs. Tomorrow night she would have Scarlet meet her at the entrance.

"What is that?" Scarlet said, pointing at a dark spirit in the window of a building they passed.

Donya narrowed her eyes. Perhaps Scarlet's dark-vision was now better than hers. She could make out the catlike shape. She would have assumed a cat sat there. Its fur shimmered in the distance, a dead giveaway. It was a genius, which she had not seen outside of a fae realm before. "A genius."

"I have seen one before in California. Why are they called that? I thought people were geniuses?"

"I have heard humans use the word. One might have a genius, but I don't know if one can be one. Can you sense it?" She paused then continued, "it would be nice if we could get a genius's help."

"Could we ask it?" Scarlet said before closing her eyes. Her forehead wrinkled up. She shook her head. "No, with my eyes closed, I don't feel anything."

"Hmmm." Donya didn't like that Scarlet couldn't feel anything from the spirit or herself. It was bizarre to have such sight but not any other sense.

Scarlet interrupted Donya's thoughts. "Where are we going?"

"I need to show you, not tell you."

Scarlet sighed but got into the other side of the cab when Donya opened the door. The cabby seemed surprised as they sat. Donya did not speak but passed him the piece of paper with the address on it. If she said it out loud, Scarlet would want many answers, and Donya was almost depleted of words for the night.

CHAPTER 31

# SCARLET

The inside of the cab smelled like smoke. Usually, this would have upset Scarlet, but she was too busy observing the brighter world around her. Initially, she compared her sight to daylight, but that was not correct. Shades stayed muted, but she could see all the details of her surroundings. It seemed more akin to a day-lit world through tinted blue-black sunglasses. The sky appeared a neon purple, and the stars shone brightly.

The cab stopped after a short drive. They were in a neighborhood of grand dilapidated dwellings that stood quiet at this hour.

Donya opened her door the moment the cab stopped. She handed the cabby a wad of cash, then told him to wait in Italian.

"You know how to speak Italian?" Scarlet asked. She knew she asked a lot of questions, but she could not seem to stop.

"I can speak most human tongues. I have found I have a knack for them."

Scarlet wanted to ask when she got a chance to hear so many languages. Was that the reason for the California trip? However, she realized they were breaking into a house, which pulled her mind up short. The lock had been tampered with, where the key hole should be there was a slightly bigger hole. Did Donya use her strong stony finger to break the metal? Scarlet stopped dead in her tracks, not knowing what to do. Should she keep following? Would standing on the street look more suspicious?

Donya pushed one-half of the double doors and waved her inside. Scarlet held her breath. They came into a hallway. It smelled like dust and stale air. Donya took her past several doors, then into a large room. It was a library; leather bindings and gold lettering winked at her. Enormous windows stood bare of drapes; they viewed a tangled garden. They went to a green door and opened it. Back in the fresh air, Scarlet whispered, "isn't this someone's house?"

"Yes, but she won't notice."

Scarlet wanted to protest. Whoever it belonged to would notice eventually, but in the face of all the magical happenings in the last few weeks, she found minor breaking and entering no longer bothered her. They stepped into the garden. Even at the end of winter, many plants in Italy were green. Scarlet could pick out the different shades in the bushes and the trees. They walked over to a thorny citrus. It was overgrown, and the thorns on the lower branches were an inch long. Underneath, a metal grate lay pushed aside. Donya stepped into the muddy hole.

"I can't go down there. Is that a sewer?"

"No, it is a catacomb."

"I'll ruin all of these nice clothes," Scarlet said, waving her hand around in front of herself. She watched as the troll looked down at herself and the mud she stood in.

"You are correct. I am used to wearing black," Donya said, nodding a bit, then asked, "you can find this place on your own the night after next?"

"Yep. Why not tomorrow night?"

"Tomorrow night, I will go to recover the sword. You will take the night to rest."

Scarlet didn't argue, needing rest. It was true, but also, she felt like perhaps she slowed the little troll down. "All the way to this hole? I don't know if I can get past the front door." Scarlet watched as a puzzled expression passed over the small troll's face.

"Would it help if I ate the human in the house?"

"NO!" Scarlet said too loud. She clamped a hand over her mouth after the outburst. Nothing else happened. No light went on.

Donya smiled at her. It was an odd smile, crooked and toothy. Troll teeth were sharp. It seemed like Donya was in a good mood, even joking around. "Okay, I get the point. You said she's old. I guess she can't hear."

"And if she does come down here, I will eat her, and the problem will be solved."

"That is not funny," Scarlet said but found herself smiling too. Was she always this morbid, or did exhaustion make her this way? Unsure, she spun her ring on her finger.

"I have a question for you," Donya started.

The pause went on for so long that Scarlet felt a moment slipping away. She realized she needed to speak first. "Go ahead. Ask anything."

"What is wrong with your ring?"

"Wrong with my ring?" Scarlet had no idea what she meant.

"As I said before, I can speak with the stones of the earth. I cannot with your ring." There was another pause, then she continued, "it sort of babbles. It is no language I know."

Scarlet puzzled over this for a moment. "I know. It's a lab-created stone." Again, she spoke too loudly. She waited for a beat before she continued, "I told Juan not to get me a traditional stone. I wanted a gem that came from a lab. I work in a laboratory, you see, and the mined ones can come from sources that use child labor or destroy the environment. And I think they all use caustic chemicals on the ore. The metal should be recycled too."

The troll's mouth opened and stayed that way. "You humans can make stone now?"

"Ya, it's not even new technology."

Donya finally closed her mouth and came out of her surprise. She regarded the ring. "Pleased to meet you, little one. You are very special."

Scarlet could barely contain herself. "What did it say back?"

"It squeaked."

"Aww, let me know if you hear any words out of it."

Scarlet slipped back into the hotel early, at around three-thirty. She washed up and hit the bed like a sack of rocks. Her eyes opened slowly; the glowing orange numbers of the alarm clock read a quarter past eight. Scarlet rubbed at her eyes. The colors in the room appeared normal now, not like when she arrived. Juan sat at the desk.

"Hey babe, why didn't you wake me up earlier?" Scarlet said.

"You looked pretty tired the last few days, and I have timecards to approve anyway."

"Ugh, timecards. What do you think the chances are that James will approve them, and I won't have to?"

He stood and opened the blinds, bright sunlight streaming in. "I wouldn't bet a burrito on it."

Scarlet wasn't prepared for the assault on her eyes. The colors were startlingly bright. And there were colors that appeared different from before. Her purple backpack in the corner fluoresced a brighter hue than violet. Her sapphire ring, she could see every detail of it, and the twinkles of light slowed inside the gem and pushed back out a different shade. A shade she did not have a name for.

Juan had his back to her. He peered out the window, stretching a bit. She was thankful he couldn't see her face. Her expression must be shocked and probably also awed. Then, collecting her thoughts, she glanced past him at the sunlight. "It's a nice day."

"Yeah, the weather is supposed to get rainy this afternoon, but I don't see any clouds yet." He turned around.

Scarlet gasped at the sight of his eyes. The whites glowed too white, and the brown of his eyes was gone, replaced by a deep, dark purple shade, almost black. His eyes that she loved were alien to her.

"What?" Juan asked with a hint of fear.

Scarlet panicked. What to say? She was a terrible liar. "You're just so handsome," she spit out with a shrug and a laugh, hoping he would be convinced. She still scrutinized his eyes. After several long blinks the effect stayed the same. They had not appeared different with indirect light.

"You want to start something?" He walked up and put his arms around her. "God, babe, I thought," he paused, "I don't know what I thought." He slipped his hand under her loose top.

She pressed her face into his shoulder, closing her increasingly freakish eyes. "We will be late for the walking tour."

"What, not late for the free walking tour."

"Or we could miss breakfast," she whispered, shifting her hands.

"Miss breakfast and eat gelato instead because of sex. This morning is my dream come true."

That made Scarlet laugh. "Close the damn window."

They were a few minutes late for the tour. Free tours wait for the stragglers as they rely on tips. Juan got banana-flavored gelato because it was breakfast gelato. Scarlet ate chocolate because she liked it.

They did not walk far at first. Their guide told them about the Piazza del Popolo and the historic northern gate, the Porta del Popolo. Scarlet gratefully stood around. It gave her a chance to get used to her eyesight. Most people's eyes stayed the same. Colors were still richer and more varied than she ever noticed, but also, something moved around them. It was easiest to observe out of the corner of her eyes, or if she stared at an object like a fountain and lost focus. It looked like the shimmer of heat waves coming off hot asphalt in August.

She still tried to catch the shimmer as they walked to the Trevi Fountain. It was close by; the sun struck the freshwater and sparkled below the massive statues. Scarlet was impressed with the sheer size. It appeared everyone on the tour was impressed. Everyone snapped pictures.

"This isn't crowded for the fountain. Come back this evening around sunset, and you will see it packed with people," called their guide over the group's head. He was small and rotund wearing a bright orange beanie. A matching umbrella for them to follow dangled from his hand.

"How do we make the wish?" Juan asked the guide.

"The wish, the one to come back to Rome—you take your right hand and throw a coin over your left shoulder. Everyone go. You have five minutes to get it done. I'll be at the top."

Their group was a dozen strong, they all rummaged around in their pockets for euros. Juan tugged Scarlet to the water's edge. "Crap, hurry."

Another tour group approached, much larger than theirs. The other guide held a magenta umbrella and a loudspeaker.

Juan offered Scarlet a coin, and they both turned around. Juan threw his right over his shoulder, but she hesitated. Did she ever want to return to Italy? It seemed like a bad idea.

She tossed the coin. Then spun around to see if it hit the water. A reaction occurred as it struck the pool. She saw the shimmer ripple through the water. Observing more closely as coins struck the water every few seconds, the shimmer reacted in time.

Magic, it was surely magic of some sort. She closed her eyes. Donya said she could sense magical creatures. This had to be one. She tried reaching out.

Nothing. Not a different sound, or presence, or even a painful foot.

"Come on," Juan said, tugging at her shoulder.

Scarlet opened her eyes as the flood of human bodies crowded the stairs, all rummaging in pockets. She would figure this out. This phenomenon needed study. And if there was one thing she was good at, it was studying.

She followed Juan to the left and wiggled up the stairs toward their tour guide. "Can we come back here tonight?"

"Of course. We left today open. I only have directions to that Etruscan Museum you wanted to see," Juan said as they reached the orange beanie.

"Great. I want to sit by the fountain."

"We can throw another coin in too."

"Yeah?"

He nodded, "I really like Italy, and I want to come back. Maybe we could buy a house here."

"Great, babe. It sounds great." She repeated herself. The sound of her voice came out strained and it felt difficult but she managed a weak smile.

CHAPTER 32

# DONYA

What does one troll have to do to get through to another realm? Donya wondered to herself as she tried the incantation again. She sat in the catacombs, repeating old words she thought would work.

"Call more shadow," instructed the tufa.

Donya would if she could. She didn't feel strong enough yet.

She sunk farther. Now she placed her brow to the earth. She summoned the shadows and darkness. She spoke the words.

She felt a warm wind on her face, a smelly wind. Then the wind reversed directions. It was not wind.

Donya opened her eyes to be greeted by a monkey-faced dog lion. "Wonderful, a chimera," she said as she sat back on her feet. She scratched behind its monkey ears.

Nothing else was in the tunnel. It came in the way she had. If it wasn't so ugly, she would worry that Heldrig sent it. But there was something sloppy about the beast, and as far as she knew, only human alchemists worked at making these amalgamations.

She stood up and walked to the opening. If she was going to get any more surprises, she wanted to meet them head-on. The chimera followed her, wagging its dog tail as they went.

When she came to the top of the hole, the old woman relaxed in a rusted garden chair.

"You keep coming into my home, but you never stop to say hello," she said in crisp Latin.

Donya nodded. This might be another time to attempt to use tact. "I thought you might be dead."

The old woman cackled. "What gave you that impression?"

"A stone in your wall." Donya sighed, "they said you wouldn't notice my coming and going."

"Your stone was correct, I never noticed you, very sneaky, but your friend last night is anything but sneaky."

"Yes, you heard."

"No-no. I felt."

"This is yours then?" Donya asked, waving at the chimera sitting between their feet.

"Brutus belonged to my master. Terrible name for a chimera. Brutus killed him. Betrayer namesake and all," she paused, "I helped, but that is beside the point."

This human felt dangerous now that she sat there in front of Donya. What was one more danger, though? "I apologize for not introducing myself sooner. I am Donya. I came through your home for remote access to the catacombs."

"Well met. I am Grazia. Humor an old woman and leave nothing out."

Donya squirmed a bit under her milky gaze, but she lifted her chin. She was a troll and could eat this woman if needed. "I need to get to the between realm where the Wolf Kings hold court."

"If that is all, you should have used the other door," Grazia said, waving her hand.

"Other door." It wasn't a question, more an annoyed repetition of words.

"In the library, the door behind the bookshelf." Grazia walked back into the house, "I'll show you. But this is no gift. You need to do me a service."

"What would you want?"

"The redhead."

Donya stopped. No, not again. She had been too dismissive earlier.

"Perfect response. I worried you would eat her," Grazia said with a happy wheeze in her voice. "I need water from that realm for my arthritis. I would go myself, but the hum is too much for me now."

"You don't want anything more than water?" Donya was still tense and stiff.

"There is much I want more than water, but I doubt you can give me back my youth."

"I might not be able to give you anything if I am killed by the Wolf Kings."

"There is much truth in that. Beware Servius Tullius."

"I thought of going to Romulus."

"A mistake for sure. What is it that you want?"

"Aid in the least, justice for a broken oath at the most."

Grazia thought for a moment, tapping at her chin. "It could work. Ask one of the Tarquinius first, either one. They might help. If you went to Romulus and he refused, which he would, then none of the lesser kings would do anything to oppose him."

"This is very wise. You know them all?"

The old woman entered the library; her steps soft and close together. The chimera wandered off down the hall. "I met two kings when my old master lived; thus, my interactions were limited. Push this bookshelf to the left, then wait for me."

Donya did as she was told. The bookshelf moved easily—dust rose in the air as it shifted. There was indeed a wooden door behind it. She considered that Grazia left much out of her story. Donya took a deep inhale of her scent as she shuffled toward the door, holding a large plastic water bottle.

"Please fill this."

Donya must have frowned at it as she took the bottle. The frown was from the lack of her scent. Donya could still smell the dust, she could smell the velvet of upholstery, wool in a patterned rung on the floor but not Grazia. It seemed this woman was barely there.

"I like it because it will not break," Grazia explained, perhaps thinking that Donya did not approve of plastic.

"Practical."

Donya opened the door and walked through. Then she was on the other side. Humming filled the air. She stood in a great grassland. Hills rolled mildly away to the horizon.

The Kraken's grotto lay south of the door. Donya found a river and swam for hours before she came to the mouth of the tributary she wanted. It was the same small stream she and Scarlet landed in. Donya stayed in the water as long as possible, as she was a faster swimmer than a runner.

She could feel the pull of the sword. It would be ready in the moments before dawn, and she wanted to be there when it woke.

Stepping up out of the water at the closest point to the sword, she instantly broke into a run. When trolls chose to move, they were very quick about it. They simply did not choose to move often. The forest whipped past Donya. She didn't dodge trees as they snapped on impact with her. She did dodge a few boulders; she didn't want to hurt any of them.

She saw the torchlight and slowed to a jog. Surprising her benefactor might not be the best way to proceed. She stepped around the tree to the watering hole. The Kraken reclined on the stone steps waiting for her. No husbands stood in sight. They were alone.

"You are early," The voices came from the water.

Donya nodded in response. She wanted to enter the water and check on the sword. She stepped up to the precipice and dropped to a knee. "May I enter and see the sword."

"It is not ready; you will know when it is." The Kraken moved under the water. "Still, come in."

Donya dropped in and allowed herself to sink to the bottom. She felt the shadow of the Kraken descend with her.

In the low light near the bottom, the sword waited. It was opal still, but nothing else seemed special about it. She looked up at the Kraken.

The Kraken's voice came from the water all around her. "You may have no luck of your own, but you certainly are lucky to me."

This made no sense to Donya, "explain, please." She held in one lungful of air, bubbles floated up out of her mouth with every word.

The image of the old woman in the garden shimmered in the water. "You have found another interesting human." The Kraken's appendages feathered out around Donya. "I did not take you into my plans before, but perhaps I will keep you around."

Donya shrugged.

She felt a tugging at her side. It was the bottle full of river water. The Kraken took it. She brought it to herself and pulled open the top. She pulled the ordinary water from it and pushed in the water from the pool.

Donya suspected this water was far superior to the water in the river. "What will it do?"

"Not everything she wanted. It will heal her joints," the Kraken responded. "It is a token. I can do more, but she will have to visit me herself. You will take the message to her."

Donya nodded again.

Another image shimmered in the water—Scarlet and the smudged spell. "It was a good spell. You did not execute it entirely."

"I know that spell. It was done perfectly."

"You learned it from your grandmother. Did she tell you what it was for?"

"You know the answer," Donya said. The Kraken had been in probably all her memories while she slept in this pool. Donya grew short on air and short on patience.

"That spell is meant for her cows, to prevent them from tripping in the dark."

Donya coughed a little, wasting more of the air she needed to talk. A spell for cows, and she used it on a magic-wielding human. She'd wondered what that spell was meant for, but her grandmother taught her many spells. She didn't always give explanations. She wanted to say, 'Another fine mess' but knew she couldn't get much out. Instead, she said, "shit."

Minutes before dawn the Kraken floated over Donya as the sword's vivification approached. Donya could feel the sword. It was like another part of her came into being, like another arm she never knew she had. It felt essential, and she was greedy for it to get here.

Donya kept her eyes on the sword, hoping to catch a glow, or other sign, like when she and Scarlet formed it.

The moment arrived. Nothing changed in the pool, but Donya felt it inside of her. She reached for the hilt and glided it out of the saturated soil.

With the sword in her hand, she knew precisely where Scarlet existed and what she did. She slept in her hotel next to her fiancé. And there lay an identical sword now in her hand—glowing and dangerous.

CHAPTER 33

# SCARLET

Scarlet still felt frazzled as they considered their options at the train station. Waking up to a sword in your hand will do that. The sword disappeared when she opened her hand and dropped it, but still, very startling. Clouds covered the sky and sun, and Scarlet was thankful for it. Juan's eyes looked normal. Everything looked normal.

"Maybe we should pay for one of the tours to get to Pompeii," Juan stated as he eyed the dismal options for trains.

"You know we could scrap this day trip," Scarlet said. She wanted to get out of the city and watch the landscape sweep by for a few hours, but she also couldn't handle one more complicated thing.

"What are we going to do then?" Juan was getting exasperated.

It took Scarlet a few moments to think about it. What did she do when she used to travel alone? Maybe a hop-on, hop-off option would be good. They hadn't seen that much of the city yesterday during the walking tour. They could get around to all the sites this way. "How about a bus tour? We can make one of those dealers' days on the street. And I think there is a stop right outside."

"Yeah, I guess that could work. It isn't the prettiest day for it, though," he said as they started to walk outside.

"Maybe there will be fewer people. We can sit on the top all by ourselves."

The bus ride was perfect. They went along the old city wall, and there was a stop near the Spanish Steps not far from their hotel. She also got to rest her foot. It didn't hurt much, but the blister-like bite on her toe continued to swell with water. She needed to ask Donya about it but didn't want to sound ungrateful to the Kraken.

The stops were numbered. They needed to get off at ten. They revisited the pantheon, which had been rushed in the walking tour. The oldest gelato place in town lay a couple blocks away; Juan hoped to retrace yesterday's steps and find it. It had far more flavors than most of the newer shops. Scarlet ate a pear and caramelized fig the first time—Juan, walnut, and cinnamon.

Juan listened to the prerecorded audio through the free headphones they gave out. He touched Scarlet's arm as he pulled them free. "It's the next stop."

"I hope we get this lucky with the next bus," she said, closing her purse and bundling herself back in a scarf. They sat at the front of the bus, toasty warm in the enclosure. At first, this spot seemed like a bad idea. You could see every time the driver almost collided with another driver or a pedestrian. But after about ten minutes, Juan and Scarlet started treating it like a roller coaster ride. It appeared their driver was competent and the bus had excellent brakes.

They pulled to a stop along a curve. The stops were usually far away from the attraction you wanted to see. Stop ten was no exception. They hopped out into the cold air, and the driver shut the door behind them. After that, they spent most of the day getting on and off buses. An entire loop completed, they admired the Circus Maximus in the morning and then traveled out to the catacombs stop they'd toured before, which reminded Scarlet of what lay in wait for her tonight.

Juan checked his phone as they walked. "I tried to drop a pin, but being offline, I don't know if it worked."

The clouds broke up. Scarlet walked silently beside Juan—the sunlight made her nervous. She wasn't sure how her eyes worked yet. The dark vision was easy. It worked like night vision goggles but in color. Indirect lighting seemed normal to her, but strong sunlight seemed to be the key to something else. She wanted to know more but felt maybe, in this case, ignorance was bliss.

"Look, there it is, Giolitti. That is the name. If I took a picture, it would have been easy to find. Come on," Juan said as he spun her around for a selfie.

Scarlet smiled up at him. Something was wrong. She wasn't sure what, but he seemed out of character. One minute short and then overexcited. "Maybe we should do the selfie after we get the ice cream."

"Both, we will get a few inside too."

He clicked away, and Scarlet tried to angle her chin down but not so far down that she got a double chin.

They went in, and Scarlet felt overwhelmed by the number of people and things to buy. One counter held pastries and one long curving counter gelato in a rainbow of colors. They both went up to the gelato. "This time, I want to get a big cup," Scarlet said. She hadn't held back before, but in the last few days, she almost overindulged.

"That table is opening up. Go grab it, and I'll order. What flavors do you want?"

"Surprise me," Scarlet said as she went toward the table by the window. The sun shone outside. She investigated the bright light and saw nothing. It lay on the other building. It wouldn't touch her here. Man, she hoped he wouldn't get her coconut or pineapple.

Juan returned in a few minutes with two beautiful glass cups overflowing with gelato. They both contained a giant hard cookie sticking up out of them. Scarlet raised an eyebrow at it.

"Yours is Chocolate because I can't go wrong with that, caramelized fig again because you said you liked it, and finally a flavor called Roman Holiday. I don't know what it is."

Scarlet laughed, "it's amazing. What's in yours?"

"Rice flavor. It's good, not too sweet, Sicilian orange, and Bailey's whiskey cream."

"Ewwwwww, babe, you're weird!" She dug into hers, and it tasted great. The mystery flavor seemed to be a sweet mild nut.

The sky cleared when they made it to the Pantheon. Scarlet tried to not be weird about walking on the shady side of the street. Even when she was okay with what her eyes saw in the sunlight, it did make walking a little precarious. The small waves and swirls of glitter sometimes startled her; the shimmer blurred the edges of buildings and other objects, occasionally throwing off Scarlet's depth perception.

The pantheon in the sun was glorious. The waves of glitter agreed, shimmering in the air around it.

"Go stand in front of it so I can get a picture of you. There were too many people yesterday—it's better now," Juan said.

Scarlet obliged Juan. The sun sat behind him hitting her right in the face. She pulled out her sunglasses. They helped with the glare, but not the shimmers. Smiling as wide as she could, she put her arms on her hips and attempted to ham for the camera.

A green blob appeared behind Juan right as she motioned for him to come to her to get more pictures together. It wasn't a large green blob, maybe iguana-sized. It was fat with bulging eyes and six legs. It quickly climbed up his leg, over his stomach, and sat on his shoulder. Its big eyes focused on his face.

She didn't realize she had turned herself down until that moment. The lizard blob startled her. She let go. The sunlight allowed her to see what happened. A bubble came out of her. It knocked the blob off Juan's shoulder and pushed away the shimmer that hung in the air.

"What's wrong?" he asked as he made it to her. "You're making a stinky face."

"Um, nothing," she said, watching the blob pick itself up and scamper away from them. She couldn't sense it even right in front of her. But she could see every detail of it. She could see the details of the bubble she and Juan stood in. The shape and the color of it reminded her of the night under the bridge. It was like a force field out of *Star Trek*. It must be her power. It wasn't that she repulsed spirits, she could make a physical barrier against them. Juan watched her. "I thought of something, um, work-related. I checked my email last night. Now I'm annoyed."

"You work too hard," he said.

"Hey, I saw you do it too," she responded as they walked into the pantheon. It wasn't very crowded here either. Maybe on Sunday, everyone went to church.

Through the central opening, up in the sunlight, she could see the shimmer. The clouds obscured it yesterday, but it, whatever it was, poured into the dome of the pantheon. She couldn't see it once inside because there was no sunlight. But she knew it funneled in, a lot of it. Where the sunlight did shine through the hole, she could see it swirling around, clockwise. The air did feel thick. Finally, I maybe can sense something she thought.

This is what she must do from now on. She needed to make sense of all this magic and the monsters. She hid from it her whole life, and now it had come back to bite her. Maybe devoting her life to it wasn't the way, but she couldn't hide from it either.

CHAPTER 34

# DONYA

She dreamed of Nera. There was no visual sense to the dream, only the smell of water and a laugh heard from afar.

Opening her eyes, she still smelled water. It was different. Water comes in many scents—this one laden with the syrupy tang of magic. The sword lay in front of her. She took it up and swam to the surface where the Kraken waited.

"That sword is lazy," the Kraken's voice emanated from the water.

Donya expelled water and sucked in air. She placed the sword on the stone steps and climbed up. "How unfortunate."

"It took three nights to awaken, and now look at it. Back asleep."

Donya touched it. She squeezed the hilt. She felt the sword stir.

"Keep at it."

Donya kept squeezing. The Kraken's tendrils floated in the water under them. The sword warmed in her hand. Minutes ticked by.

After three full minutes, she felt it awaken. She slashed out at the night air above them. Nothing happened.

It could do something. Donya wasn't sure how to access it, and there was not much time to learn about this new tool.

"Try earth," instructed the Kraken.

Donya stood and pointed down at the ground. She could feel it moving with the sword. She brought down the sword in a wide arch, and the ground crumbled away underfoot. That was an impressive interaction with her earth magic. How could the sword interact with shadow? She needed to stab a body and see what happened when the sword pierced into the darkness inside all living things. Leveling a gaze at the Kraken, she asked, "is there a tree you are not fond of?"

The Kraken raised her tentacle, pointing to one on the rim of her glade. Donya could see this one was different from many of the spectacular trees which surrounded the grotto. It resembled the trees in the rest of the forest, with green needles, small pinecones, and a sharp sap scent. The trees closer to the Kraken were larger, with broad leaves of silver and gold, and bright flowers that perfumed the air with spice. Walking up to the thick conifer, she jammed the blade into it.

Nothing happened. Donya pulled the sword free. As she did, the tree turned black as night and began to dissolve. The shadow funneled into the sword tip.

"How pedestrian. It amplifies your abilities," said the Kraken.

"It can do more, but for now, this will be enough."

"Mmm, you are most likely correct. I thought I felt a ripple in Scarlet's room. She is too far away from Venice. It is difficult to communicate when I am unfocused."

"I will confer with her soon. Goodbye, now, Lady."

"Give my regards to that alchemist."

Donya felt a broad smile on her face. This sword might be lazy, but it sure was strong. With it, she knew they could defeat Heldrig. With it, she might be able to defeat anyone.

The swim and run back South took even less time than the first trip. Donya felt solid and robust as she made her way back to the door in the hill. Those feelings let her drop her guard. So she was taken quite by surprise when a howl erupted behind her as she jogged up to the door.

She spun around, hand grabbing at her sword hilt. She squeezed but did not pull it free of her belt. Her eyes caught the sight of a wolf—a large gray wolf with squinting eyes. The wolf appeared similar to those who roamed her mountain home, but not the same.

Donya took a knee, reaching into her shirt front where she kept the scroll of introduction tucked in its glass vial. She held it out to the Wolf King. "My lord, a formal introduction."

Was it customary to keep one's eyes downcast? Donya could not be sure. She opted for the middle interpretation and watched the wolf's feet as they approached. First, there were four paws. In the space of a breath, there were two feet. When Donya peered up, there was a naked man in front of her, taking the scroll from her hand.

He was not tall but had a full head of dark hair streaked with gray. His eyes still squinted. Like he forever looked into a bright light or laughed. He read the letter, not a single emotion flickered across his face. Donya waited. She felt sure he would speak to her eventually.

Finally, his eyes came up from the paper; he stared down at her. "We will hear you tomorrow at the eleventh bell."

Even Donya needed more information than that. She formulated a question. "You are very kind. We will be here. How many will attend? I would bring you tokens."

This did not change his face. "Who can say? At least myself, at most all seven," he paused, nodding to himself. "You should hope against seven."

That was a big risk. "The woman is on the other side of this veil; we could meet now if it pleased you?"

"Impertinent. I gave an hour," he said, the words sounded almost amused.

"My apologies. I do not want to waste your valuable time."

He turned, changing back into a wolf, and ran off with the scroll in his teeth.

Donya stood up, the sword dangled at her side. It still slept. With a strong possible enemy mere feet in front of it, nothing changed. It really would not awaken until she held it for a full three minutes. She'd hoped the Kraken had been wrong, but it was she who was wrong about the sword.

The door remained on the side of a green hill, slightly obscured by long grasses and tall flowers. It would be missed if one didn't know it stood there. She slung the water bottle off her back and pulled the door open.

The library on the other side glowed with electric light. Scarlet and Grazia sat sipping tea. Neither spoke. Scarlet exhibited a large crease in her brow.

Grazia rose as Donya stepped through. Donya proffered the bottle to the elderly woman, then in Latin said, "from the Kraken herself. She requests a visit if you would like more."

Grazia cackled. "We will see how good it is, then I will consider. I am liking this young woman. Too bad she knows almost no Italian and no Latin. The youth today are uncivilized."

"You could not speak to each other? What a shame. You probably could explain better to her than me," Donya said. She understood magic but from a troll's perspective. Grazia and Scarlet were both human, so she assumed they would have more in common.

"Perhaps yes, Perhaps no. I trained in lore and power from a very young age. She is a natural. I can feel her, a bit like a furnace."

Finally, Scarlet could take it no longer. "Could you please tell me what is going on?"

"This is Grazia. She is not a random woman who owned this house, although I still don't know what she is. Best not to ask when we need her help. Probably an alchemist from the chimera I saw."

"Tell the girl she needs to learn Latin," Grazia interrupted. She opened the bottle and sipped it.

"She wants you to learn Latin," Donya faithfully interpreted, then said first in English, then in Latin, "We don't have much time. Let us go over the sword and the Wolf Kings." Donya pulled the sword from her belt. The moment her hand touched it, a shadow of the original appeared in Scarlet's hand.

"That keeps happening!" Scarlet yelped, standing up. She dropped the sword, and it dispelled. No true substance.

"Put it down and have young Scarlet pick it up," Grazia said.

Donya set down the sword on a dark wood table. "You pick it up." She gestured for Scarlet.

Scarlet stepped forward. When she grabbed the hilt, the same effect occurred. Now a shadow sword lay in Donya's hand.

"Such a thing of beauty," Grazia said, dabbing at her eye. She continued, "I am delighted I lived to see this day. Magic is waking back up. You two are all the proof I need."

Donya watched Scarlet, but what Grazia said struck her as very odd. "What do you mean? Magic has always been here," she said to Grazia. Then to Scarlet, she said, "hold it for a few minutes 'til it wakes up, but don't swing it around."

Grazia continued, "you do not know. I would assume those with magic inside them would sense this. The cycle restarted in 2012. From there, it will rise for 5,125 years."

"I am not a very old troll. I am around two thousand years old. Perhaps elder trolls would know."

"A teenage troll you are," said Grazia, "translate it for Scarlet; she must know these things.

That was how the rest of the night went, Grazia gave them pieces of wisdom which Donya translated. They stayed too late. Donya would need to sleep in the catacombs, and Scarlet would barely make it back before Juan woke up.

"You can make it here by ten-thirty tonight, right?" Donya said before Scarlet ducked into the cab.

"I said yes. Don't worry about me. I promise to make it." She held a book Grazia pressed into her hand earlier in the night.

Scarlet waved as the Taxi pulled away. She had changed. Whatever resistance that persisted in her was reduced. Donya walked back up the stairs. Grazia's spine appeared straighter. Her white hair boasted a few black strands now. The water worked.

"I am not excited about the meeting. I do not want to grovel for their assistance," Donya said.

Grazia shrugged. "Groveling never helped with those Wolf Kings anyway."

# CHAPTER 35

# SCARLET

Juan sat on the edge of the bed, watching the door when Scarlet walked in. He spoke quietly on the phone, his jaw tight. The muscle that ran along the side of his face stood out. Scarlet startled. It was still dark, and she only carried an old ornate book. Reading would not work as an excuse she could do that in the room at the desk.

She had no reason to walk around in the wee hours of the morning in a large ancient city. Her heartbeat sped like a hummingbird's. She felt herself lose control of her magic. She could feel that. Her mind seemed to be running very fast and yet empty of anything useful.

Not knowing what to say, she kicked off her shoes and sat next to Juan. She wore the clothes Donya had gifted her, which he would have never seen. She checked her foot. It didn't glow. Apparently, the Kraken wouldn't help with mundane matters.

Her heart still flopped around, but the thought of the clothes cleared her mind. She could still take them off. He couldn't see in the dark like her. She wriggled out of the fine warm sweater and pants. Then she crawled up into the bed. The squawking on the other end of the phone went silent. Juan didn't speak.

Finally, Juan exhaled. It was loud, long, and slow. "Listen, it isn't that bad. I'll deal with Todd when I get back. Have the vehicle picked up from the impound lot. It's only a few days. He can keep working until then. I don't believe this is a fire-able offense, just a bunch of really bad decisions."

Scarlet wasn't used to hearing him speak in such a clipped manner. His words and his tone didn't match. She wondered who he spoke to. Probably Lucinda. Whoever it was, they rattled off a bunch of words again. Scarlet moved around the back of him. She could see his shoulders tight and bunched up too high to his ears.

In a very uncharacteristic move, Juan interrupted the speaker, "I hear you, but I have to go now. International call, you know. Bye." Juan pulled the phone away from his ear. The light from the phone illuminated the room for a moment, then went out.

Juan didn't turn around or say anything. In the silence, her heart pounded. A little part of her brain felt her magic expand. She heard a squeak from outside the window, probably a spirit got burned. Her magic did feel strong now that she knew how to hold it in.

Then she heard it, a sound far worse to her than if he yelled. Juan sniffled. His shoulders shook. No one at work or any of their friends knew this—Juan was a crier. He worried about people and cried when he got upset. Scarlet thought it was a character trait he got from losing his dad. Juan had been twelve. His dad went to work and died of heatstroke.

Scarlet got up out of the cover and wrapped her arms around him from behind. "I'm sorry," she said because she was. She was sorry about this whole situation and dragging him on this trip.

"I thought you were in the bathroom," he started, his voice gravelly, "but then you didn't come out, and I was on the stupid phone." He sniffled. "Why can't the guys even haul a simple load to the dump while I'm gone?" He moved his hands and wiped at his face.

Scarlet knew it wasn't healthy but right now, distracting him with a work problem worked best for her. She latched on to the silly problem. "You know how I am, sweetie; I can never sleep. I went for a walk around the piazza, all well-lit. I should have left a note."

"Or taken your phone," he croaked.

"I'll take my phone if I need to do it again. I really wanted to tire my brain out so I could sleep before we went on our tour today."

"I know. I thought that was it. But you could've been dead in the street. You didn't take your passport either. No one would have known who you are."

"Nothing happened. When I traveled alone, I did way worse."

"That doesn't make me feel better." He stopped shaking but still sniffled.

"I know. How about you tell me what happened at work?" she asked, breaking her hold and moving back under the covers. She patted his side of the bed.

His eyes focused on her in the dark room. She noticed what a pretty crier he was. His eyes glittered, and his cheeks glistened with tears. She always got red patches on her neck, and her eyes would swell shut if she cried for more than thirty seconds. He stood up and walked around to his side of the bed, and got under the covers. She cuddled close to him, placing her ear to his collarbone.

"I played it down, but I am one hundred percent firing Todd when we get back."

Scarlet laughed. A short outburst but it possessed joy. "Oh babe, you did not play it down that much."

The day was bright and cold. A wind blew through the streets. It was bad on their way to the Vatican and while their tour group stood in line—a fairly short line, shorter than the line for the David. Their tour guide seemed drunk, drunk at ten am. He bobbed his head and swung to a tune no one else could hear. Finally, the giant walls of the Vatican blocked the stiff wind. They started the tour in the gardens, learning about the history of the place. Scarlet found she didn't care about any of it. She hadn't cared before she came as she suffered no religion to speak of, and given all that happened to her, she cared even less.

She was also incredibly tired, more tired than in college when she would pull all-nighters to finish a paper on time. Because even during finals, she only needed to miss maybe a couple of nights of sleep. That morning at breakfast, she took a coffee and chewed Tums to help with the acidy feeling in her stomach.

The tour guide rushed them through the large building. At the tour's start, he said he wanted to get them to the chapel early. There were times when more tour groups would hit, so this company tried to schedule their tour slightly before that. It all sounded very clever at the time, but now Scarlet suspected he wanted to get out of there and back to a bar.

Out of the sunlight, her vision was the most normal it could be. She thought she saw things in shadows, not spirits, and not the glitter, but something else. It gave her the feeling she missed important information again. Like she had the entire time Donya and Heldrig tried to capture her and Juan. Her vision wasn't supposed to be what she focused on. She needed to be better at sensing magic, like Donya. In all her practice, though, nothing much came of it.

She followed the group. Juan didn't seem interested either. He'd been quiet all morning, and they hung back in the group. In all their other tours, they stood at the front, asked questions and actively participated. Scarlet took his hand and gave it a little squeeze. He squeezed back but did not turn. He studied the painted maps on the walls.

"No questions once we enter the chapel. Take your time and admire the ceiling. The center is always the most packed. I will be waiting at the back, but I am not meant to raise my green flag. You will have to watch for my beautiful face," the tour guide said slowly into his radio. They all wore cheap earbuds to hear him.

He wasn't wrong. Scarlet had thought the Vatican wasn't as busy as everyone said. But in the Sistine Chapel, people stood packed tighter than a can of sardines. Amazing artwork surrounded them. However, Botticelli and Tucci were overshadowed by the ceiling. Scarlet craned her head to get a better view of the vast work. Many people stood in the center of the room where God reached for the reclined Adam.

She remembered a quote about the amount of work one person could do in a lifetime. Michelangelo finished this vast masterpiece and still had time to do the David. She searched the figures, trying to find her favorite. But the bright colors and perspective kept her eyes moving. She felt grateful to see this after its cleaning and restoration. The teal robes looked magnificent without centuries of soot and grime.

The crush of people got to her. She peeked at Juan, his face still tilted up to the ceiling. "Which one is your favorite?"

"I don't know. It is so big. Maybe the one with the serpent." He pointed with his hand.

Scarlet looked up as a wave of people moved beside her. Another group left, which gave her more breathing room. A golden serpent wound around a tree. The top half appeared to be a woman. She wondered if that meant the devil was a woman. She frowned. "Why do you like that one?"

"Because other than the finger-touching one, I know what it is about," he responded.

"You don't know the rest? I thought your mom took you to church a bunch when you were little."

"Yeah, but I was little. I haven't been to church in at least a decade. And I never paid attention."

"Do you mean to say kids don't like Church?" Scarlet said with mock sarcasm. "We better buy your mom holy water on the way out."

"I need to get it for her, my aunties, and my sisters."

"I didn't think your sisters would want any."

"Lettie won't care either way. Bertha likes to put on a show. She will probably post about it."

"I wouldn't know. She unfriended me last month," Scarlet said. She kept it neutral. She disliked Juan's middle sister. This wasn't an unusual situation; it seemed like most people disliked Bertha.

"She did?" Juan asked, but his tone let on it was rhetorical. They moved forward toward the last Judgment.

Scarlet gave the work a once over. It was supposed to leave an impression as you walked out of the chapel. But she didn't feel anything about it, except maybe a bit thankful to have more breathing room at last.

After the people press, it felt good to walk around outside again, even in the cold. The guide led them back to the tour headquarters, probably to try and get them to sign up for more packages. But this was it for Scarlet and Juan. They had one full day left, reserved for the Colosseum and Roman Forum. Also, this tour had probably been the worst they attended; not a great selling point.

Others in the group felt the same. Three split off and walked away down a side street. The guide didn't notice or care. Juan held Scarlet's hand and pulled her up to the front of the group.

"Scusi, where can we get good food around here?" he asked the guide.

"Great question. We are in a nice neighborhood to eat. Here, I will lead you to the place," The guide lit up at the question about food.

They turned left at the next corner. A few of the other members of the group looked more interested again. Scarlet wondered if they felt the same about this tour as she did. The diminished group of nine turned again, causing Scarlet's sense of direction to scramble. The streets were old and narrow.

"This is the place. Best food around. Stay here if you want to eat. They will close in about an hour."

"Thank you, Señor," Juan said with a smile and nod.

"Wait, see on that corner… good gelato."

"Perfect, you are a mind reader," Scarlet added. The thought of good food put a smile on her face and gratitude in her voice.

Scarlet and Juan walked into the small restaurant, followed by about six others from the group. The man behind the counter boasted bushy eyebrows that rose high at the large group. It wasn't busy, but with all these people, the place would be packed. Scarlet eyed the sunny tables in the front. If they sat out there, hopefully, no smokers would sit next to them, and they could be warm. Scarlet ordered the *tagliatelle al ragù alla Bolognese*, and Juan ordered *ravioli en brood*, then went to sit outside.

A Wi-Fi password was hand-painted on the wall. Juan typed it in and scrolled through work emails. Scarlet watched as his jaw tightened again. She couldn't read his eyes in the sunlight, pearlescent and strange. Even though a few other strangers possessed interesting eyes in bright light, no one had the same effect as Juan. She needed to ask the little troll when this vision would wear off. She didn't want to be an extra freak forever.

Juan sighed. He could be worried about work. She couldn't find it in her to care about work stuff. James could go suck a frozen whale turd for all she cared.

With Juan distracted, she worked on her control. After the early morning outburst, she thought she had a good idea of how to unleash her power at will. She regarded Juan—he read through an email. Then she studied her hands in the sunlight. It felt like exhaling deeply.

The barrier was ball-shaped and red. It expanded out of her midsection in a perfect sphere. She watched it move out. The red light had a similar shimmer to that in the air. It expanded out quickly, displacing any shimmer. If this was her magic, then the stuff in the air must also be some sort of magic, she thought. It could be someone's or, more likely, something's. She would have to ask about it tonight. She pulled the sphere back in. It was a few inches outside her table range. She concentrated on its size when Juan sneezed.

She looked over at him. "Bless you, babe."

She'd lost control of the sphere. She knew it got large quickly, but besides being startled by the sneeze, she saw something strange. The iridescent shine from Juan's eyes. It was steam, vaporizing, swirling very much like the shimmer. It swirled out. When he sat in her magic field, she could see it dissipate and become part of the sphere. Was it feeding off of him? Was that what all the spirits wanted from him? And was she no different?

The waiter placed steaming bowls of food in front of her and Juan. It smelled delicious, but Scarlet's appetite was gone.

CHAPTER 36

# DONYA

Donya knew this presence. Someone familiar entered the catacomb network. Above her, the sun shone. Nera. It was far off, but she was acquainted with her energy now. It resonated through her body. Donya scrambled to her feet and barreled forward.

Why she moved with such purpose remained unclear to Donya. Did she want to help Nera or get help from her? Nera assisted her before; she would do it again. Donya was almost sure of it. Nymphs, even part nymphs, were not fully capable of hatred. Nera was better than Donya, and she would not hold the push against her, especially if Donya killed Heldrig. If Nera *could* hate someone, it would be him.

Daylight persisted, but the sun hung low in the sky. It didn't matter. Donya could move faster through the catacombs anyway. She picked up the bone she brought with her before. "Where are we going?" it asked sleepily.

"On a fool's errand," Donya replied.

She picked up the pace, running through the darkness. She was low to the ground and heavy. Cornering in the tight space was no problem for her. She pounded along, running through the maze with ease. She came to a new body of water and splashed into it. Nera wasn't here, but she felt closer. She powered along the bottom of the cistern and came up on the other side.

"That was cold," whined the little bone.

Donya kept moving. But now that she neared, she could feel her path might be obscured. Nera was in the catacombs, but not one connected directly with her. Also, Nera was not alone. Donya pulled up short. Could this be another trap for her?

No, she doubted Heldrig considered her still in this fight. But he didn't understand the depths of her spite. Besides, she doubted Nera before—a mistake. This time she would be cautious, and not run into another bad situation.

Her new clothes dripped, making a puddle in the darkness. "How do you feel about participating in a spell?"

"Me?" asked the bone with so much glee she almost squealed.

Donya nodded. This would be faster and safer, but if she wasn't cautious would use up a lot of her precious power. Earth magic always did.

She leaned down and mixed the water on the floor with the tufa dust. It made a good paste. The bone set well into the mixture. Stopping to take off her clothes, she left them in a sodden heap on the ground. She could always get new clothes, but maybe those would be salvageable. She especially liked the pants.

Then she began to hum. It produced a sound like a milling stone grinding flour. Picking up the bone, she scooped mud up with it and spooned it into her mouth. She worked it around, still humming all the while. She reached out to the tufa and used her strong fingers to grind out a shallow crescent moon, large enough to fit the bone. It was Monday—homage to the moon could help. Spitting the mud into her hand, she began to paint the inside of her carving. When she finished, she got another scoop of mud and repeated the process. It wasn't fast, but she could feel it work. The sun set far over her, and she knew her abilities increased.

"Many things are best taught by doing. It's your part. Are you ready?"

"Yes, yes, I am ready."

Donya placed the bone into the mud. She could feel the little one release energy; the young could be potent. A fog of tufa dust wrapped around her, then she was in the stone, enveloped in the spongy mass. The smell of magic stuck in her nose. In here, she could not breathe to clear it. She knew where she wanted to go. It wasn't a direct path through stone; there was dirt in the way. She passed through with ease.

Her destination rested inside the stone next to Nera who floated in the water. She stayed undetectable as at this moment she existed as part of the stone. She could sense the consciousness of the bone there with her as well, as it should be. Technically, she powered this magic. Donya procured the physical elements for it.

"This is so exciting. Look at her. She is the most beautiful thing I have ever seen!" said the bone.

"I agree."

"What is she doing?"

"That is what I will figure out."

Nera floated in the water. Mars watched her from the perch. His face showed nothing. His lips stayed parted. One of his arms hung bandaged. The dressings were dusty with dirt and grime. Something was wrong with this water. Donya could taste it seeping into the rock below her. What were they doing? It wasn't a spell, per se.

"Sister, it's time again."

Nera dove into the water; she swam with a grace and speed Donya hadn't witnessed in her lifetime. She shot out of the water by Mars. He reached into a bucket. Nera turned her back to him. He took out a paintbrush and anointed her. She flinched at the first touch. Donya could not see from her angle. She needed to move. She pushed through the rock, wishing she didn't have to. The bone was strong, but she needed to get back, and if this process took long, she would be pushing it.

They moved to the top of the cavern. The symbols were small, in the same script Mars used on the spell under the bridge. Instead of making a circle, he dictated from a notebook. The substance he wrote with was oil, explaining the flinch. It couldn't have felt pleasant to her sensibilities. What could they be doing? If it wasn't a spell, what was it?

She guessed it was the third round of application. She completely watched the second round, and then Nera bathed herself. Most of the text was unfamiliar to her, but she recognized Irrlish and old Norse words thrown in. Watching Mars work helped her decrypt the text. It serpentined, as many old languages did. The first round she missed probably called to the sun to lend no aid. The second, a plea to the moon. This one for the air, the wind specifically. Donya suspected Heldrig must be vulnerable to the wind—wind purified.

Everything they appealed to had to do with the sky. Heldrig would want to attack when Scarlet couldn't call on any help. He would use the flight to California. He knew the exact date from the seer. He'd obtained their names. He could build a very exact spell, tailor-made for Scarlet and Juan. Could she follow Nera and Mars back to their refuge? Would Heldrig have been fool enough to stay in a stone-walled structure? If he had, she could stay in the walls like this. She could learn everything.

And if she missed the Wolf King meeting because of it? They were an uncertainty. They might not assist them. But this, this would be more helpful, and if Heldrig and Mars left, maybe she could talk to Nera alone, apologize even.

Minutes ticked away. Mars finished the last of the writing around Nera's left foot.

"Done," he said from a kneeling position.

Nera let out a sigh of relief and jumped in the water. She twirled and scrubbed under the water. Donya wondered if Nera's skin seemed raw from the harshness of her movements. When she floated to the surface and held still, the iridescent oil slick on the surface of the water looked foul. The water was thoroughly contaminated. For just a moment, she saw Nera's eyes linger on the spot where she existed. If she could feel Nera strongly, maybe the nymph could sense her.

"Mars, I can walk myself back. I would like to stay here for a while. I am tired now."

He snorted. "Are you mad? Father would rather kill you than leave you alone now." He took a few steps toward the water. "Do not make me drag you out."

Donya bristled. That little shit. How dare they treat her like that. If she could push through the stone… She felt herself move forward in rage. She must come back out where the crescent existed, or she would have killed the boy. Nera could run away. Heldrig couldn't recover from such a loss quickly. Scarlet would be safe.

"I don't like him," whispered the bone. Donya could hear the tiredness in her voice. The spell went on too long, hours too long.

"Do not worry. He will get what is coming to him."

"I'll help."

"You will be rewarded if I survive."

"This is already enough."

"No, it is not," Donya said. The hardness in her voice leftover from the rage.

They watched as Nera got slowly out of the water. She dried her abraded body and wrapped it in another loose dress. Mars walked ahead of her, so sure she would follow.

"We will need to track them; do you think you can handle it? I can get us to the crescent afterward, I think," Donya said.

The little bone flared up, "I can do this. I can."

Nera glanced over her shoulder again at the spot on the wall where Donya would be. That secured it in her mind. Nera could sense them. Mars couldn't. It must have been the bond they formed under the bridge. In the span of a week, Donya developed many more ties. One human. One Nymph. Perhaps even the fabled Kraken.

Nera quickened her pace, bumping ahead of Mars. Good, this was good. If they hurried, then Donya could make it back for the eleventh bell. The hour grew near, but she could push her power into the spell and get them back to the crescent.

Mars and Nera came out of the catacombs in a church courtyard. Donya could see two priests crumpled in the corner. They must have been around earlier. Donya pushed herself closer to Mars, wondering how he had done it. A blood puddle pooled under the priests, seeping through the cobblestones; it could have been as simple as a knife.

They exited a side gate onto a peaceful street. Donya could feel the energy in her spell strain. Nera almost stomped to a busy street. She hailed a cab on the corner. An old black car came to an abrupt stop by her. Mars got in too.

Traveling through the tufa had been easy. Even the church stones did not try her. But the dirt, cobblestones, and occasional asphalt under the taxi were difficult. The media changed quickly because of the speed of the car. But the spell held.

"I do not feel right," said the bone. She understated the truth.

"Here, let me help more." Donya tried to release some of her strength into the spell. It marginally worked. She organized the physical means; the spell didn't want her power, but it took a bit. Magic could be finicky.

The car left the city limits, which made it easier to move. The country contained more dirt, which was consistent.

"This is what it used to look like," the bone uttered as they passed green rolling hills.

"I'm sure all those buildings confused you."

"The monster we follow is more confusing than the colorful fires and tall buildings."

"That is a car. It's a machine, not a monster," Donya explained.

The car sped around another bend and pulled up to a rustic home. Beautifully trained olive trees lined the property. Donya rushed to keep up with the car, almost not noticing the painted blood ring around the outside of the home. She stopped short. It was an easily recognizable and quickly built ward. Heldrig would not have been acquainted with more complicated wards. He remained overconfident. A better-constructed ward would have caught her out.

"I will take the moonlight," Nera said as she stepped from the car. She walked a bit and flopped to the ground barely inside the circle.

Donya could see Mars watch Nera, then he turned back to the cabbie. The inside of the car illuminated because of the open door. It appeared Mars would hand over cash. Instead, he lashed out with a blade, stabbing the man in the chest.

Mars got out of the car, then got the dying body from the front. He dragged it to Nera. The corners of her mouth turned down; her brow wrinkled.

"Fresh heart blood to repaint," Mars said.

"I know what it is for! I'm too tired to participate. Do it yourself."

Mars's face never reacted. He got the heart from the body and walked the circle counterclockwise. Nera waited till he slunk around the corner and drew a line at the dry part of the circle.

"Hurry," she whispered in Donya's direction.

Donya dragged herself forward past the now broken ward. They had till Mars made it back around to Nera. Then, hopefully, he wouldn't notice the smudge in the old blood.

Inside the house, a decayed taste penetrated the stone walls. The stones were ancient but took notice when Donya and the little bone entered them. They stayed awake. They watched. It wasn't a large place. Heldrig worked by a sizable western window, thrown open, probably to help with the rotting smell. Like his children, he had bandages. He wore many more. His head was bandaged, and his whole left hand and arm. A few wounds he didn't wrap; angry purple burns, mostly on his neck.

It was useful to note his condition. He hadn't wanted to waste the magic to heal his wounds. He must know a healing spell or two. Books lay spread out on the walls, pages and pages hung out. His notes stood open. The notes focused on dreams, dreams of forests, dreams of water, how to enter a dream and exit a dream, and forced sleep.

A star and sun chart hung up for the coming Wednesday. He made a great effort to get the positions correct. He arranged them plotted with the airline flight times. Two airlines flew into San Francisco that day. He wasn't sure which one they would be on. That was somewhere to strike. If the airline stayed a mystery to him, his spell wouldn't be as precise.

Mars passed by the window. Heldrig looked up at him. He tapped his fingers on the table. Donya took that as her cue and raced along the wall and out of the house.

She paused outside, in front of Nera. After soaking in the moonlight, the script scrawled on her in oil became more visible. It was light, but every space on her exposed skin lay covered, the skin slightly raised, like welts. Those scripts pulsed as if alive. Nera fiddled with something small in her hand.

Donya must get back. It was almost eleven—she would be late for the meeting. Somehow, she doubted the Wolf Kings would like to be kept waiting.

"I'm sorry," she said to Nera, who watched the spot where she existed. Nera didn't react, but Donya hoped she heard. She would say it again when she saw her in person, and she would prove it to her.

CHAPTER 37

# SCARLET

Where could that little troll be? Scarlet waited on the library side of the door to the other realm. It was almost time to step through, and there was no sign of Donya. And Scarlet couldn't talk about any of this to Grazia because they didn't speak the same language. Grazia appeared unfazed by the development. Grazia wandered slowly through the rooms of her home, picking up books and small objects. She placed them all in an old suitcase.

Scarlet checked her watch, five minutes till eleven. They needed to go. What would happen if they stood up the Wolf Kings? Would they go find that Heldrig character and let him know? People were vindictive, and these kings used to be people. And from the googling Scarlet did, they seemed to be not very nice people.

Grazia surprised Scarlet by fiddling with her pockets. The old woman poured coins into Scarlet's pockets, and then lit a sickly gray candle. She then perched in a chair opposite the door. "Partire, Partire," she said, making shooing motions at the door.

"But Donya?" Scarlet whined.

Grazia's eyebrows bounced a few times, which Scarlet interpreted as 'Oh well.' She wished the lady could come with her, or at least give her a pep talk right now. Scarlet glanced at the doorknob and then over her shoulder at the woman. Grazia nodded her silver-bunned head, then picked up the candle and closed her eyes. Scarlet pushed the door open.

The other side was another warm night, with the hum in the air. It wasn't as shrill as insects but annoying in that same way. A figure waited for her. Scarlet blinked. She would have felt confused at the sight but recalled everyone else knew magic. Grazia stood there holding the same candle.

"Come on then. We should have left earlier," Grazia said, walking up the hill.

"I can… I can understand you!" Scarlet said, astonished. What a practical use for a spell.

"Everyone can understand everyone in fae realms. My gracious, you have much to learn." She stopped at the top of the hill. A warm breeze flickered her candle. She did not raise a hand to shield it.

"I'd thought after all of this I wouldn't have to worry about magic stuff when I get home. But life keeps getting weirder, so I will need to learn, I guess," her voice trailed off. She wanted to ask if Grazia would please teach her. Maybe they could video chat? Scarlet noticed Grazia's clothing did not move in the breeze. "You are not here. Why didn't you walk through with me?"

"As I said, learn Latin, then you can have access to all the great teachers. It will take you one hundred years to get through the books, but it is a good start." The grassland around them shivered in the moonlight. The two women were alone. Grazia peered into the darkness. "Of course, they are late. They want to make a grand entrance. Get those coins out of your pockets."

Scarlet reached into her pockets—ordinary two Euro pieces filled her hand. The older woman ignored part of her questions. Perhaps she shouldn't pry. Learning from her was more important in any case. "Where can I find those books? And I thought if I do learn Latin, maybe we could talk on the phone, and you could teach me?" She jingled the coins in her hand.

"I packed the first of the books in that suitcase by the door. You can take it when you leave later. I will be happy to teach you, although I doubt I will be able to do much over the telephone."

"Over there," Scarlet said, pointing. The tall grass moved in the moonlight. It was a way off; only Scarlet's eyes could see it from this distance.

"They will be here soon. Let me do the talking."

"I think there are three of them." Scarlet squinted at the movement. Then she was sure. They broke out of the grass and stood in a clearing at the bottom of the hill.

"Do not look directly into their eyes either," Grazia said in a low tone.

"Was it insulting in Roman times?"

"No, it makes mean dogs bite and snarl."

Scarlet saw the wisdom in this. She glanced at the coins in her hands. She picked out six coins, slipping the rest back into her pocket. They jingled softly; the metal sounded strange here. Two for each wolf, all the coins shone, the metal gleamed like liquid in the darkness. The old kings probably wouldn't be that impressed—they might expect gold.

In the moonlight loped a gray wolf with eyes like Donya had described, followed by a deep espresso brown wolf, and finally, an almost white wolf. They approached in a single file. Scarlet watched them but never met their bright eyes. Grazia stood in front of her. Under closer inspection, she noticed Grazia was slightly transparent. You could see the candle flame through her torso. Why had she not come through in person?

A breeze blew from behind them, the wolves stood in front, and Scarlet saw them sniff at the air. The gray and the white wolf shifted and shimmered into human form. Now two men stood there, fully naked, which caused Scarlet to blush deeply.

Grazia cleared her throat. "Wolf Kings, we have come here tonight to ask a great good favor."

"And who is this 'we?' You are not the one I met last night. You have not even come all the way," the King with the full head of hair answered. The white wolf turned out bald.

"I am Grazia, known as the golden sealer some time ago."

"The golden sealer, I recall you, but you were a great beauty. Men from far and wide asked, nah, begged your hand, and you refused them all. Yes, I have heard of you," the bald one spoke up. Somehow he made all this sound like an insult.

"I was a great beauty, almost three hundred years ago. I believe I have aged gracefully, not as gracefully as you perhaps," Grazia's voice stayed smooth, her gaze level on the leader's chest. "Dear girl, the coins."

Scarlet stepped forward with the coins in her hands. It did not escape her attention that Grazia failed to introduce her. The Wolf Kings made no introductions either. She gave over two cheap coins to each man, then leaned over, placing two in front of the wolf who had not changed. His mouth came down, and he licked her hand. It took all of Scarlet's discipline not to pull back. Any wolf would have startled her, but this wasn't a wolf. It was a wolfman. She did glance up at the contact, right into his eyes. Nothing happened. She stood up and took a stumbling step back.

Grazia cleared her throat again, lowered her eyes, and began speaking; she seemed very regal. "We ask for your assistance in ridding Rome of a vile interloper. His name is Heldrig. He is from the north—"

The lead King raised his hand. "Your whole party has not arrived. Why do you rush through this grand occasion?"

"Late, very late," said the bald one, circling around the back of the leader.

Scarlet knew that behavior in dogs. She didn't like it. These men were not here to help. She felt down inside of her. The fire was right there. She could get Grazia and her out of there. She should interrupt right now, and call the whole thing off.

"All trolls move on a slower time scale than any other magical being. Much to my disappointment, our troll seems to be the same. I will not make excuses for her; this is simply the truth. She will come. I can feel it," Grazia said.

When Grazia stopped speaking, the tension in the air did not melt away but shifted. Nevertheless, the moments of silence did not feel perilous. Scarlet watched the men's feet.

They stood like Roman statues, keeping their weight on one leg and relaxing on the other. Perhaps they tried to give the impression of nonchalance, but it did not quite work.

Grazia seemed to grow tired of the silence. "Would you happen to be Ancus Marcius?" Her hand in front of the candle dropped a tad as though she relaxed too.

A sparkle flashed in the Wolf King's eye. He liked being recognized. "It has been a long time since I have heard my name from a human mouth." He smiled and nodded. In a minimal movement, those eyes moved to Scarlet. "Tell me, what do you know of my reign?"

For the briefest second, Scarlet got a wave of gratitude so strong for Google that her knees felt weak. "You were the first Roman King to declare war. Sadly, there is not a lot of information on the Kings of Rome because records from that time are few and far between. Also, a few of the records appear to contradict one another. I hope to learn more about ancient Rome. Tomorrow I am going to the forum, and maybe eventually I can come back and spend more time here." She shut her mouth with a snap—that felt like a ramble.

"We should not have allowed the barbarians to sack the city. But, back then, we never thought anything as great as our achievements could be erased," Marcius said.

"Time and barbarians will take their toll," Grazia added with a smile.

Scarlet got the feeling Grazia meant to cajole these Kings into helping her and Donya. It might work. Though Grazia was old, older than even Scarlet thought, she enjoyed a presence. And it looked as though Marcius took notice.

Emboldened by the sense that events were turning their way, Scarlet spoke up again, "it does not even take much time. I can't name most of the leaders of my country, even the great ones that led in more recent wars. Or I remember their names, but not what they did, like why was Roosevelt beloved? I have no idea. People are quick to forget."

"Very wise. Perhaps all the time humanity spends trying to wheedle themselves to power is wasted," Marcius said with genuine merriment.

The bald man seemed to be frowning more and more from all of this. Scarlet had almost forgotten he was there. The brown wolf, on the other hand, sported a big dog grin on his furry face.

"Pursuing power might be a waste, but pleasure pays its weight, I have learned. To be young again," Grazia added.

"Now I know what you want, golden sealer, but what about you?" Marcius let the smile drop from his face. He had a way of changing the tone of his voice. He manipulated the mood deftly.

Scarlet let the silence stand for a moment. It always helped in a meeting at work to collect herself, and not rush in with the first thing that came to mind. "Like Grazia said, we ask—"

A howl erupted in the dark distance. It was an angry howl if ever there was one.

The bald King fell to all fours as he morphed back into the white wolf. The brown wolf tucked its tail. Instead of seeming cowed, Marcius quickly stepped forward. He grabbed Grazia by the wrist and took the candle from her hand. He placed the taper in his mouth; extinguishing the flame on his tongue, he bit off the tip of the candle.

"NO!" Scarlet shrieked, but she was too late. The Wolf King scooped up Grazia in his arms, her form shimmering in his tight grip. He bounded back a few steps. Scarlet let the burning heat of her anger escape. The white wolf who stayed closest to her yelped and moved back.

Too much happened simultaneously. Scarlet could see movement in the grass, but she darted her eyes back to her one ally who transformed rapidly. The wrinkles smoothed. Her tight white bun came loose. Curls of dark mahogany hair spilled over slender shoulders.

Then a black wolf appeared on the hill. The other Wolf King took a knee and bowed his head, muttering, "All hail Romulus."

CHAPTER 38

# DONYA

Donya left the little bone sleeping in the muddy crescent. Eventually, Donya would thank her, but it might be years before she woke again. They used too much energy running after Nera. It should not have gone that way, but what Donya got was valuable information. She crashed through the opening of the Catacombs and up to the spot where her sword rested. It was placed under the orange tree. Brutus sat next to it. She scooped up her weapon and pounded through the courtyard door.

A clock on the plaster wall read eleven twenty. Grazia's body sat in a chair, an extinguished candle in her hands. She appeared dead, but Donya saw her chest rise. It wasn't too late. If the Wolf Kings were tardy, then none would be the wiser. Donya knew in her heart her life never played out fortuitously. She rushed through the waiting door. The night lay dark and noisy, but she could feel Scarlet. Magic clung thick in the air. It smelled wild, with hints of smoke and musk. And through the sword, she knew Scarlet was agitated. Thankfully the sword stirred in her hand.

She stopped for a moment, noticing the direction of the breeze. Scarlet stood upwind and at least a few Wolf Kings. She skirted the bottom of the hill, staying low. The grasses around her barely stirred.

When Donya or Scarlet picked up the sword, a double of it would appear in the other's hand. The double was not real. It would not continue to exist if put down. It was merely a shadow of the original but still as potent when wielded. Donya came out of the grass to see Scarlet holding the sword in not such a bad stance, facing off against four Wolf Kings. Three were wolves. One stood as a man holding the shade of a lovely young woman.

The black wolf was strong. Scarlet let her own power pour out of her, but that dark wolf could be a big problem.

"Put her down, and we will leave. This wasted your time, and I apologize, but put her down," Scarlet threatened.

Donya squeezed on the sword. They couldn't win, not against the ancient incredible power of old Rome. They needed their help, not their wrath. What could she do? Gods, redhead, stop threatening them.

Scarlet's eyes flicked to where Donya crouched. Of course, she could see her. It was a foolish move; the dark wolf could quickly spring for her throat. Donya stood, blowing her element of surprise. This also seemed to be a foolish move, as the Wolf King had not moved a muscle.

"There you are. Now the party is all assembled. We should formally begin," said the Wolf King she had met before.

Scarlet did not relax. If Donya didn't know better, she would think the human was used to standoffs. Donya walked forward. She held her sword in her hand. It would be awake in a few more seconds. She passed into Scarlet's fiery magic, but the sword absorbed the energy. Right now, they were linked. "I am honored so many of the old Roman Rex have gathered to meet for our meager plea of assistance." She tried to keep her tone flat, but still, it came out as a bit of an accusation.

"I, Ancus Marcius, welcome you all. Never before have I known a troll to enjoy the eternal city. And we are all deeply privileged that the great Romulus has descended the hills to be with us tonight," his voice cast out into the night like others listened and watched.

Donya pulled up short. The very founder of Rome was here with them. If they could get his help, Heldrig would be a pile of blue dust on an old Roman cobblestone. She needed to choose her words carefully, and she needed Scarlet to lower the sword.

Then the sword awoke in her hand. The shadow image awoke in Scarlet's. Both shimmered in the moonlight. Donya glanced at Scarlet and reached out, "relax, we are here to speak."

"I'll relax the moment they put Grazia down. We don't need to talk about anything; I can tell they don't plan on helping us," Scarlet said loudly.

The young-looking woman was Grazia, but she had seen her back at the house. This magic she did not know, astral projection perhaps.

"I would like to be released. Although my dear, I can't leave until I get the candle back and lit by Marcius," Grazia said.

Marcius nodded and set Grazia on her feet. "The candle is mine for now. Is this not what you asked for?"

"Keep it too long, and my body will die back in Rome," the younger Grazia said.

"Enough," said Romulus, still in his wolf form. The voice came out like a growl. "Show me what the weapon can do."

The crafty old king noticed the awakening of the swords. "Certainly, my liege," Donya started.

Scarlet didn't say anything, only raised the sword and struck out. Blue fire sliced out of the top right toward Romulus. He caught the wave in his jaws, deflecting it.

Then he sat back on his haunches. The brown wolf to the side of the action tucked his tail again, and Marcius' mouth hung open. Everyone stayed quiet.

"You are overconfident. It was right to beg our assistance," growled Romulus.

"My apologies for the human," Donya began again, "she is impetuous."

"Reminds me of myself when I was human," Marcius said.

Romulus turned his head to glare at Marcius with dark eyes. "You should have alerted me of this happening. I will make the ruling." He turned back to Scarlet and Donya. "We will give you no additional aid, but neither will any Wolf King ever do you harm."

"Your generosity is much appreciated," Donya said, unsure if it was correct. Grazia said begging would do no good. Also, from the way he worded it, they'd already given them aid. Scarlet stood with the sword down, but her arm did not relax.

Romulus rose. He strode a few long paces and melted back into the high grass; the two other wolves followed. Marcius watched them go, and Grazia stood by his side.

"I will keep my eyes to the north for you." He raised Grazia's hand and planted a kiss on the back of it. Shifting into a wolf took seconds, then he trotted away.

The sword in Donya's hand fought to stay awake. However, as soon as the Wolf Kings were away, it went out like a light. The whole performance lasted four minutes tops. It was still a young sword, but this did not bode well for their upcoming confrontation with Heldrig.

The young version of Grazia smiled at the troll and human with her now full lips. The moonlight shined through her a bit. The dress she wore hung off her frame. She retained the same basic shape, but her weight carried differently. "Hurry back to the door," she said quietly.

Scarlet let go of the shadow sword, and it evaporated into darkness. Her shoulders fell. Donya could see in the moonlight that she appeared ashen and had a fine sheen of sweat on her face. Donya could also smell a slight bitter smell from her, perhaps she had been afraid. Scarlet moved toward the door. Her steps were low, her eyes studied the ground.

"When you go through, change into my old clothes. You will find them in the upstairs wardrobe," Grazia said in her low tone. "Scarlet, take the bag I have packed for you by the door. Do not forget it. It may not help you right away, but it is essential for your future." She seemed rushed. "What do you see out there in the dark?"

Scarlet raised her head, "a few of them followed Marcius and the other wolves, small spirits, many of them round and sort of yellowish. More showed up with Romulus, a lot more. He is followed by a small army. They have almost all left now," she said, scanning the area, "oh, I recognize him. Hey there," she said, waving at a high stone sticking out of the grass on a neighboring hill.

Donya saw one of the Kraken's husbands step out. His face seemed stretched tight over whatever scaffolding his kind had. "One of the Kraken's husbands," Donya muttered for Grazia's introduction. They had one more day; they could turn this around, still, couldn't they?

The husband shambled down the hill. It was the faster, taller one. His seaweed body was still not quick though.

"This is excellent. I needed to get to the Kraken. He will speed up my trip," Grazia said.

"You're not coming back with us?" Scarlet asked.

"I can't even if I wanted to. Marcius tied my soul to his when he ate part of my candle. He knew it was a seal. He knew who I was before this even started," Grazia said.

"What do you think he wants with you?" Donya asked. Had none of this night even been about her and Scarlet?

"I can think of at least one thing he wants to do with me, but he did give me what I asked for. I regret stealing his assistance for myself. My youth lasted long enough the first time." Grazia shook her head.

"They weren't going to help us. I've seen plenty of people like them before," Scarlet said quietly.

The husband made it to them at the bottom of the hill. The door was in sight on the bottom swell of the next hill. The wind picked up. "Greetings. That could have gone better." He eyed Scarlet with his larger eye. "Still, they didn't take a bite out of any of you," he said with a nod of his gelatinous head.

"Can you give me safe passage back to your lady?" Grazia asked without an introduction.

Donya jumped in, remembering how easily irritated the husbands could be, "this is Grazia. Your wife invited her, and gifted her water." The events of the night started to have an effect; Donya could feel herself slowing.

"I shall take you, living dead girl. We should leave. Too many eyes on this place," the husband said.

"Agreed. Scarlet, don't forget the bag. Tomorrow, find salt, any salt. Mountain salt would be better, of course, put it in your first scar and sleep that way, your young lover's as well. Do not wash it out until this predicament is over," Grazia instructed.

"My first scar?" Scarlet repeated, her eyebrows raised.

"Your navel, dear. It will tie your energy to your young man's. You can use whatever makes him special and add it to your energies," Grazia rushed out.

"I think I already do that," Scarlet said then paused. "I saw it today. I think my magic steals his magic. I can see it in the sunlight. It is in his eyes too. Then it swirls up and goes into the ball I make around us." She sighed, "I bet I take it all the time. What if I'm like all the spirits? That's probably why they want to be around him. What if it is why I like him too?"

"Sounds like a problem for another day. If you saw it, I believe you are right, but taking his power is not a misstep.

On the contrary, it will help you both get out of this dire situation," Grazia said.

Donya agreed with the wisdom of this statement. Scarlet's energy formed a ball, she pondered the possibilities. "If only we had a few more days..." Donya said, almost to herself.

"From the looks of you two, I doubt you could take more of this," the husband said. His eyes rested on Scarlet. "On that, should you make it to California, our lady has a favor to ask of you."

"Okay." Scarlet's voice cracked. Her eyes widened at something behind him, then her expression shifted. "Oh no," was all she got out.

A large Kludde hopped through the grass at them. Scarlet's warning gave them a bit of extra time. A blue flame flickered around its toad head, but these beings could diminish it for extra stealth. Donya always wondered how they snuck up on their prey, and now she knew.

Donya squeezed the sword handle, but it did not respond. As fast as she could, she shoved Scarlet toward the door while turning on the great beast, its shape that of a giant toad, with claws the size of daggers.

The husband grabbed onto Grazia's shade, and they scrambled up the way he came. Neither of them would be any good in a fight anyway.

Donya struck at the great Kludde's foreleg next to her. That leg was roughly the same size and girth as her whole body. Scarlet pulled the door open but didn't run through. Instead, she turned, searching for Donya.

"Shit!" she heard Scarlet yell.

The toad's great mouth could easily have scooped both up. Donya moved to the other leg and hit as hard as she could. She couldn't cast a spell to help, she was too drained from earlier, and none of her magic was fast enough.

"Smash its foot!" Scarlet yelled.

Donya jumped into the air and landed with all her stone weight on the large toes. The foot quickly pulled back, causing Donya to lose her balance. She scrambled to her feet and toward the door.

Scarlet let off another blast of heat. Donya peered over her shoulder at the toad. It worked. He backed away. Donya swore after she dealt with the Heldrig problem, she would find this damn Kludde and make it pay. Taking her largest of strides, she grabbed Scarlet by the forearm and hustled her through the doorway.

Grazia's clothes were not to Donya's taste, nor did they fit properly. Scarlett tolerated them better. The human smelled unwell when Donya sent her back to her hotel in a cab. Rest would do both of them good. And Scarlet seemed pleased when they moved Grazia's body up the stairs to her bed and laid her under the covers. The body could survive three, maybe four days. If Grazia's soul did not return by then, it would perish.

Donya suffered a sinking feeling. She was back to square one despite all they accomplished. She sat alone in Grazia's big house. The sun peeked over the horizon. Every time she thought she had a good plan or an opportunity, it was snatched away. Why did she keep trying? If she walked away now, nothing would happen to her. Nothing of hers was on the line. Yes, she was connected to Scarlet now through the sword, but not mortally connected.

Nera, she had only met, and things did not seem to be off to a good start. If she headed back to her mountain, Heldrig would most likely never bother her again. Donya dragged her feet as she walked through the empty house; a large wooden wardrobe stood in a small north-facing room. She opened it and climbed in among two stacks of books. The sun would not bother her here.

The smell of old paper and ink reminded her of leaves. She closed her eyes. She could not run away and keep even a semblance of honor. The truth was she began this. This fate befell everyone because of her. Seeing it through was the least she could do. Her decision should have been a burden, but instead, she felt solidified. She needed rest; what she did last night drained her. Then the failure with the Wolf Kings drained her short stock of emotions. She drifted off to sleep, feeling uneasy and weak again.

CHAPTER 39

# SCARLET

It was Scarlet's last day in Italy, maybe her last day anywhere. If Donya was right, tomorrow something big would happen. Today Scarlet and Juan walked around the Colosseum. The sun glared brightly, and his eyes appeared strange again, which still unnerved her. When they walked into shadows cast by the enormous arches, she found herself drinking in the way he looked, normal and safe. Staring at his warm brown eyes made her feel teary, partially from her fear of tomorrow and partially from exhaustion.

They decided to leave the Colosseum and check out the Roman Forum. The space was much more open in the forum. Green plaques to read stood in front of the ruins. She was happy to have a reason to stop. Her foot ached again, and she would have to ask the Kraken why tonight. Probably because the Kraken helped her even now. Their two energies were dissonant. The Kraken hadn't known that when she put the mark on her. It saved Scarlet all the same. Donya told her about the plan at the train station.

"Let's get pictures up here," Juan said, breaking into Scarlet's thoughts.

"Sure," she responded, pulling off her beanie and fluffing her hair. Today her hair had curls from the bun she had kept it in.

Juan held up his phone and got a few selfies of them together. A vast temple initially dedicated to Empress Faustina and then co-dedicated to her husband after he died once stood behind them. The massive columns still existed from the original temple, but a church had been built on them. When she tried to read more on the plaque, her eyes did something funny to the text. She blinked, and it faded. Her eyesight was still changing. Or she was still figuring it out. Warm white columns almost shone in the sunlight. Everything was painted the most lovely colors by the soft light—brick red, saffron, buttercup yellow, the sky that white-blue of early spring.

They turned, and Scarlet took pictures of Juan in front of an old brass door patinaed turquoise with time. He kept his beanie on. The sun stayed out, but a chill hung in the air.

They did not speak much; it was their last day, and Scarlet could not muster the energy to try and smooth things out. She felt stressed because they might die, or be captured, or who knows what. He felt stressed because of work and his family. Juan's mother bombarded him with messages about traveling safely. It got worse now that they would be flying again.

Scarlet stopped on another promontory and snapped pictures of free-standing pillars. The light green of the spring grass, the dark green of the cypress trees, and the blue of the sky made taking good pictures easy, even for her. She snapped a lot of them, a lot with Juan, walking, and candid. She got one of him giving a longing look at another tourist who had gelato in a cone. She would send them to his family tonight, just in case. Her eyes prickled again with tears at the thought.

In the dark cypress trees, she could see a few spirits—multi-hued and long-bodied. One of them saw her stare and took flight. It glided through the air, coasting smoothly until it hit an upwelling of the simmering sparkles. It gracefully pulled up, then swooped around to land on a low crumbling brick wall near where Scarlet and Juan walked. After being in that other realm and talking with so many spirits and creatures, Scarlet didn't feel anxious about the tiny thing. It cocked its head to one side, and six-blue beady eyes peered back at her.

She felt off. She decided to run an experiment, reaching for the warmth she usually felt nested around her lungs. You would think one's power sat in the heart, but she found hers to be more spread out and closer to her ribs. She wanted to expand it around her and Juan.

Nothing happened.

The warmth was there, not as much as usual, but she could feel it.

She took a deep breath and tried again. Nothing happened.

Tomorrow was the big showdown, and it struck her. Magic might be deserting her.

They stood above the Spanish steps again, twilight on their last day in Italy. Scarlet tugged at her ring while Juan kept his arm around her. Whatever bothered him earlier had melted away. In the darkness, she could still see. It amazed her how many young couples were emboldened by a little less light. She counted at least five sets with their hands slipped past zippers and buttons.

She averted her gaze from the distractions and gazed out at the city. She could see the dome of the Pantheon from where they stood. "I'm glad we made it here for sunset, to finish our Roman adventure where we started it."

"That first day was such a long walk, and on your foot. Next time we get a cab," Juan said.

"Next time? What do you mean? We already have our subway tickets for tomorrow."

"No, I mean when we come back again. We didn't make it to Pompeii or Naples and Sicily. We'll have to come back."

Scarlet failed to respond. After what happened with Grazia last night. No, they shouldn't ever come back; it was too dangerous. She concluded that the reason she always avoided learning about her power could only be that she was a coward. She felt the distinct pull to ignore this painful thought. She took in Juan's bright brown eyes, thankful she could see all the details of them.

"Don't you want to go home?"

"Yes, I didn't say that. I like traveling with you a lot. But now that you mention it, I am homesick," he said as he pulled on her hand. They descended the crowded steps and headed for the same restaurant they'd eaten at for several dinners. The inside was gaudy with giant blown glass chandeliers, but the pasta was fresh, rich, and delicate.

It felt warm for late March. People milled around out in the street, enjoying the first wisps of spring weather. They kept walking. This place came recommended by their hotel and was a bit off the tourist path, not by much, though; the restaurant still boasted English menus.

Scarlet ambled slowly, not because of her foot and the throbbing pain, but because she wanted to drag this out. If she was honest with herself, she didn't want to meet with Donya tonight, and it wasn't cowardice. Last night had been a genuine betrayal. She showed up late to the meeting with the Wolf Kings. Scarlet remembered her giving a reason once they got back, but the reason escaped her now.

Hadn't Scarlet made it to all their meetings on time, on time in a strange city, while dealing with a whole new set of problems, most of the problems brought on by the little troll? This was all her fault, and at the last minute, she botched up their hard work. The Kraken said Donya was unlucky. In Scarlet's experience, luck was partially created, by hard work, staying focused, and being observant of changing conditions.

Warmth stirred in her lungs. She reached for it the minute she felt it. The heat responded, rolling in a slow wave. She felt the moment the power left her skin and enveloped her and Juan. Apparently, it liked her righteous indignation. No wonder she usually contained so much power then. She was in that state about half the time she stayed awake. She couldn't even watch or read the news because she felt she might start yelling and frothing at the mouth.

They sat at the same table they had the first night they came here. Several other tables held patrons, but the restaurant was mostly empty. Juan and Scarlet ate earlier than the Italian crowd. Thus, they got a spot right next to the window.

Juan ordered a whole bottle of wine, which rather pleased Scarlet. Maybe a hangover tomorrow would feed the fuel of her fire even more.

Her phone pinged in her purse; she must have left the Wi-Fi on all day. She pulled it out, happy to send out pictures before they got back to the hotel. It was probably her mom.

*'Hey Scar, I wanted to warn you, Bertha is on the warpath. I guess she thinks you should have A. already asked her to be a bridesmaid, and B. let her plan an engagement party. Sorry. Welcome to the family, lol.'*

Scarlet wanted to growl and laugh at the same time. It was a message from Lettie. She studied at Davis; the poor thing should be worrying about her parasitology class, not her annoying sister. Bertha was insufferable. But right now, it was such a mundane problem to have. Too bad her magic couldn't shield her from annoying humans.

A shield. Scarlet stopped. Her other property wasn't just some barrier, it was a protective shield.

CHAPTER 40

# DONYA

Donya waited outside when Scarlet and Juan walked past. Scarlet made eye contact. They couldn't meet in the lobby as they did in Florence, as this was a boutique hotel. The lobby was small, and the staff attentive. They would eavesdrop, which in and of itself wasn't a problem unless Mars used some sort of spell on any of them. Donya couldn't be sure she would pick up on it. Maybe the smell, but Donya doubted everything now.

Donya couldn't see their hotel window as it faced the inner courtyard, but she knew when Scarlet was on her way a few hours later.

Her eyes were bright again, although shadows hung under them. Fatigue in humans happens quickly. Donya accepted the exhaustion was, in fact, her fault. Donya rose as Scarlet approached; they walked silently along the piazza back to the fountain. Scarlet sat down on the edge. Donya reached into the briefcase she brought from Grazia's. She handed Scarlet salt. It came from a mountain in the far east. The packaging hadn't claimed it, but she asked the crystals.

"I completely forgot to get salt. It was a weird day. For a long time, I couldn't get to my magic," Scarlet said.

Donya was not surprised. Scarlet expended much of it yesterday. It was exceptional she had anything left at all today. "You can get to it now, I hope?"

"Yep, but it's still not all there. Also, I think I have a precise idea of what my other magic is. It's a shield."

"We could ask the Kraken." Donya cast her voice to the fountain.

The Kraken's singular voice came through the water, "a peculiar power to have, one which would normally not pair with fire."

Scarlet stared at the water. "Have you never seen it before? Is Grazia there with you?"

"My husband will arrive with her later. It has never happened that I have seen your combination of affinities. I have known shields and earth, and I once kept one that was another barrier and water. She worked efficiently in the canals," the Kraken answered.

"How has your practice been? Can you sense my location during the day yet?" Donya asked Scarlet, leading the conversation away from her less-than-optimal magic pair. It worked well enough for what she'd done all her life. If they noticed it earlier, maybe they could have worked with it more.

Scarlet sighed. "No, I can't sense you; I can't sense anything, even in the other realm. Maybe I can sense my power, but when it's in my actual body. I can only see things. Since you gave me the dark vision, I can see farther, and I think I can see spirits through walls. I suspect I might even be able to see raw magic floating around, but all my other senses are normal."

"That's fine. With your eyes, I don't doubt you will see them coming." Donya did feel sure of this. It wasn't an exaggeration.

"Tell me more about what you called raw magic," instructed the Kraken.

"With my new vision, I can see in the dark, but during the day, I can see other things. I've been keeping a list of everything different. Most of it's not important, like seeing spirits through walls, but during the day, I've noticed shimmering particles in the air, moving around spirits, coming from Juan. I remember my Auntie Lou saying magic is in everything. This stuff seems to be on or in everything, so I'm hypothesizing it is magic," Scarlet said.

"When this is over, you must come back to Venice. I would like your opinion on where magic is pooling. Donya and I can sense it, but if you're correct, you could be more precise," instructed the Kraken.

"You should have told me of this before. We could have tested it," Donya said.

"It works in sunlight. Don't you die in the sunlight?" Scarlet responded with a bit of edge in her voice.

Donya had not thought of that detail. Humans were very good at details; Scarlet seemed no exception. Donya nodded, thinking that this would be their last meeting, possibly ever. What else could she give Scarlet which would help tomorrow? Donya needed to leave if she would get up to what she wanted and get back to the catacombs in time for dawn. "Last night, where did you learn your stance?"

"I took some martial arts classes as a teen. I saw a movie and wanted to be a black belt. I wasn't very good," Scarlet said.

"I heard you wielded the sword better than to be expected from a flying imp," the Kraken interjected.

"Sadly, I do not know much about using a weapon in a fight. But your feet were well placed, a good connection to the earth. What I do know is to keep the sword low and come from below. Last night your downstroke worked because you are taller than Romulus in his wolf form. Besides your shield and fire abilities, try to use the sword for defense. I should be the offense," Donya said.

"The best defense is a good offense," Scarlet retorted. She appeared spunkier as this went on.

"She is correct, but dear, you are no swordsman, nor have you been working with magic for more than a week." The Kraken's voice was gentle.

Scarlet shrugged, which the Kraken couldn't see.

"Donya, on the other hand, arrived late, and for what reason?" The Kraken asked.

Donya bristled at the accusation in the Kraken's voice. The meeting with the Wolf Kings—she chose to be late. She thought following Nera more important, it felt more important at the time. How to explain that now, after what happened with Grazia? "I found Nera, and I found where Heldrig—" Donya started.

"I am glad you feel compelled to finally find Nera, but no direct action against them will help without the Wolf King's assistance. That was wasted effort. You should have known better." The water of the fountain rippled with the force of the Kraken's voice.

Scarlet's spunk rubbed off on Donya. "It may be true that I did not do the correct action, but still, I saw what they evoked. Given what I know of Heldrig and what he is working with, I am confident of what he plans. I am also confident of what I need to do to throw that plan off."

"Enlighten us then," the Kraken said.

"All the appeals were to the wind, sun, and moon. All elements of the sky… the attack will come in the sky. Scarlet's flight will take place during the day, so why the moon?" Donya asked.

"Maybe the moon will be out tomorrow during the day," Scarlet answered.

Donya felt pleased she paid attention. "If the moon is out during the day, it has very little influence as the sun rules the sky. However, the moon always has sway over dreams. Mars uses dream magic, Nera will be assisting him, and they plan to pull you under in a dream. Then Heldrig will scoop you up and carry you off."

"You can't be sure of all that," Scarlet said.

"No, she cannot, but it is all very likely. Magic is unpredictable and can be used in many ways, but for the best success, controlling time, place, and influences are essential. Those assumptions are, in fact, quite good." The coldness in the Kraken's voice drifted away. "You should hurry off then, Donya, so we can all be connected through the swords to aid Scarlet."

"I don't think I will have time; I need to throw off the airport schedule for tomorrow, but not to the point of flight cancellation. Getting to California will make Scarlet harder to take in general. You will still be connected through the mark, and I can be connected through the sword," Donya said.

"What are you going to do at the airport?" Scarlet sounded startled.

"I don't know yet, but time is of the essence. The airport is outside the city, so I should be off."

"Did Grazia use all of my spring water? If you can obtain some and take it to where you plan to set up for the day, we may be connected as well," said the Kraken.

"Excellent idea. Scarlet, we should get you back to the hotel. Is there anything else you want to ask me before we leave?"

Scarlet peered down at her, light brown eyes narrowing in the dark. Donya remembered the first time she looked into those eyes on the plane. If she must be bound to a human, at least it was a formidable one.

"How likely do you think we are to win this?" Scarlet asked.

Donya turned her eyes up at the obelisk in the piazza. "Last night, I thought it not very likely, but throughout this conversation, I have felt hope. I would give us even odds. Now Lady Kraken we take our leave, goodnight and I am in your debt."

"Goodnight troll, before you leave this place please wet one forearm with the water of this fountain Scarlet too," said the Kraken.

"I want you to know how much I appreciate your help. We would be lost without you. Goodnight," Scarlet said.

They both dabbed water on their arms and took leave of the fountain. Donya was relieved to see more of a spring in Scarlet's step. She'd thought the odds would bring Scarlet down.

"I know you got me into this, but thanks for helping after. I've been thinking something of this nature would have happened eventually with me and Juan," Scarlet said as they walked.

They stopped outside the hotel. "Go rest. You must try your best not to fall asleep on the plane."

"If I can stay awake, would I ruin their plans?" Scarlet asked.

"Probably not, but it is worth a try."

"We aren't going to make anything easy for them," Scarlet said. Donya felt the woman's magic pass over her. In the first encounters, it was horribly hot and dry. Now, to Donya, it felt like a warm summer breeze.

Donya got a cab out to the airport. It took thirty minutes at this late hour. She gave the cabbie a hundred euros and slunk out into the darkness. She did not walk into any terminal, but opened a cheap chain-link fence with a quick pull and walked out onto the asphalt. Everything lay covered in asphalt or cement, which could tell her nothing. She needed a proper stone. She kept to the shadows away from security. They couldn't stop or catch her if they saw her, but it could impede her progress.

She walked and walked until she came to the end of an area with older tin buildings. Near a doorway sat a boulder, cigarette butts scattered around it in the darkness. Humans used it as a perch for a smoke break.

Donya picked up the litter. "Good evening. Could you give me information?"

"Certainly," the large stone said in a high and happy voice.

"Where would be the best spot to open up a small sinkhole if I wanted to delay international flights by an hour or two?"

"Go to terminal three, the busy one. I wouldn't say to do anything to the runway. The humans could shut down for days doing a safety inspection. Open up a pothole right in the way of the baggage haulers."

"Perfect. I hope your home smells better now." Donya walked to a small trash receptacle outside the door and dumped almost fifty cigarette butts into it.

"For now, it does. Much appreciated."

Donya hurried to the terminals. It became harder to keep to the shadows. She circled the place, finding the route the baggage came out of most often, where there were several ports. Scarlet's flight left at nine-thirty. Donya would construct the enchantment to start at dawn, just enough time to cause delays.

It was after midnight. Flights landed and departed. If she injured a security guard and took his clothes to get the spell done, that could cause severe delays. It was much easier to destroy than create. Donya sighed into the night. There were a surprising number of people around. If she appeared purposeful, maybe no one would notice her. She stayed on the side of the painted lines and walked out into the fluorescent lights. No one stopped her, although one baggage driver did scrutinize her but continued to buzz by.

Her new bag held several important items, one a chunk of chalk, found in a planter under dense ivy. She dug it out and kneeled at the spot best for the hole. Drawing quickly and sloppier than she would have liked, she got a light octagon on the asphalt. Standing, she strode a direct line to a puddle of darkness. She inspected her work from a distance, it would do. Time ran short, she hurried to the nearest opening in the cement. She needed contact with the earth. It was the dirt she would cast a spell on.

Kneeling between two runways on bare earth and grass, the words came naturally to her. It barely counted as a spell. Earth magic needed only a word or two and a little push from her. The spot under the octagon would give way as the last darkness fled at dawn when a cart drove over it. Easy enough.

Another cab ride got her to Grazia's, where she found the bottle with around a cup of the Kraken's water left in it. Grazia saved some for a rainy day, perhaps. Before Donya left, she went up to the empty body and gently poured half down her throat, careful not to drown her in the process. She couldn't be sure it helped, but maybe.

Donya took to the streets. It was the easiest way to get her bearings. The cistern where Nera washed off the oil… she knew it would bring her closer to whatever they contrived. She could piggyback off the residue and perhaps drain away the effectiveness. Whatever it took to get the edge on them, she would try.

Dawn approached yet the streets remained quiet; she felt weak again. She rounded a corner, knowing she closed in on the fouled water. It was across the city from the catacombs by

Grazia, not connected to that system. In a darkened flower shop window, she saw a display that caught her eye, a dried arrangement that included lotus pods sticking elegantly out of it.

She had time for a snack. To cause no damage, she asked her way through the rough stone walls. They parted for her without question. The interior of the florist smelled pleasantly dry, like fresh hay on a midsummer night in the valleys around her mountain. She snagged the pods, and the seeds rattled in them as she lifted them to her mouth. They tasted starchy and good.

On a back wall wrapped in silk ribbon hung more seed pods, papery and transparent. She snagged those too and swallowed the whole bushel, silk, and all. It tasted like eating air, but she felt more solid after taking them in. They were not her exact seeds, but like the cattails, they did something. After all this, maybe she needed to spend more time foraging for different seeds unless she didn't survive today's encounter, which was possible.

CHAPTER 41

# SCARLET

Their plane ended up delayed three hours; they got the text moments before they left the hotel. The train ticket was open time, the Leonardo Line out to the airport from the central station. Juan still wanted to check out and get moving, but Scarlet talked him into staying in their room an extra hour. Hunger compelled Scarlet to finally check out. The morning sun warmed Scarlet's face as they walked to the subway station.

"We could get one nice breakfast before we leave," Juan said as they walked past a café bustling with life.

"Uh-huh, sounds good," Scarlet stayed quiet all morning. Donya's plan worked. The fight was delayed by a few hours. She could not relax though. Were they delaying the inevitable? She did not want to get to the airport early. She suspected being unpredictable and hard to find right now was the best course, and taking a big breath of the sunlight-warmed air, she said, "we should drink lots of coffee too, so we stay awake through the whole ride."

"Ugh, but all that caffeine will dehydrate us," Juan said with a frown. He hauled their luggage again as Scarlet's foot caused a slight limp.

"But think of all the movies you could catch up on," Scarlet cajoled him.

"I guess I could get one espresso with you—which cafe was best?"

"The one I liked best was next to the gelato place you liked. But it is kind of far."

He looked at her. They both knew there were things not being said. "Let's do it."

Scarlet positively buzzed with caffeine. Her stomach and her foot ached. She still did not like the flavor of a coffee bean, and her stomach protested something about it. But in the last week, she used the source of caffeine as a crutch. She needed it to get through this flight. Magic was all well and good, but real physical substance was useful too.

Her thoughts pinged around in her mind like spilled rice grains on a kitchen floor. She tried to think of and chronicle everything that happened on this trip, everything she learned about herself and the mystical world around her. And she searched her thoughts. She knew a revelation or epiphany was in there. Her gut told her, but also her mind.

It's like when you misplace the book you're reading in a dark house; you check by the table with the lamp. You turn more lights on, you search in the kitchen by the teapot. The book could be anywhere, not only the most obvious places.

So, she searched around, poking at bits of her mind, opening her notes app, and scrolling through her meager notes on spirits she'd seen. She longed for more information, hoping in the final hour something would come through. Isn't that how it worked in movies after all? Didn't the hero need to get bashed up and then, at the last minute, find a secret reserve of strength and pull through?

Scarlet didn't feel like a hero. She would need to do this the way she always did, hard work. After they checked in, she made sure she paid for the Wi-Fi on the plane. She could spend the plane ride working. Grazia gifted her a grand book, all written in Latin. Her new vision helped her translate parts already, she could look up any word she didn't know. She wasn't afraid of hard work.

They sat at their new gate. They hadn't even made it to their original one when their phones pinged with a notification, which sent them walking in the opposite direction. It was not an easy airport. Getting confused, Scarlet insisted they go back to the other terminal on the tram, which turned out to be wrong. Juan seemed annoyed at her—one more thing she didn't need pinging around in her head.

"Here it is, finally," Juan said.

"We'll get our steps in even with a long flight," Scarlet said. Juan made to plop down with everyone else. She kept walking to a sunny window past their gate. A potted plant sat by a low cushion. It seemed as good a spot as any. With her back to the window, Heldrig probably couldn't sneak up on her. Juan sighed as he relaxed into a chair next to the plant.

Scarlet got an apple out of her backpack. They couldn't bring it to California. No fresh produce. It was a little after eleven AM. Their flight left in an hour. Nothing appeared out of the ordinary, just a lot of pissed-off humans. Whatever Donya pulled last night sure caused havoc. But not so much that her flight got canceled. The whole of the flight would be in daylight. If Donya was going to help, Scarlet didn't know how.

The flight began boarding, with families with small children first. Their group had a while. Scarlet stared hard at everything, she swore the walls occasionally became transparent. She searched every face in the crowd around their gate. She concentrated so hard, Juan noticed and asked her what was wrong. Perhaps she scrunched up her nose when she studied her surroundings or something that gave her away. He let it go when she shook her head and said nothing.

"I'm going to go use the restroom before we get on," Juan said, eyes still on the game he played on his phone.

"Good idea, I'll go too."

Scarlet looked in the bathroom mirror as she scrubbed at her hands. Light purple bags showed under her eyes. This last week took probably a year off her life. She wiped her hands on her jeans; she wore her regular clothes again. Unfortunately, wearing different garments wouldn't help keep her hidden today.

She made it out of the bathroom before Juan, just in time to see two people run up to the line waiting to board at their gate.

Sweat puddled on the older man's brow. He dabbed at himself as he stood in the back of the line. She saw him peer around nonchalantly.

"Come on, let's get in line." Juan grabbed at her hand, squeezing it.

"No, wait." Too late. Scarlet wanted to stand back. They were in the last boarding group. They didn't need to line up. But she saw it happen. She saw the older man recognize her.

He didn't know. He didn't know Donya explained everything to her. What did he think happened that night? She squeezed Juan's hand and let her shield out around the two of them. Juan brought her right up to the pair. The younger one, who appeared blond, did not speak to the man or even flick his eyes toward them. He was smartly dressed. Everything on him appeared clean and new, all Nike brand.

Nike for victory, Scarlet thought with a frown.

CHAPTER 42

# DONYA

She felt the pull like a tremor before an earthquake when Scarlet met Heldrig. He did not strike. Donya waited. The water still smelled and tasted like oil. She sat in it fully clothed.

There would be no rest for her today. After the last few nights, she again felt mortally exhausted, weak, and chalky. She must not give in to the weakness. Like Scarlet, she could not avoid this confrontation. At first, it had been about taking revenge against Heldrig. But something more grew out of working with Scarlet, working with the Kraken and Grazia too—Fellowship. Trolls were solitary, but the more Donya thought about it, the more she realized she wasn't such a good troll.

That was fine. After today, she would do what she wanted and what felt right. She would follow her curiosity and see where it led her. Probably into more trouble. Surely into more trouble, with her luck. And no more eating humans, even if it was easy, and they had been tasty, just in case Nera was right.

She loved stones but did not much like the idea of turning into a standing one.

Donya had become very good at sensing what the human woman did with her power. Sitting under the oil-slicked water, she opened her eyes and scanned the water above. She swore she could see the image playing out in her mind. Heldrig could be clever. He kept them all guessing. Scarlet's fiery shield reached out and singed him. Donya needed that contact. Now she could sense both Heldrig and Mars. Sitting in this water worked as she hoped it would.

No Nera though.

What would he do? The time of the flight was far different. Whatever he worked on must be weakened. Hopefully, that would be enough for them. It had to be.

Hours passed. The bond between Donya and Scarlet stretched thinner through space. Although it felt elastic, in being stretched, it did not weaken but grew taunt. Their sword lay in front of Donya, ready to grab. In the few nights they had, she spent all her free hours holding it, practicing with it. She was no swordswoman by far, but she knew its limits.

Donya kept herself open, but Scarlet didn't encounter either Heldrig or Mars again. She hoped she hadn't been wrong, and he would follow her to California to attack there. If he suspected the forces building against him, it would have been the safe thing to do. But, hopefully, he did not suspect.

Because Donya sat in this water, she believed she would feel it when Nera made a move. She must be part of the plan.

But why had she not felt her get on the plane? Could she be alone? Would they have left her sitting at that house? If they did, Nera could get up and walk away. She could ruin her father's whole plan all on her own.

Heldrig wasn't the type to leave that loose of an end.

Donya lost her diamond-edged focus on Scarlet, her mind wandering to Nera. She blinked, her eyes still focused on the oil above her. It did seem like shapes swirled in them, the residue of magic, a vast amount of magic. Mars had brought the attention to the moon, to this place. The moon loved water folk.

"Nera, did you hear me when I apologized?"

The oil slick floated purple and green in the darkness. For a moment Donya saw Nera. Her face appeared as she'd first seen it, eyes sewn shut. Donya blinked, still gazing up at the oil slick. She was sure she saw it, the shape of a delicate hand, but something dimpled in the flesh along the forearm. It had not been a trick of her tired, sandy mind.

She saw a leg, but an extra joint bent between the knee and ankle.

No, Heldrig wouldn't have left loose ends. He would have made sure his daughter would help and could not get away.

She felt the Kraken pushing power toward Scarlet. It hurt the human. Power is more important now than comfort. The Kraken contained much power.

When she closed her eyes to the swirling oil, she could smell the water from the Kraken's grotto. She could sense

Grazia there. The two worked on a pattern in paint on a rock. Their energy felt frantic and rushed.

Donya wondered at how long it took Heldrig to enact his plan. She pushed back the plane's schedule, but if he'd always meant to start his spells late in the flight, then perhaps she had not done as much harm to him as she thought. His position on the earth would be a bit off.

Donya felt doubt prickling at the base of her spine. Perhaps Scarlet would be taken, and Nera lay broken and hurt someplace she didn't know. Would her bad luck spread to everyone associated with her?

CHAPTER 43

# SCARLET

That thing had tried to make conversation with them. Heldrig. Even Juan noticed something off about him. His teeth were black. Juan said gray. After they boarded the plane, they discussed what was wrong with him for his teeth to turn that color.

Evil, Scarlet kept to herself. Evil was what was wrong with him. She didn't know if his brand of evil felt more terrifying or less than the human type. Probably less, at least he was a monster. When a human killed his pregnant wife, it had to be darker. Humans could understand misery and pain; maybe whatever Heldrig was couldn't.

Scarlet slowly convinced herself walking into the confrontation could be worse. Donya had the sword and would help her when the time came. That little troll helped out of spite, but spite was a fine motivator.

She hadn't been reading for fun since the weirdness began after Pisa. And now wasn't the time to get distracted, but she pulled out *Good Omens* anyway. Flipping the pages would keep her hands busy while she concentrated. They were at the back of the plane again, not all the way back but near enough. And thankfully, this time, the third seat remained open.

Heldrig was not as clever as Donya. He could have walked back and made this seem like his seat. Or perhaps not as bold. It had been something when Donya began all of this by snatching up an empty seat. In all the questions Scarlet asked her, she forgot to ever clarify that event.

The thing is, when you are ready for a fight, excited, or even afraid, it can only last so long. Anyone can get used to anything. Scarlet went through many strange situations and perils lately that she lost enthusiasm for this. What was in her head was the boss fight. She sat, flipping through her book for hours, and nothing happened. Keeping herself a bit extended, with Juan safely inside her shield, came easy. She'd done it naturally her whole life. It felt as easy as breathing.

Her foot hurt, though. A dull ache shifting occasionally to a radiating throb. It spread up her shin and almost to her knee. The Kraken seeped energy into her. It helped even as it hurt. Scarlet had no other perception of her allies on this flight. Her eyes could see farther and better than ever before, but they couldn't see back to Italy.

She checked the flight time, six more hours, and they would be home. She closed her fantasy book and slipped it back into her bag. If a demon and an angel could work together, surely she and Donya would make this work. She pulled out one of the items Grazia packed for her. It was an old book, filled with the secrets of magic. She deeply regretted denying what she saw her whole life. With more time, she could have been prepared for this encounter.

The lights were off in the cabin, but she saw something move. Her vision wasn't stable. She noticed the instability more and more. Even on the failed night with the Wolf Kings, she saw phenomenon the spirits themselves could not pick up. Donya had done a real whammy on her eyes.

"What's that?" Juan asked.

She mistakenly thought Juan concentrated on the action movie playing in front of him. She carefully set the book on her tray table and opened it to the middle instead of the beginning, where she'd started to translate pages using notepaper from the hotel shoved between the yellowing vellum. "Oh, this, I got it from a bookstore. Don't you remember when I bought it? In Venice?" she lied through her teeth. Venice did boast a lot of bookstores, and it was the farthest thing back on their trip.

"Hmmm, no. You shouldn't handle that paper with your hands. You should use gloves or tweezers."

Scarlet couldn't explain that the book seemed to like being handled by her. The more she used it, the more it felt like her book now, and the faster she could translate it too. Probably something to do with magic transference, like what Donya explained with the clothes, but more so because this was an actual magic item. "I'll try to touch the cover and the edges 'til we get home. I feel like the cover could use the oil from my hands."

"I have leather conditioner at home. You can use that, but spot-test it first."

"Of course, darling." She leaned over and kissed him on the cheek. He still nagged her a bit. Something bothered him. Probably her.

"*Facramento* means fragment. That font and ink are cool." He kept examining the page.

"I like picking out the words too. I'm getting better. Maybe if I learn Latin, I'll finally be able to learn Spanish." She paused and scanned the page, which looked normal now. When she stared but didn't focus, the meaning seemed to float up above the words. "*Virtuetez*, means virtue." She pointed without touching the page.

"Then you can finally talk to my mom."

"Yep, and maybe understand when your grandma tries to teach me cooking."

"You don't need to learn any of their recipes. You don't even like most of them."

"I like fresh tortillas—need to learn at least that." She left her eyes on the page. The writing did the thing… over the brown letters. A shadow seemed to appear. This passage was about not fragmenting one's virtue and intellect but rather studying one discipline as humans did not live long enough to master more. Not every word would come away perfectly. The brown script was the most accessible, but many sections were written in indigo ink. It took her longer to work her trick on that script.

She took a few notes on her phone. The text was too small for Juan to see, and she loosely translated it if he asked.

She hadn't been sleepy at all. That was why it seemed odd when her eyelids felt heavy, and her head lulled forward.

Out of the corner of her eye, she saw it. It moved like a mist along the ceiling. It disappeared anytime she focused on it. So that's what a spell looks like, she thought. She was sure, even though her strange eyes still changed, seeing new odd things. This moved ominously in a slow yet jerky way, sick, and noxious.

How had it gotten to her? She pushed out. She knew where the edges of her shield were. It shouldn't be able to affect her inside of it, right? Right? That's how she stayed safe all this time.

Most of the other passengers slept. The lights were low in the cabin. Juan sat awake, his eyes wide open. Was the spell coming for her, like the time at the bridge? Her magic hadn't been enough then either. If the Kraken hadn't interceded, who knows what would have happened that night.

She still had the Kraken kiss now, and they obtained the sword. If sleep was what Heldrig wanted from her, she might as well give in. Donya thought she should avoid the confrontation, but to what end? Was there a point in dragging this out? She couldn't master anything more in maybe the month it would buy them. Donya said it would be dream magic. She'd been right. Hopefully, Donya could join her in those dreams or nightmares.

She kept one hand on the book, reached up, and turned off her blinding reading light. Juan's hand sat on the armrest between them. She gave it a squeeze. He glanced at her, "I love you," she whispered. He couldn't hear her with the headphones on, but he knew what she was saying.

"I love you too," he whispered too loudly.

Scarlet regarded Juan's profile one more time, focusing on a freckle on his ear. Then she swept the dark cabin eyes straining to see the magic in the low light. She hoped the salt thing worked. She wanted a connection to Juan in this. Not too close of one; she didn't want to put him in danger too. He didn't seem sleepy at all to her. Good, it would be only her in danger. She loosened her seatbelt all the way and swung her feet up into the empty seat by the aisle. Hopefully, no flight attendant or Juan tried to wake her. She doubted this would be a Sleeping Beauty moment, and a kiss would work. Nothing would work if she didn't win.

There's no going back now, she thought. Scarlet closed her eyes and mumbled Donya's name.

The feeling of being pulled under made her want to scream, but she held it in. It felt like every nightmare ever smashed into one moment. When she opened her eyes, the scene was strangely serene. A kelp forest waved around her. It was dim like you would expect at the bottom of the sea under the shade of so much algae. And she felt the pressure all around her. Had the Kraken done this, pulling the dream into her area of expertise?

Scarlet swam along the bases of the swaying stalks. She was utterly alone. Did she need to call Donya again? Their bond should be strong enough to pull her into this place. A glow followed her through the forest. It came from her foot. Her power sputtered… perhaps the Kraken hadn't done this. Water, could she use her power in this much water? It worked at the bridge before she knew what she was doing.

Swimming up seemed the best option. In this dream place, she could breathe underwater. It did not feel the same as the Kraken's home, though. Maybe at the surface, she could see something. But, down here, there were no landmarks. She was lost.

Up and up she went, but the kelp kept going. The sword, her sword materialized in her hand. This gave Scarlet a boost. She kicked harder.

Donya must be here now too. She stopped kicking, swimming around in a circle. She reached out to see if she could feel the troll or any other magic. It didn't work. It never worked. But besides the water, which felt wet, she felt something dry. The book held firmly in her hand on the plane. She stayed connected to the real world.

Inside a spell would be the perfect place to see magic. Her eyes stared into the dark blue and brown-green around her. The color of the magic was the same as the mist, gray with a hint of heather. She'd been swimming for nothing. It came from not above or below but from her right. She dragged herself through the kelp. It was like following a path or a poorly marked hiking trail.

Something was out there; she saw it move in the undersea forest. It moved slowly and seemed big. It sported a prominent dorsal fin, triangular, and its pectoral fins hung down. A shark. Of course, there swam a shark in the sea of a nightmare.

Scarlet doubted a dream shark would be deterred by a sharp bonk on the nose like a regular shark. She swam faster as it circled. The sword buzzed in her hand; it woke up. Was she close enough to the source? It had to work.

The shark turned sharply as she lifted the sword; it was a massive shark. It could bite her in half. Did Heldrig want her dead?

She slashed out with the sword. Fire worked. It didn't go far, but the front of the shark charred in mere moments.

Then everything went black. Donya wielded the sword nearby.

CHAPTER 44

# DONYA

It was cold. Donya didn't realize she was with Scarlet after hearing her name. Donya had been sitting in water, and she was still sitting in water. It all contained the same oily smell. But she sensed Scarlet, and upon opening her eyes, kelp floated and swayed all around. She grabbed up the sword and hurried along the sea bottom.

Scarlet moved the wrong way, which was fine with Donya. It would be preferable if she did not interfere. Donya could smell the hint of the oil in the dream.

Her revenge would be sweet. She would cut off Heldrig's head. Too bad she wouldn't have the real thing to display on a spike in front of her cave.

She closed in on the source. Scarlet shifted her direction and swam in from the other side. Donya ran and rolled along the bottom when enormous jaws clamped shut on her.

Struggling, the pin teeth ground and snapped on her stone flesh. The sour smell of poison fouled the water around her.

With no wounds, it wouldn't bother her. She grabbed at the top of the mouth and pushed it open. Falling out of the gaping maw, she caught sight of what tried to eat her.

It was a thirty-foot moray eel, dark green with splotches of chartreuse. A dream apparition, she had not sensed it. She couldn't sense it now. The sword woke up in time. Scarlet brought it to attention. She used it too.

Donya slashed, and a razor of shadow sliced from the sword, cleaving the eel in two.

Scarlet needed to hold her own. Donya must get to the source and end this. It wasn't far, and the sword would not stay awake for more than five minutes. She felt sure she still held the element of surprise. They didn't know about her connection to Scarlet and this place. That eel possessed no real power.

What would give her more surprise? She smiled as she invoked darkness. It wouldn't bother her; she knew where she needed to be. And hopefully, it would give Scarlet more cover.

Unfortunately, at that moment, a shift occurred. The dream changed. The water pressure dissipated. Donya crouched; now would be a good time to see. The ground shook. Air completely replaced the water. This didn't come from the right direction, though. It came from above. It contained the feel of the Kraken.

This was the problem with not having a real plan. Their efforts were chaotic.

She ran through the darkness—her direction had not changed. The ground quickly dried. Donya's footfalls, which initially made a terrible squelching racket, now pounded on dust. Donya could feel the power of the Kraken creeping around her. Her arm itched furiously.

Shit, Scarlet made it to the source first. What was happening in the dark? Then, as if to answer her question, the darkness faded. The sword was too young to use more than one ability at a time.

The landscape turned into a wasteland, huge dry cracks ripping through the earth. Donya saw Scarlet and what appeared to be another colossal eel. Or maybe it was a sea serpent. Clearly, out of its element, the goliath's head moved slowly.

The cracks got larger as she approached the battle. She suspected something. She stopped for a moment. The fissures formed a pattern. The earth was not real, but she used her magic anyway and it came. The pattern formed a seal. It wasn't active, yet.

She held a pretty good idea of what would activate it; the blood of whoever cast this place. Even if they didn't manage to kill them, they could trap them here. A well-laid trap, but she did plan to kill Heldrig. She checked her arm, the one that itched strangely. It had a seal on it, too, not one she recognized. The inside contained an isosceles triangle and twisting vines. She didn't need to understand it now. It was beneficial. A few of the fissures were large enough for her to fit into. She wedged herself in one and moved as fast as she could.

She passed under the tip of the sea serpent's tail. That wouldn't be a killing blow. She turned left, and fire blazed across the top of the fissure. Scarlet moved behind her.

The enormous serpent moved, rattling the earth around her, and then its belly passed over her. She raised her sword and plunged it in. Dark, poisoned blood rained on her. The behemoth wasn't dead yet; in a rage, it looped its massive head under itself and grabbed her by the leg. Its fangs were tougher than the eels. One punctured her skin and pain seared below her knee.

Trolls don't really have blood to poison. But there is moisture in them. This wouldn't kill her, but she slowed. It flung her. She landed not far from Scarlet.

She felt herself getting lighter and frail, chalky again. She couldn't withstand another blow from the snake. She peered up at it, neon yellow bands blazed in the sunlight. It prepared to strike at her again, but the blood worked.

Donya hadn't noticed that the dream took place in daylight. The sky was blue-white, a color she had never seen before the air sizzled with heat. Scarlet rushed up to her. The woman's hair shone a brilliant red in the sunlight.

"We need more time, the seal," Donya said.

Scarlet looked around. Then she laid her sword on top of the one Donya still clutched. The Kraken's power flowed through Scarlet into Donya. A blackout activated, not by Donya but by Scarlet. Donya felt Scarlet's hand on her forearm. She dragged her through the darkness. They didn't get far. Donya was too heavy. Donya kicked her legs to help.

The serpent moved in the darkness. She heard the thump of it striking where they were.

The sword fell back to sleep, and the darkness broke like a mirror would. Great chunks and splinters of darkness fell, shimmering into nothingness on the descent.

Enough time passed. The seal in the ground was complete. Chains came up from every crack and wrapped around the serpent, which shrunk and morphed.

Mars sat cross-legged, bound all around. Donya propped herself up. She didn't know if she could move. And the dream crumbled now, too, the landscape shattering.

"Where is the old guy?" Scarlet asked.

Donya shook her head.

Scarlet shot up and headed toward Mars. "You followed me back in Florence. Where is the other guy? Where is Heldrig?" She shouted.

"Not here. Never was," he said, clutching at his injured stomach.

Donya could barely hear him. Scarlet kicked him in the shin and turned back toward Donya.

"How do we get out of here? Heldrig isn't here, so now I have to keep dealing with him." Scarlet's voice shook.

"Getting out of here is easy. You made good allies." Donya tapped the seal on her arm; she could see the one on Scarlet's shine a light gold. It was almost the same but with the rune for fire at the center. "Close your eyes and concentrate on your body."

She watched Scarlet do it. One minute she stood there, and the next, Donya was alone with Mars, just the way she wanted to be.

It was hard, but she got to her feet and ambled over. Their sword would get stronger as time went on. But killing one's enemy was the best way to strengthen a sword.

"Any chance you will tell me your father's next step? Or where your sister is located?"

The young man shook his head.

Donya ran him through. It was good she had a lot of weight to put behind the thrust. A sword made of opal isn't that sharp.

CHAPTER 45

# SCARLET

Scarlet came to, feeling unhinged. The final showdown hadn't been the final showdown. Donya arrived and gave almost too much to the battle. Scarlet could see bits of her flaking off before she left. The seal from the Kraken and Grazia saved them both. But would the Kraken still help now? Did she know Scarlet still needed her? She couldn't feel her leg, the one with the mark. Her other leg tingled too from being up in the seat, but the way her right leg felt was all wrong.

She hadn't opened her eyes yet. It was all too much without any more information flooding into her. She could hear, though. "Is there a doctor onboard?" came through the communication system. It wasn't loud. But a hint of panic wavered in the flight attendant's voice.

She heard footsteps rush past her. Mars had been on board. What happened to his body when he got stuck in those chains? And what had Donya done after? Scarlet couldn't see the future, but she saw the murderous look on the little troll's face. It gave her a hint of doubt about their future alliance. The shadow magic in Donya was backed up by real darkness.

Scarlet cracked open her eyes. The cabin lights were up. Passengers opened their window shades. Daylight streamed in through the far windows. It wasn't as strong as outdoors, having to go through several coatings of whatever a plane window consisted of, but the magic particles glimmered and danced in it. In the bars of light, Scarlet could almost make a pattern out of them.

"Good, you're up. I need to get out." Juan's voice broke into her rattled mind.

She turned her head and drank in the sight of him. His brown eyes were beautiful behind his glasses; she wanted to cry with relief at seeing them again. Not crying in public had been ground into her though, so no tears spilled over. Silently she unbuckled her seatbelt and stood up.

She clutched the book to her as she moved into the aisle. Her leg moved awkwardly under her. She waited for the pins and needles to start, but they never came. It occurred to her that maybe she'd been damaged by absorbing vast amounts of water magic through a small spot on her foot. She stayed standing in the aisle as no one disturbed her. Finally, she checked her foot.

Nothing. Her foot did not glow. It appeared normal, even when she stared at it, although it did not feel that way.

Another flight attendant rushed through the other aisle. Sweat wet his brow. It might have been the same one as before. Scarlet couldn't tell. She'd stayed so focused on trying to locate Heldrig that humans blended together.

Juan came back, and she sat next to him. She closed her eyes. Now that her mind quieted, she noticed she suffered a splitting headache and felt thirsty.

She kept the book on her lap, leaning forward, pressing her forehead against the seat in front of her. Then she passed out.

She woke up mad at herself for what she thought of as falling asleep. However, the rest did seem to do her good. The headache pounded less, and they were landing. Juan gazed out the window. When the plane circled, the sun came in and hit his face. His eyes shone as she'd become accustomed to. If she wasn't startled by it, then she could see its beauty. The iridescence twinkled a bit like a star.

Although the horrible situation wasn't over, she seemed to be settling into a tranquil state. Juan's eyes seemed beautiful. The sun on the rain-cleaned roofs seemed beautiful. Even the light winking off car windows from the parking lot impressed her. Or maybe it was finally being on her home turf, well, almost.

They deplaned slowly, presumably because of what happened with Mars. There was no sign of him or Heldrig as they got off the plane. Juan and Scarlet gathered their bags without incident. Did this mean she would have to keep an eye out forever, 'til the day he decided to come for her?

Donya described him as impatient and greedy. He couldn't set a proper trap as she could. Would he wait as Scarlet feared? The uncertainty made her skin crawl. He knew their names and where they lived. If she didn't defeat him today, she would never feel safe or probably be safe.

Juan got both of their bags, and they headed out to where their shuttle pickup stood. The air outside was cleaner and fresher than what they breathed in a while. A lone smoker stood outside, polluting the sunshine. Scarlet took one last look over her shoulder. There he was. Heldrig.

He'd waited outside the doors. He leaned on a cement pylon. His arms were crossed. He noticed her. It didn't seem like he tried to hide it either. His eyes locked with hers.

She relied heavily on her fire, the shield used in tandem with it. But in her broken and tired state, she felt it, the minute part of her that was solid that wanted to protect. Would it be enough on its own? She hoped so. She must keep Heldrig away.

They needed to cross the street for the pickup. The old book's first section had been about protecting oneself when using magic. She uttered a few words from the book hoping they would work with her shield. They seemed right, and if they were wrong, maybe they wouldn't hurt.

Tires screeched.

Juan stopped next to her.

She looked back, too, worried at what she saw. She sensed her shield. It hadn't spread out of her like usual but sprung up back where the screeching came from.

A maroon SUV's tires spun, trying to go forward. Scarlet could see the magic framework in front of it. Probably no one else could. The man cartoonishly tried to correct the wheel. Moving hand over hand spinning it.

Heldrig was right there. Scarlet repeated the words. Concentrating on what she wanted to happen, the shield split in two, funneling the SUV back toward the airport entrance.

Part of the shield was behind the pylons. Heldrig stood between it and the vehicle.

She let go of the shield in front, and the SUV smashed into Heldrig. Several nearby people jumped back. Heldrig didn't move. He couldn't.

Whatever he was made from, it wasn't the same as a human. For a moment, his splatter seemed wet and stuck to the shield. Scarlet let go, and the blue streak fell to the ground, but not with a wet sound. It moved like powder. A breeze came and blew it away.

People screamed.

A short woman and her two children walked behind Scarlet. She grabbed the kid's hands, saying, "we have to go try to help."

Juan stood open-mouthed. Scarlet eyed him, then the street, they stood in. They were right in front of the scene. "We should move in case that guy does anything else," she said, knowing it wasn't fair of her, but she needed an excuse to get out of this place.

"Do you think anyone is hurt?"

"No, he didn't hit anyone," she responded with so much conviction she almost convinced herself. Mercifully, their shuttle pulled around the corner. "Oh my god, hurry we have to get on that one. I bet they are going to close the whole airport in a few minutes." She tugged on Juan's arm, and he moved with her.

She didn't think her numb leg could move fast, but she managed it. They hurried onto the shuttle as the blinking light of an ambulance could be seen in the distance. In the sunlight, the man in the maroon SUV sat on the sidewalk, his head in his hands. She hoped he wouldn't get into very much trouble.

Juan tuned in to a news station on the radio when they made it to their car. He wanted to hear if they reported what happened at the airport. Scarlet googled the nearest McDonald's. Her stomach felt hollow. Her headache throbbed again. She wanted normal plain boring fast food.

It was a short drive.

After eating one cheeseburger and gulping half a soda, Scarlet felt unsatisfied, she knew it was the moment. She denied herself for a long time and look at what ensued. Now she'd become a murderer. Heldrig had been a bad guy, but that didn't change the fact. It was easy to go along with trolls and sea monsters. Maybe she was a monster too.

She needed to be honest. She would tell Juan. Probably there would be a better time. But if she waited, it would be the old pattern of her life repeating itself.

Could this be self-destructive behavior? He could leave her. What if this was the last straw? He proposed, and she instantly got weird.

She reached across the table and took his hand. He still chewed on his double-quarter pounder. No onions because she didn't like onions. He did many things for her. She could do this for him. Let him decide.

"Babe, I've got something to tell you. It might take a while, but I want to get it out."

CHAPTER 46

# DONYA

Time was up. Donya carried Grazia's body through the spirit world. They couldn't put her back into it without the candle, and the Wolf King never reappeared.

The elderly body reacted quickly to the magic of this place. As she carried it through the forest, coming up on the Kraken's grotto, the skin appeared more and more bark-like. Sometimes that happened—it was why humans couldn't stay here too long. Their humanity left them. The place got into them. And the hum drove them mad.

She felt like she might go mad. The image of the room where Nera was held flashed in her mind. A dank place for how dry it stayed. Nera's blood on the ground, drag marks in the dust. She was alive, but in what condition?

How would she find her? Because she must.

The trees parted. The Kraken lounged in the pool while her husbands labored over the stone blocks which surrounded it. Grazia's shade stood nearby.

"There you are," came the thousand voices of the Kraken, "place that over to the northeast, where it will not block the moonrise."

"The body?" Donya was confused. How could such a tiny body block anything?

"It won't be a human body for long," the Kraken said.

Donya headed to where she directed. The Kraken's eyes watched her. Grazia observed as well. The husbands took no notice. Donya was not fully recovered. The short trek took too long. Some help now would have been nice.

"To the left two more steps," the Kraken continued to issue commands. Grazia's shade wandered over.

Donya put down the body. Its hair became less like gray strands and more like golden leaves. A tree, the body would become a tree. Grazia's body used to be almost devoid of scent but now it had the faint smell of water. Donya had always been in a hurry at the Kraken's grotto, or miserable, for the first time she really observed her surroundings. Could all these trees be human bodies?

"Would you mind crossing my hands and bending my ring fingers?" Grazia asked.

Donya nodded. The body grew stiff. It stood on its own. A husband got up, bringing a pitcher of water with him. He watered the feet, and roots sprang forth.

"I'm a willow, how lovely," Grazia said with a smile. "I tried to make my body immortal for hundreds of years, but in failing, I have succeeded in extending my existence."

"Are you trying to be inspiring?" Donya asked.

"Maybe. Will you let Scarlet know what happened?" Grazia asked.

"Yes, she gave me her number. I will call her tomorrow. She killed Heldrig for me. It was prophesied that he would die. I wish it could have been by my hand," Donya said.

"Do not call from my house. My disappearance will be suspicious. I left my worldly possessions in her name and sent the deed to my home with her to California."

"You did what?" Donya asked.

"I had no other heir."

"I do not think she will want to come back here."

"You are probably right, but she must. Of course, you are welcome to use my home. But I cannot legally leave my possessions to you," Grazia said with a smile.

"What about your Chimera? What can I do with him?"

"Dear, I did leave a few loose ends. He loves the catacombs. Leave him loose in there. He finds his food easily."

That didn't sound like the best idea, but she held no better one. The Kraken observed them. Donya turned her attention to the mighty force. "My lady, how will I find Nera?"

"You will do as you have done. Search, and I will aid you as I can," the Kraken responded.

"She did not come to you here?" Donya asked.

"I suspect she does not want to be found. You have centuries. Give it time," the Kraken said.

"No," Donya snapped too loudly.

The husbands both eyed her. Grazia cleared her semi-transparent throat, "you are very young. I know it is hard to wait. It will be easier on you if you do."

"I don't want the easy way," Donya said.

Both Grazia and the Kraken sighed in unison. Then looked at each other and smiled.

The Kraken spoke, "do what you will, but before you leave, come ask these stones if the makings please them."

Donya came closer to the hollow. Every other stone was decorated with golden paint, and intricate seals of an old type, but with a newer Italian script. One with a beautiful ray pattern spoke up first, "if it pleases our lady, it pleases us."

"I second that," came another stone, "and the paint is most handsome."

"They are happy with the changes," Donya relayed.

"There are going to be many changes. Do prepare yourself," said the Kraken.

Donya breathed in the air; the warm forest smells mixed with the magical waters here. She thought of the road ahead. She sat. There was much to learn here. There was much to learn everywhere. "I do intend to prepare myself. Can we please begin now?"

# EPILOGUE

Donya climbed up her mountain. In it was a small cave. Summer months had begun. At this latitude, the summer nights grew short or nonexistent. She would hibernate. Her cave was a good place to sleep off her exhaustion. She asked the boulder she'd placed in the cave mouth to move, and it did. All her rocks seemed happy to have her home. She heard them chittering and calling out.

"Let me sleep. I'll tell you all about it when I wake up," she said, patting a big blue chunk of lapis. She placed the little bone next to it. Wouldn't it be surprised when it woke up, big change of scenery. She laid her sword behind her.

She closed her eyes, using her arm as a hard pillow. Sleep didn't come. Nera's smile by the river in Florence haunted her.

Donya searched far into spring after asking the Kraken for help. Everywhere she could think of. No sign of the part nymph. Finally, she came home, too exhausted to continue. Now she breathed in the scent of her damp hollow. It smelled of moss and wet rock. When winter finally came, she would try again. She must try again.

Scarlet checked the phase of the moon one more time. A Monday night was not a great night to stay out late, especially since she started this new job, but what could she do? A baby Kraken hatched when a baby Kraken hatched.

She still couldn't feel her foot, but she made do walking out onto the sand, which was particularly difficult. After this, she hoped she could wear sandals again. Closed-toe shoes all summer had been terrible. But the blister that contained the small spirit didn't grow much at least.

Not many people wandered the boardwalk. The rides closed on weekday nights in the fall. But the arcade stayed open, and people played volleyball on the beach. There was a nice pier that sold good ice cream, although nothing as good as the stuff in Italy.

She slipped off her shoes and left them in the fluffy sand, then waded into the water. It was always cold. The zing of a shiver climbed up her spine. Her foot, of course, glowed again. The Kraken, although far, must give a bit of energy to get her progeny out and on its way.

Then the glow moved outside of Scarlet's foot, a tiny ball of yellow light in the water. She watched it through the foam and sand particles. It differentiated itself. It resembled a miniature squid with enormous eyes. Fully unfurled, it was no bigger than a house key. Another wave came, and it tumbled around. Scarlet leaned down and scooped it up in her two cupped hands.

"Alright, little one, you're free. I scoped this place out, and it's pretty fun. I think you will like it here. I'll be by to check on you." It twirled around in what she hoped meant understanding; it was a baby after all. She gave it a big smile and added, "oh yeah, I'm Scarlet, your human godmother."

THE END

# ACKNOWLEDGMENTS

There are so many people to thank, so many of my friends and family members helped me. Here I go.

My eternal gratitude to Erin and Tara for editing this book. Analynn for beta reading. Ivan for sitting patiently as I read the third draft in its entirety to him. He said it was good and he enjoyed it, but I'm sure all the long pauses where I stopped to fix grammar issues were very boring. Leo for taking naps long enough for me to write, edit, and/or read out loud to his father. Nicki for all the help through the years, she has been in classes, writing groups, and listened to me whine about self-publishing.

Infinite thanks also to Sarah and Val for the early reads. Henry for all that professor's patience and encouragement. Patric for doing writing sprints with me at the beginning of this journey. Everyone in the MPC novel writing classes I took. Many of my classmates helped shape this manuscript. And a few didn't but were super mean and that helps a writer build thick skin (I am not salty.) Also, thanks to all my friends I griped, grumbled, and/or whined to.

Thank you to Dave for the wonderful exterior design of my book. And thank you to Danna who did all the interior design. They were both very patient with my new author's quirks and questions.

Thank you to my niece, Panda, who has not read my book but thinks it's cool that I write.

And thank you to all my friends who help me promote *Traveling Monsters* by posting on their feeds. I am not good at social media (really social anything). The assistance is needed and appreciated.

I am sure there are those I forgot. Let me know and I will make a proper apology in the sequel acknowledgments.

FINALLY, THANK YOU
TO ALL THE MONSTERS,
TRAVELING, AND OTHERWISE.

Printed in the USA
CPSIA information can be obtained
at www.ICGtesting.com
BVHW030849230823
668790BV00002B/160

9 798988 516903